{00:00}

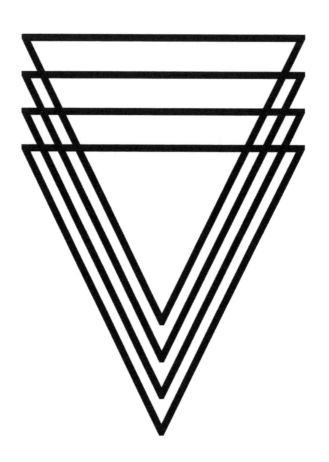

{00:00}

D. I. Richardson

ISBN: 152274956X
ISBN-13: 978-1522749561

Dedications

Dedicated to:
Michelle "Mitchy" Munro

"He is terribly afraid of dying because he hasn't yet lived."

— Franz Kafka

{Chapter: **One**}

I still hate Christmas. But regardless, I woke up on New Year's Day, feeling groggy as all hell. This wasn't a hangover groggy, this was just a natural state of "where the hell am I" and confusion. I rolled myself over and looked at my wall. I sighed and rolled back and looked at Evan's cute face. His eyelids were still tightly shut over his pale blue eyes. His short black hair was still fluffed up from yesterday. Whatever hair product he uses works super good, his hair is never not styled properly.

I poked his cheek a few times, hoping that it might wake him up. I don't know how long he's gonna sleep for and I'm gonna have to go pee soon. I kept poking at his cheek until his eyes fluttered a little under the eyelid. Was this it? Was this Evan's grand awakening?

"Good morning, gingersnaps," he mumbled to me.

I kissed his forehead. "Morning, loser."

"How's the New Year so far?"

"Warm, cozy, slightly hungover, and looking good."

Evan smirked. "You're just talking about me."

"I might be."

He pulled himself closer to me and kissed me on the lips. "The first and last one of the whole year."

"Pfft." I grabbed him and kissed him, making that two on the year so far. "I just made you a liar."

"Darn, rats, toots."

"You're an unbelievable dork."

He smiled. "I know."

"What are we gonna do today?" I asked.

"The coffee shop opens at one today. We could go there again?"

"Yes," I replied. "I actually did like that coffee shop. Plus there's the added benefit of being able to sit in comfy seats instead of just getting a coffee and coming back here to sit around and do nothing productive. It's also past noon already, so…"

"Um, how is sitting in a coffee shop productive?" Evan asked.

"It just feels productive. Y'know?"

He shook his head and mouthed the word "no."

"I know, I'm weird," I said. "And I also have to pee. Aww, my first pee of the New Year."

"Didn't you get up at four to take a pee?"

"Shut up," I snapped. "That one didn't count."

"Whatever. Do you need me to move or can you climb over me?"

"I'll climb over you," I said.

"Don't crush me."

"No promises," I said, wrapping my arm over him and pulling myself over. I plopped over him and got out of bed. I let out a yawn as I stretched my arms up to the ceiling. Even though I couldn't touch it, I still tried.

"Aww," Evan said from behind me. "You're so cute."

I turned around and stuck my tongue out at him. "Get alive, bud. We're gonna sneak out before all the other drunk kids wake up." I grabbed my phone from the nightstand and headed off for the bathroom.

Urinating. Pretend this is a paragraph about the joys of that first morning pee. The feel of the relief of release or something.

I washed my hands and face and headed back into my room. Evan was still lying in my bed. I walked over and sat down on him and fell back into my spot between him and the wall.

"Five more minutes," he whined as I climbed back under the blankets.

"I wanna go get food and coffee and I sort of need you for that."

"Why?" he asked.

I kissed his forehead. "Because I don't wanna spend *my* money."

"You're a dick," he said with a soft chuckle. "But you're a cute dick."

"You know I'm a girl, right?"

He nodded. "God, I hope so or else this relationship is gonna be awkward for me."

"Why's that?"

"Because I'm into girls, Spencer."

"Oh... I totally forgot," I joked. "Anyway, let's get up and at it, starshine, the world is waiting."

"Gingersnaps," Evan grumbled.

"How can I help you?"

"You smell kinda nice."

I blushed a little. "Yeah, okay, thanks, anyway, let's go!" I pushed him off my bed and he plopped onto the floor. "Let's go, go, go."

"No, no, no," he said, sitting up against the edge of my bed.

I rolled over off the bed and sat down next to him on the floor. "You're not lying down anymore at least, so at least there's a little progress."

Evan yawned and rubbed the sleep from his eyes. "Okay. I'm up. Let's go do stuff."

"Do they have a good breakfast at that coffee shop?"

"Well, I think it's a great breakfast, but I don't know if you're gonna like it or not."

"That's fine. Either way, it's food," I said, standing up. "And ya girl just needs some food."

"Okay, let's go and get some." He stood up and stretched out, cracking his back several times as he did.

"I'm not getting a new bed because of you," I said firmly.

He turned to me and cocked an eyebrow. "Why would you get a new bed because of me, anyway?"

"I heard all them back cracks."

"That happens all the time," he replied. "I actually think your bed is hella comfy, so never get a new one, unless it's the same mattress as this one."

"I can agree to that. I love my bed."

"I do too," Evan said. "So let's just sleep all day instead of going anywhere. Sound good to you?"

"Nope, I still love food more than my bed." I pulled my phone from my pocket and checked for texts. None. "Let's go now. Nobody else is awake."

"How do you know that?"

"They would have texted me asking if I was awake," I replied. "They do that if they ever sleep in a different room than me. And they haven't texted me yet."

"At least they respect your privacy."

I tossed his beanie at him. "Let's go." I walked over to my door and looked down the stairs. I listened closely, but I couldn't hear anyone walking around or talking.

"Are we good to go?" Evan asked from behind me.

I nodded. "Roger that. No tangoes in sight. Stay close behind me, rook." I walked out of my room on the edges of my feet so as not to wake anyone up.

"Why are you acting like we're in a spy movie?"

"You think this is a game?" I asked, glancing over at him. "This is life or death, soldier. If the enemy spots us, we're gonna be stuck in a morning conversation that could drag on well into the PM hours."

"My girlfriend is an absolute dork," he said, sighing softly.

I smiled. "Yeah, your *girlfriend* is."

"Just get down the stairs, nerd."

"We must bide our time, for silence is our only friend," I stated.

He groaned and walked past me. "You're a dork and you whining about being hungry got me hungry, so let's go."

"Fine," I grumbled, following him down the stairs. "Why you gotta ruin my fun you big jerk?"

"I just want coffee. I'm still half asleep, Spencer." He turned to me and with pleading eyes said, "Spencer. I need it."

"Okay, okay."

We reached the bottom floor and moved in silence to the front door. We slipped our shoes on. I grabbed my coat and then remembered that Evan's coat was still upstairs. Shit. I went to go back up the stairs, but Evan grabbed my shoulder and pulled me back

4

quickly.

"It's fine. I don't need it," he said. "We're just walking to my car and then into a coffee shop."

"Your funeral, bud," I said, opening the door and stepping outside. "It's pretty cold."

He stepped outside and closed the door behind him. "I'm Canadian, *eh*. I'll just adjust to the weather."

"Let's just go. Where'd you park your car?"

"Just up the road," he said, pulling his keys from his pocket.

"When did you get your keys?"

"They were in my pocket all night. I never took them out and then we got all comfy in your bed and I was too preoccupied with kissing you and eating those gummy worms."

I frowned a little. "You owe me a bag of gummy worms now."

"Oh, I see how it is. You just want me for the gummy worms I can supply you, huh?"

"No, I want you for you," I told him. "The gummy worms are gonna be an added benefit."

"Mm-hmm, okay, whatever you say, buds," he said, walking down a driveway and onto the road.

"Where did you park, seriously?" I whined as we crossed over the slush-covered street.

"Right here," he said, walking over to his car. Well, SUV, but whatever. I still think he would be better suited with a two-door grey sports car or something, not the dark orange SUV that he drives right now. It's not character fitting.

I sighed. "This is so far."

"It's not even a two-minute walk from your house."

"I like to be lazy," I told him. "Being lazy helps me to conserve energy for when I need it."

"That doesn't even make sense. Just get in the car."

I pouted at him and walked around to the passenger side of his best friend's ride— Um, sorry. Anyway, I opened the door, hopped in, and buckled myself into the seat. I punched Evan in the arm. "It's been too long since I did that, sorry."

"I'm gonna have a permanent bruise on my arm because of you. You do know that, right?"

I shrugged. "It'll be a cute bruise. It'll remind you of me."

"I don't bruise easily," he stated. "Plus it doesn't even hurt."

"Right, right."

"Hey, I know we haven't talked much about this other than that one time or whatever—"

"I won't tell anyone." I scoffed. I was a mind reader. "It's not their business, it's yours."

"You're scary good," Evan said with a perplexed look on his face. "But thank you. It means a lot to me that you understand where I'm coming from with the whole C-word thing."

"Fear of the word only increases fear of the thing itself," I said, quoting Hermione Granger.

"Did you just quote—"

"Yes," I said, cutting him off again.

He smirked. "I think you might just be a keeper."

"I am a keeper," I said. "I am keeper of the keys and grounds at Hogwarts."

"You can stop that, you nerd," Evan said, smiling softly.

I leaned over and kissed his cheek. "At least I'm cute."

"At least you're cute," he repeated.

"So how much longer?" I whined. "Are we there yet?"

"Soon, just close your eyes and listen to the radio."

I let out a groan and lolled my head back on the seat and watched the houses flutter past us as we drove down the streets. The radio was a minor comfort, it's not like it was anything good, but it was better than nothing at all, so it's not a total loss. I watched the houses get nicer and then get more mediocre again. I watched the houses turn to businesses and then back again. Finally, after what felt like forever, we pulled into a parking lot and Evan shut off the car.

"We're here," he said, poking my face lightly.

I swatted his arm away and groaned. "I hunger so much."

"I know. I could hear your stomach rumbling pretty much the entire time we were driving over here."

"*We* were driving?" I asked. "Don't you mean while you were driving? I was half asleep in your passenger seat."

"Same shit, Spencer." He opened his door. "Now let's go get some food and coffee, okay?"

"I want an omelette du fromage, please."

"You can get a ham and cheese omelette," Evan said. "And for the side?"

"Bacon or sausage, either or."

"Both?" he asked.

"Why not," I said, getting out of the car. "Today's a cheat day."

"Atta girl, what a way to start off a brand new year."

I pushed him toward the front door of the coffee shop and scoffed. "I'm in better shape than you are, okay, buddy?"

"Okay, buddy," he quipped.

"I am," I said, pouting.

"It's so nice and warm in here," he said as the door closed behind us.

I slipped my coat off and sighed. "I could have gotten your coat for you, dumbass."

"I was cold for 30 seconds, relax."

"But you're my little baby, Evan. But it's whatever, I'm gonna go get us a seat. Get me an omelette."

He smiled at me as I walked away. "Will do, boss."

I walked over to the table we had sat at last time and sat down. I liked this seat. It was neat. It wasn't to be beat. Did you like my rhyming? I try to make my mundane life a little cooler for you. Sorry.

I waited a solid five minutes for Evan to walk over to my table with our coffees. I gave him a small pout as he sat down. "What took you so long?"

"Oh, they asked if I wanted a fresh batch of coffee, so I obviously told them that we wanted a fresh batch of coffee, and so then they made us a fresh batch of coffee," he stated. "And we were having some minor chitchat."

"Pfft, wow," I grumbled. "How long till our food's ready?"

"Ten minutes or so?" he said with as shrug. "I'm not psychic."

I nodded slowly and winked at him. "Sure you aren't."

"Shut up," Evan snapped.

"So, remember how I said I wanted to come along to your chemo?"

Evan nodded. "Yeah, what about it?"

"When's your next session?"

He shrugged. "I don't know. I have to call them and set up a time for a scan and then a session. It'll probably be in a couple weeks or so. Or maybe even sooner than that. It just depends on their openings."

"Hopefully it's sooner rather than later, right?"

"Well, sure," he said, shrugging slightly. "I don't really care either way. It's just one of those things for me."

"Mm, so what are you doing tomorrow?" I asked.

He cocked an eyebrow at me. "Why? Is there some social function you're trying to drag me to?"

"No, I just thought maybe we could do this again. Maybe we could hang out with Charlotte. You guys seemed to get along pretty good," I said. "You guys do get along, right?"

"Oh, yeah," Evan said. "Charlotte's a cool time."

"So you wanna hang out again tomorrow, huh?" I asked, kicking at his feet under the table.

He sighed and nodded. "Yes. It's too early in the relationship to disappoint you."

"You wouldn't disappoint me," I said. "You'd just make a me a little bit sad, but I'd get over it and have a girls' day out with Charlotte instead."

"So what are gonna do tomorrow?"

"Just hang out." I shrugged. Shit. I hadn't really thought that far ahead. I'm not good at planning sometimes, okay? Sue me.

He nodded. "Why don't we go shovel my street off?"

"Is it still bad where you live?"

Evan nodded. "It's nice you live in the area of town that actually gets their roads cleared of snow."

I laughed softly and he smiled back at me as the waitress came over and laid our plates of food down onto the table.

{Chapter: **Two**}

"Ding dong," Charlotte's voice rang out into my somewhat empty house. Way to use the actual doorbell there, bud.

I turned my head over to see her walk into the kitchen. "Yeah, no, just walk right in like you own the place."

"Well, you knew I was coming over, so it's not like this is a huge deal or anything," she said, taking her coat off and swinging it onto the back of a chair. She sat down and glared slightly at me. "Where's my cereal?"

I put a spoonful of the Fruit Rounds in my mouth and smiled. "In my belly."

"Rude."

I started sipping up the milk from the bowl and she just shook her head at me. "What?" I asked, setting the bowl down.

"The taste of milk after having fruity cereal in it is gross."

"You're gross," I barked back.

"So is Evan coming to hang out today?" Charlotte asked as she got up and walked over to the counter.

"Yeah. He said he would."

"Nice. Evan's a cool time," she replied, clicking the kettle on.

I chuckled softly. "That's exactly what he said about you when I asked him if he wanted to hang out with the two of us today."

"When's he coming over?"

"Soon," I replied. "I texted him to come over whenever he wants. My parents are at work and Jordan's off at her friends, so we have the house to ourselves all day."

"What about Taylor?"

I shrugged. "What about her?"

"Where's she gone?"

"No clue. I don't keep tabs on her. She's her own woman."

Charlotte nodded and then pulled a cup from the cupboard behind her. "You want me to make you a tea?"

"Please," I said. "I forgot to make one when I was getting my cereal."

"And you're too lazy to make yourself one now," she teased, grabbing a second cup and putting some sugar in it.

"You better believe it."

"Your resolution this year should be to stop being so lazy," Charlotte stated. "Imagine how much cooler you would be."

"Imagine how much smarter I would be," I said with a soft sigh. "Ah, but these are only dreams, Charlotte."

"I know it is," she said. "There's no way Spencer would ever not be lazy."

I nodded. "Yeah, so how's that tea coming along, buddy?"

"The water is still boiling," she replied. "Relax. It'll be done when it's done."

"Make it boil faster. I require tea."

"I would if I could."

"Be a superhero and have your superpower be the ability to heat things up at will and in an instant."

Charlotte scowled slightly at me. "Come on, if I was gonna be a superhero, I'd have a way better superpower than that."

"I don't know," I said. "I feel like you would have a really lame superpower and then you'd just be stuck with the feeling of regret. Or you'd misuse it."

"How would I misuse the ability to heat things up?"

"You would just heat up all of my food to be way too hot for me to comfortably enjoy it," I explained. Before Charlotte could reply to me, there was a knock at the door. "Come in!" I shouted.

The door opened and after a few seconds, Evan walked into the kitchen. "Hello, hello."

"Do you want me to make you a tea too?" Charlotte asked as he took his coat off.

"Um, yeah, sure. Thanks," Evan said, walking over to me. He smiled at me as he grabbed the seat across from Charlotte's so he could sit close to me.

"How are ya, buddy?" I asked. I had told Charlotte that Evan had slept on my floor last night. I didn't want her to know we were together yet, but she probably has her ideas that we are.

He pouted. "I could be better."

"How so?" I whispered to him.

"I mean, I don't even get to kiss you hello," he whispered back.

I smiled at him. "I'll make up for it later, nerd."

"You better."

"So how are you?" Charlotte asked, interrupting our whispered conversation.

"I'm good. How are you?" Evan replied, glancing over to her.

"I'm good," Charlotte replied. "But, uh, quick question, how do you take your tea?"

"Any way. Just make it how you're making hers."

Charlotte nodded. "Makes my life a little easier."

"So what's new?" I asked him.

"Nothing," Evan replied, shooting me a weird look. "Nothing new has happened since yesterday."

"Well, you never know. Maybe something super cool happened to you last night, man. I don't know."

"I don't know. I slept. Is sleeping cool? Well, I know sleeping is cool, but does it qualify for being worth of talking about?"

I shrugged. "Did you have a cool dream?"

"Nope."

"Stop being boring," I whined.

Evan pouted at me. "What about you? Did *you* have any cool dreams last night?"

"Yep," I replied.

He waited a moment for me to keep going, but I didn't. "Okay,"

11

he said. "What happened in the dream?"

"Well, it was a dream," I told him. "And in the dream, I was selected to be a member of the Justice League and my superpower was the ability to conjure up mangoes and other fruits at will."

"Oh, but my superpower was lame?" Charlotte butted in.

Evan looked over to her. "What was your superpower?"

"She said I would have the superpower of heating things up on command."

"Yeah," I said. "It'd be helpful. You could boil water and cook food!"

"That's what a stove is for!" Charlotte barked.

I let out a loud groan. "But you would be able to do it *on command!* It's not just heating it up, it's heating it up *instantly.*"

"Still lame, Spencer," Evan said, taking Charlotte's side.

"Shut up, you!" I barked at him. "My superpower is lame too, but it's still useful. Who doesn't love a good mango now and then? Right?"

"Shut up. Yours is lamer," Charlotte snapped. "What about Evan? Now give Evan a lame superpower so we can be the world's shittiest superhero trio."

"Hmm," I said, thinking for a moment about what lame superpower would suit Evan the best. "I got it, Evan's power can be the power of massage."

Evan chuckled softly and shook his head a little. "Now *that* is one really lame superpower."

"It's not lame, it has its uses," I protested.

"Like what?" Charlotte asked.

"Like when I've had a long day and need someone to rub my goddamn back, that's what."

Evan scowled slightly and sighed. "Well, lucky for you, I already actually do have that power."

"Do you?" Charlotte asked.

"I do," Evan replied.

"Prove it."

"How?"

"He's proved it to me," I replied. "In the mall, he massaged my back for me and it was just heavenly."

Evan winked and clicked his tongue at me.

Charlotte walked over with two cups of tea and put them in front of both Evan and me. "Maybe you should toss a massage my way."

"Maybe," Evan said, sliding the tea closer to him. "Thanks for the tea, by the by."

"No problem," Charlotte said, going back over for her own cup of tea.

"I get dibs on him, he was my friend first," I said with a pout.

"I made you tea, you can rent him out to me."

Evan sipped his tea and tried to hide a smile stretching across his face. He must enjoy getting fought over.

"Tea doesn't get you the right to have Evan massage you."

"But he's not your *boyfriend*, so I should be allowed." She turned over to Evan. "Right?"

"Yep," Evan said, flashing me a teasing look.

"Evan," I growled.

He smirked at me. "What? I can't massage and caress your best friend's bare back?"

"No," I said with a pout.

"Why can't he?" Charlotte asked.

I sighed. "He was my friend first, so I get dibs."

"Oh, yeah?" Evan asked.

"I came to have a good time and I'm honestly feeling so attacked right now."

"Is little Spencer getting jealous?" Charlotte teased.

I scoffed. "Jealous of what?"

"The thought of Evan's hands exploring my body," she replied breathily.

"No," I lied. The though actually did make me a little hot under the skin.

"So, Evan," Charlotte said, turning to him. "Wanna maybe take me on a date tomorrow night?"

Evan shot me a look and then smiled at her. "I'd love to."

"You can pick me up at seven, yeah?"

Evan nodded. "It's a date."

"You know, I'm notorious for giving it all up on the first date," Charlotte said with a wink to him.

"Lucky me," Evan said back, narrowing his gaze on her.

I felt my blood actually boiling. My boyfriend just agreed to go on a date with my best friend right in front of me. He could have said no. What the hell? My jaw got tense and my hands started to get me clammy. Even though I know it's most likely a joke, it still pissed me off.

"You'll help me get ready for tomorrow, right?" Charlotte asked, turning to me.

"No!" I shouted. "I will not help you get ready for a date with my boyfriend!"

"There it is," Evan said.

"There what is?" I shouted at him.

"Evan bumped into me when he went to the bathroom on New Year's and we had a little talk," Charlotte explained. "He slipped up and said you two were dating, so the two of us decided to have a little fun at your expense."

"That was *not* funny, assholes," I said angrily. I could feel that my jaw still tensed up.

"You get pretty red when you're angry," Evan said, leaning over to me. He cupped my cheek in his hand. "And your jaw is so tense."

"I thought you were about to go on a date with my friend, you dick."

He smirked and kissed me.

Charlotte made a loud coughing noise. "Not in front of me, please."

"Why not?" I asked as Evan sat back in his seat properly.

Charlotte pouted softly at me. "It just makes me all sad 'cause I don't have anyone to kiss."

"Good," I said. "You purposely make me all jealous and shit and think I'm gonna care about how you feel. You meanie."

"I'm sorry," Charlotte said, standing up and hugging me. "You know I love you."

"Yeah, yeah," I mumbled into her shoulder.

"So my little Spencer has a boyfriend," Charlotte said, sitting back down. "It's crazy how fast they mature. Notice how I didn't say grow, because Spencer hasn't grown since she was eight."

Evan chuckled so I kicked him in the leg.

"I might be vertically challenged, but I can still beat the both of you up, so I'd suggest that you both hush it," I threatened.

"You can't beat me up," Charlotte said, scoffing at me.

I sighed. "Yes, I can. I'm 108 pounds of pure scraptastic goodness."

"You're so tiny," Evan said with a smirk.

"I'm scrappy," I argued.

Evan nodded. "Okay, sure you are."

"I am," I argued. "Charlotte, tell him about all the asses I kicked throughout high school."

"It was Mindy. She beat up Mindy," Charlotte said. "Mindy's the same height as her and she always took it easy on Spencer to boost her confidence. Spencer isn't a very physical being, she likes studying more than fighting."

"I hate you," I said flatly.

Evan smiled at me. "Fight me, nerd."

"Maybe later," I said, sipping some tea. "This tea is wonderful."

"Thank you," Charlotte said. "I tried my best to make it taste good."

"So what now?" Evan asked. "What's on the planning board for the rest of the day?" He slouched back in the chair and let out a soft sigh.

"We could go for breakfast?" Charlotte suggested.

I shook my head. "Nah."

"Why not?"

"We went for breakfast yesterday," I said, nodding at Evan. "Plus I just had a bowl of cereal."

"Why wasn't I invited?" Charlotte asked.

I shrugged. "It was a couple thing."

"Oh, I see how it is."

"I'm sorry, maybe later we can all go out for coffees or dinner or something."

Charlotte sighed. "Fine, yeah, whatever."

"Don't get sassy with me," I barked. "Maybe we should go for lunch instead. And then after lunch, we can go find something fun to do."

"Like?" Evan asked.

"I don't know, bowling or something," I suggested. "I haven't been bowling in a while."

"A nerd like you *would* suggest bowling," Evan teased. "But I'm fine with it if you two wanna go do that."

"But we only have three people," Charlotte said.

"So what? We just won't do teams," I told her.

"Your funeral," Charlotte said. She glanced over to Evan. "I'm kind of the bowling master. Spencer hasn't beaten me. Ever."

"That's gonna change today."

"How?"

"Evan's gonna tutor me," I stated.

Evan shot me a look. "What the hell do you mean? I'm not even that good at bowling."

I rested my hand on his. "I have faith in you, babe."

"You shouldn't about this," he said flatly, frowning a little.

I scooted my chair closer to him and looked him deep in his dumb blue eyes. "I have faith in you."

"I'm a bad bowler."

"Don't care."

"Stop being weird," he said, moving some hair from of my face and brushing it behind my ear.

"But—"

"Shh," he said, quickly cutting me off.

"But, Evan—"

He quickly shot his hand up and put a finger over my lips. "Shh," he said, sounding a little bit angrier this time.

"But, Evan," I said, mumbling slightly because of his finger. "I'm just weird. You know that already."

"You guys are sickening already. You haven't been together long enough to be sickening," Charlotte butted in. "Please slow down."

"You have friends, right?" I asked, turning to Evan.

Evan nodded. "I do, yes."

"You should set her up with one so she can shut up about us."

"Hey!" Charlotte whined. "I do not need help finding a boy-friend."

I lolled my head back and then looked over to her. "Really?"

"Okay," she said. "Maybe I could use a little help, but that doesn't mean I want to be set up on a blind date or something. I want it to be natural, not forced or anything."

"I'll get you a cat instead," Evan said.

"What?"

Evan shrugged. "Well, cats are cute and cuddly. Cats won't break your heart if they sleep with your best friend."

"Don't get me a cat," Charlotte said.

Evan nodded. "Okay, okay. No cats."

"Well, okay, maybe you can get me a cat."

{Chapter: **Three**}

It's been a week since the year started, and I already felt like a month had passed. It felt like everything was moving so slowly all of a sudden. And I couldn't tell if I liked it or not. Well, it's probably because I've just been sitting around my house with Evan or Charlotte. And we never really did anything, mostly because there's not all that much to go and do.

"I will let her know," Evan said into his phone as he walked back into the living room.

I rolled over from my spot on the floor so I could look at him as he sat down on the couch. "Who was that? What do I need to know?"

Evan sat down and put his phone back into his pocket. "That was the chief. We're gonna go clean up the mess we made in a bit."

"Oh, goddammit, I forgot about that," I groaned, rolling over and plopping out like a starfish.

"Get up," Evan groaned, getting off the couch and coming over to me.

I shook my head and pouted at him. "I don't wanna."

He sighed and lied next to me. "Fine. Then I'm gonna stay right here next to you and we just won't move for the rest of the day."

"I'm cool with that."

"Spencer, get up."

I let out a loud, groaning whine. "But you're lying down now too."

"I only got down on the floor because you were down here, you weirdo," Evan stated. "Now please get up, we have to get ready to go clean the store."

"But it was your fault," I groaned.

Evan sighed and sat up. "I did offer to do it by myself, but you wanted to help."

"Shit," I muttered. He had a point. I did offer to put my name and stuff down for the cleanup detail. It wasn't just Evan's mess to clean up, I mean, I probably spilled way more paint than he did.

Evan stood up and reached a hand down for me. "If you get up right now and get ready, I'll buy you an ice cream cone."

"I'm not a four-year-old child," I barked.

Evan rolled his eyes. "I'll buy you a coffee."

"Okay," I said, reaching up for his hands.

He pulled me upright, which must have taken no effort at all. He quickly pulled me in for a kiss too. Sneaky.

I pulled away from him and motioned to my outfit. "Isn't what I'm wearing good enough?"

"No," Evan said flatly. "You cannot wear a bright pink onesie to go and clean up paint."

"Why the hell can't I?" I asked.

"Because it's weird."

"You're weird!"

"And you don't want to get paint on it, do you?"

"Dammit," I muttered. "You make a good point."

"So go get changed," Evan said.

"Fine," I groaned, walking towards the stairs. "But I'm not gonna enjoy it."

"I don't care if you enjoy it," Evan called after me. "You can change right back into your onesie when we get back home. I promise."

I mumbled something back, but even I don't know what I said. I just kept heading my way up to my room. I made it up the stairs and

19

started peeling the onesie off. Nobody else was upstairs to see my bare bum, so I don't give a rat's ass about my rat ass. Get it?

Anyway, I walked into my room and dressed up in a random shirt and pair of jeans from the closet. I would love to be more organized with my outfits, but Evan's gonna get cranky if I take too long. I tidied up the mess I made while ripping my clothes out of the closet and then grabbed my phone and keys and shit. I threw my hair up in a messy bun and spritzed some perfume around me so I didn't smell like ass and sleep. I grabbed a pair of socks and slipped them on as I walked out of my room. I headed downstairs and into the living room where Evan was *patiently* waiting for me.

"You look good," he said as I walked over to him.

"Oh, shh," I said, sitting down on his lap and kissing him. "I think I'm gonna go take a nap now."

"We're going to clean a floor now," Evan said, standing up and picking me up as he did. Why did I sit on his lap? I knew he was gonna do this too. I am not thinking straight today.

"Nap with me later. I'm feeling super out of it today," I grumbled as he walked us towards the door. "You know, there's something calming about being carried like this."

"Could it be the fact that you don't have to use your legs?"

"Yeah, that might be it."

Evan set me down at the front door and then grabbed my coat and handed it to me. "Let's go get this out of the way."

I took the coat from him and started sliding it on. "Now let's get *you* out of *my* way," I said, pushing him out of the way so that I could slide my feet into my shoes.

"You're a little pushy today."

"Yeah. You made me get out of my onesie. Prepare to die."

Evan shook his head and opened the door. "Let's just get over to the mall so we can get this thing done. I wanna take you out for a coffee."

I smiled. "Nice."

"Okay, let's go," Evan said, walking out the door.

I stepped out and got smacked in the face with the force of a thousand winters' air. It was so goddamn cold out today. "I don't wanna," I yelped.

"What's wrong?"

"It's too cold."

Evan sighed and kissed my forehead. "Even more of a reason to get to the car."

"Right, let's go," I said, waddling my way down the driveway towards his car, well, his SUV.

Evan opened the door for me and headed around to his side as I got in and buckled myself into the seat. I shut the door closed. He got in and started the SUV up and then we were off. He pulled out of the driveway and started towards the mall.

A lot of the roads were cleared up now. Each house we passed by had a massive snowbank at the end of their lawns and all the way up from where they had dumped the snow after shovelling. And so many people still had their Christmas lights up too. It's probably because there's too much snow to bother with trying to take them down, but they still looked funny and out of place.

We started getting close to the mall and that's when the real pang of regret hit me. Why did I volunteer myself for this? We pulled into the mall parking lot and parked close to the front entrance where two cruisers were parked.

"You can make it. The doors are right there," Evan said as he pulled the keys from the ignition.

I shook my head softly. "I don't know, babe, those doors are pretty far away."

"You can do it," Evan said, opening his door. "I believe in you."

"I don't believe in me," I muttered under my breath, pouting slightly as he got out of the car.

He walked over and opened my door. "Let's go."

"Evan," I groaned at him. "I don't wanna. I wanna go home and sleepy time."

"You can do that later." Evan unbuckled my seat belt for me and pulled me out of the car.

"I hate you," I groaned, pushing my coat up and my face down to try to shelter me from the cold wind.

"I know," Evan said, closing the door and leading the way to the front doors of the mall.

"There you are," the chief said as we walked through the doors.

"You'll have to use chippers to get the bulk of the paint now that it's dried to the floor. The rest can be mopped up with paint remover and the works. It's all in the store and ready for you guys."

"Thanks," Evan said. "We'll go get to work." Evan continued to drag me along as I unzipped my coat.

"This is gonna suck," I whined.

"What?" Evan asked. "You're not used to being on your knees?" He smirked at me.

I punched him fairly hard in the ribs. "Don't be an asshole."

"Sorry," he said, still smirking.

"I don't know how I let your good looks woo me into dating you," I said. "You're such a dork."

"Random," Evan said. "And slightly hurtful."

"I mean it in a loving way," I said. "Like, he's a dork, but he's *my* dork. That sort of thing."

Evan scoffed. "You're the dork."

"You!" I shouted back.

"Do we need to have another paint fight or boxing match to settle this, you little dork?" Evan asked, stopping us and looking down at me. His eyes were narrowed on me and his jaw was slightly tensed and I was slightly turned on. Only slightly. The slightest bit of a lot.

"Yes. And I think I need to kick your ass for the final time to really get it through to you," I said, leaning in closer to him, "that you're the dork."

"You wanna catch these hands?"

"Swing first," I said, leaning my chest in. My chest was closer to his stomach though, so this was kind of embarrassing for me. Why do I gotta be so short for?

Evan pushed me back and laughed. "You're not even the least bit scary."

"I'm a fiery little ball of horror," I said, walking after him.

"Your breath in the morning is, but that's about it," he teased. "Besides, I shouldn't be scared of you. Being scared of the person you're dating isn't a very good thing for the relationship, now is it?"

"You make a good point there," I stated. "But consider this for a moment, the fact is, I could kick your ass if I wanted to."

"I'd let you kick my ass."

"Why?" I whined. "I just want the gratification of being able to beat someone up if I ever need to and you're seriously harshing my mellow about it."

"You're five-foot-one, Spencer. I'd be surprised if you could beat up a poodle."

"I guess that makes you a poodle, huh, chump?"

"You're so sassy today," Evan said, turning back to me and picking me up in a hug.

"Let me down so I can beat you up," I whined at him.

He smiled at me and kissed me, all while still walking and hugging me. I was pretty sure we were gonna trip at some point, but he kept his balance. I finally wiggled my way free of his hug as we stopped at the entrance of the hardware store.

"Okay, let's go get cleaning," Evan said, noticing a flatbed cart full of cleaning supplies.

"At least the actual store lights are on this time," I mumbled as Evan started pushing the cart.

I followed him over to where we had made the mess, and it was a big one. There was so much paint strewn and splashed all over the floor. Evan immediately started chipping away at the paint and eventually coaxed me to get on my hands and knees and scrape with him. It took us a few hours to get the bulk of the paint off the floor and into the buckets they had given us. Then we started with cleaning up the rest of the smaller and thinner bits of paint that we couldn't chip off the floor. Even that process took a couple hours to do.

After all was said and done, six hours had passed by. Evan tidied up the cart and cleaning supplies and then we pushed it back out to the main entrance where the chief and a few other officers were talking to what I could only assume was some manager or landlord for the mall.

"All done?" the chief asked, turning to us.

Evan nodded. "All cleaned up."

"Alright, good," the chief said. "Now, this would normally just be classified as volunteer work, but I figured I owe you something a little extra." The chief walked over and handed the two of us two twenties. "It's not much, but it's a thank-you for cleaning up your mess and not completely ruining the mall."

Evan smiled a little. "Thank you, sir."

"Yeah, thank you," I chimed in.

"No problem. Now get out of here, it's already pretty dark out there," the chief said.

"Getting dark and it's only seven," Evan said with a slight scoff. "Winter months, am I right?"

"Cold, long nights," the chief said with a laugh. "If you ever need some crimes to be solved, give us a ring."

"Will do," Evan said with a small laugh, opening the door for me.

"Bye," I said, waving. I zipped up my coat and looked outside. I was not ready to go back out there to that frozen hell.

I led the way back to Evan's SUV, more like ran the way back, actually. I opened the door and hopped in as quickly as I could to get out of the wind. Evan hopped in and turned the car on so I could turn the heaters on full blast.

"I'm so cold," I mumbled through my coat. I had pushed it up in my face so my hot breath could keep my cheeks warm.

"Well, warm the hell up," Evan said. "I don't like my gingersnaps cold."

"Shut up. I'm trying. My hands feel like snowballs with popsicles for fingers," I whined.

"You were outside for literally 30 seconds," Evan said as we started driving away from the mall.

"I don't care. I get cold quickly," I snapped. "So shush up and get me a hot cocoa."

"Bossy."

"I'm not bossy. I just know what I want."

"But you're asking for it in a bossy way because you're not actually asking, you're demanding, which is what makes it bossy," Evan explained.

"Pfft, all well, you know what I mean."

"We should probably grab something for dinner first," Evan suggested, looking over at the time being displayed on his car's radio.

"Food would be a good thing right now, yes," I said. "Let's just go to Burger King or something."

"And then we'll grab a coffee on the way home," Evan said,

turning onto a different street.

"Sounds like a plan, homie."

Evan groaned in disgust. "Don't call me your homie. That's weird."

"Why can't I?"

"I've graduated from homie status, that's why."

I nodded. "Right, right, you're fam status now."

"I'm gonna beat you up," Evan said with a sigh.

"I'd like to see you try."

He sighed and shook his head. "What am I to do with you?"

"Love me and cherish me forever," I replied. "Or just buy me food. I can't talk if I'm eating."

"I think the food one sounds like a good alternative," he said, winking at me.

"That's mean," I barked. "I'm cherishable."

"Charitable? That's cool. I donate to those little coin boxes by the cash registers sometimes," Evan said, smirking at me.

I punched his arm. "You heard what I said, you jackass."

He glanced over and smiled at me. I swear, this guy is gonna drive me crazy someday, but he is a good driver, so at least I'll get there safe.

{Chapter: **Four**}

Well, there go all of my plans for the day. I put my phone back on my nightstand and fell backwards onto my bed. Charlotte just *had* to bail out on me today. I pushed myself back up and grabbed my phone to text Evan. I figured that if my best friend was gonna bail on me, I could use it as an excuse to guilt trip Evan into coming over. I don't feel like being alone all day. It gets boring so fast lately.

I texted him and laid myself back down on my bed, resting my phone on my chest. He better not tell me that he's busy too. Charlotte just wasn't feeling very well, so whatever. She just better not have also gotten Evan sick. After a few moments, my phone did its little beeping and booping. I checked the message, and luckily for me, it was Evan telling me that he could come over today. My hero. I sent him a message back telling him to get his ass over here with a hot coffee and a chocolate bar. God, I really do love having my own personal bitch sometimes.

I got up and put some proper clothes on. I don't think wearing mustard-stained pyjama pants and drool-covered shirts are a good look for me... or for anyone at that. I tidied up my room a little bit while I waited. I even brushed my hair so it looked decently good today. I still put it in a bun, but at least it wasn't as messy a bun as normal. I grabbed my phone and put it in my pocket and then headed downstairs. I figured that he would probably be here soon. Cleaning up and getting dressed took me longer than I expected, probably because I get distracted easily. I sat down on the couch and waited. I waited some more. I did some more waiting. I want you to understand just how annoyed I was with waiting. I was waiting. And I kept waiting. I waited patiently. I waited impatiently. And then he finally texted me to tell me that he was outside.

I got up and opened the door for him. "Bonjour," I said, taking the coffee from the tray in his hands.

"Hi," he said, smiling at me. "Can I come in? Or do you want me to freeze out here?"

"Come in," I groaned, stepping out of the way. I peeled the tab of my coffee open and took a sip. "So how was your night?"

"It was fine," he replied, setting the tray down on the little table by the door and slipping his coat off. "I mean, it could have been better."

"How so?" I asked as I started off toward the living room.

"Well," he said, following me, "I could have been sharing a bed with you, which I wasn't doing, so there's that."

"Aww, babe, you're such a loser."

He shrugged. "Yeah, I know. I'm lame." He sat down next to me, so I lifted my legs over his lap and laid myself backwards against the armrest of the couch.

"You are pretty lame."

"Granted, but you're lame too."

"Also granted, but you're lamer."

He scoffed. "Not in this life."

"You *are* the lame one though."

"Whatever you say, nerd," he said. "Anyway, I've been thinking."

"That's never good."

"Shush," he snapped.

"So what have you been thinking about?"

"I've been thinking that you have a surprising lack of piercings," he stated.

I shrugged. "Yeah? So what? Maybe the thought of having my body get hole-punched is a little scary for me."

"Do you want a piercing though?" he asked.

"Why are you asking me?"

He shrugged. "No reason."

"I do," I replied.

"Good," he said. "I have a coupon for half off of any piercing and I figured you'd look pretty cute with something pierced."

"Like what?"

"It's up to you, ya dingus. It's your body, not mine."

"But you want me to get a piercing?" I asked.

"No, I'm asking you if you want to get one," he stated. "But I do think you'd look cute with a piercing or two. That's just my opinion."

"What should I get done?"

"What do you *want* to get done?"

"Hmm," I said, pausing to think for a moment. "Got it!"

"Alright, shoot. What do you want?"

"I want a nose piercing. Every girl looks good with a nose piercing," I said. "Look at all those Tumblr girls and Scarlett Johansson in that one photo and my friend Mindy's friend Emily. She's really cute, actually. Sorry, off topic, but it's still true."

"So you want a nose piercing?" he asked.

I nodded. "That's what I said, innit, doofus?"

"Okay, drink up."

"What do you mean 'drink up'?"

"Well, we'll head over when you finish your coffee," Evan stated.

I sat upright. "Whoa, whoa, whoa. This is a today thing? I don't even get any time to ponder it?"

"Nope," he said, smirking at me.

"Why not?" I asked.

"We live but a short time, Spencer. Stop living in fear of doing things and making memories," he spoke softly. "Besides, what's the worst thing that could happen? You get left with a little pinhole scar that won't even be noticeable unless you're right up in your face."

"I don't know. I still don't think I'm grown up enough to do this.

"You're pretty mature," Evan said. "So yes or no?"

"Ugh, let me think some more."

"Come on, Spencer. Do it, Spencer. You know you want to."

"I know that I want to punch you," I snapped, lying back down on the armrest of the couch. "You should gimme a foot massage or something while we wait." I took a sip from my coffee and raised an eyebrow at Evan.

"But they stink," he whined.

"They do not!" I shouted. "I am utterly offended that you would say such a thing."

"I'll give you a back massage instead," he offered.

"I don't know. How will I drink my coffee if I had to lay on my stomach?"

"Sit in between my legs and I can do it while you sit."

"Let's go up to my room so I can remove my shirt while you do it, then."

He winked. "Right."

I sat up and punched his arm. "No boob touching… yet."

"Yet?"

"If you do a good job, I'll let you have a little boob touching," I told him as I stood up from the couch. "Now let's go." He stood up and followed me up to my room. I took my shirt off and shut my door closed.

"I'm blinded," he teased, shielding his eyes from my pale stomach.

"Piss off," I said, making an angry face at him.

"Sorry," he said, sitting on my bed. "Now come sit here." He motioned the section of bed between his legs.

I sighed and took my seat. "No lotion this time, just go in dry."

"Always," he said. He clicked his tongue, so I elbowed him gently in the ribs.

"Don't be a nasty, ya nasty."

"Sorry," he said, taking a sip of his coffee. He put the coffee on my nightstand and then went to work on massaging my back. Even while sitting up, this massage was still so heavenly. And his hands were warm from holding his coffee cup.

"Where'd you leave that tray?" I asked, taking a sip of my coffee.

"On your coffee table," he replied. "Was that bad?"

"Well, it could be worse, so no."

"Better sip that coffee quicker. I wanna go poke a hole in your cute little nose."

"I don't think anyone has ever called my nose cute."

"Mm, well, I just did."

I rolled my eyes. "No shit. What makes it cute?"

"It looks like a Scarlett Johansson nose," he said. "When you brought her up downstairs, that's what got me thinking."

"All this talk about my nose today is making me feel weird," I stated.

"Sorry."

I took a sip of my coffee. "Ah, whatever, it's fine."

We didn't say anything after that. I just let him massage my back and he let me enjoy the massage and coffee. It's nice that I can sit in silence with him and it not be insanely awkward or jarring. After a while, I did end up sipping the last of my coffee and he stopped massaging my back, which sucked, because I was enjoying it.

"Time to go," he said, pushing me off the bed so I would stand up.

I let out a groan as I bent over to pick up my shirt. "I don't wanna leave my warm house."

"We'll go out and poke holes in your face and then grab something to eat and then we can come back here and watch TV or something. Okay?"

I nodded, slipping my shirt back on. "Sounds good. Just make sure you keep me warm. A cold Spencer is a cranky Spencer."

"Any Spencer is a cranky Spencer," Evan said with a scoff. "Have you ever met you? You're very... *feisty*."

"Feisty is cute," I said, furrowing my eyebrows a little.

"Yeah, and you are pretty cute," he said, standing up and kissing my forehead. "Now let's get going?"

I smiled and blushed slightly. "Okay." I walked out of my room with Evan close behind me. I led him back down the stairs and to the front door.

Evan opened the door. "After you, my fair lady."

I stuck my tongue out at him as I walked past him and outside into the cold winter air. "It's so cold out."

"I know," Evan said, walking out after me and closing the door. "It's wintertime. It's usually cold during winter months here,

Spencer."

"Don't be a smartass," I barked as I put my hand on the handle of his SUV's passenger side door. "Now, unlock your car so I can get in. I'm cold."

"You've been outside for 30 seconds, Spencer," Evan groaned, clicking the button on his key fob to unlock the doors.

"I know," I said, opening the door. "And I get cold fast. You still need to learn to deal with it."

"I'll keep you warm," he said, getting in on the other side. "Just not right now."

"Then what's the point?" I asked, closing the door and buckling in my seat belt.

"When we get back here later," Evan said, glancing over at me, "I'll warm you up."

"I won't be cold later, I'll be in pain because of the hole in my face."

"It's not gonna hurt that bad," he said, pushing the key into the ignition and turning it.

"I'm a little baby though."

"You'll be fine," he said as we backed out of the driveway. "And besides, the pain is worth the gain."

I sighed and lolled my head back against the headrest, okay, barely against the headrest. It sucks being short sometimes. We drove all the way across town to this little tattoo and piercing shop that was squished between a supermarket and a dollar store. Evan led me into the place, but everyone was busy, so we just decided to take a seat on one of the couches placed in the front area of the store. For a shitty couch, it was pretty comfortable.

"Nervous?" Evan asked, sitting next to me.

I nodded. "Just a little."

"It's okay," he said, wrapping his hand over mine. "I'll hold your hand the whole time."

"Promise?"

He smiled softly. "Promise."

"My hands are probably a little clammy," I said. "Sorry."

"It's fine."

"I'm such a wuss," I mumbled. "Why am I such a wuss?"

"It's part of your charm."

"Man, people say that about anything. I could shit myself and say that it was part of my charm."

He shrugged. "Well, I mean… it would be, wouldn't it?"

"How?"

"Maybe you would remind people of a baby or something."

"I swear to God if you say it," I muttered.

"What? Say what? That you're small enough to be a baby?" he asked, a big stupid smile on his face. "'Cause I totally wasn't thinking that."

"I hate you," I muttered.

"No, you don't."

I glanced at him and cocked an eyebrow at him. "The day is still young, Evan."

"Are you guys here for tattoos?" a lady asked, walking out of the back of the shop.

"Uh, no," Evan said. "We're here to get gingerbread's nose pierced."

"Okay, well, shouldn't be too long until someone's freed up," the lady said. "I'll let them know." She walked back to the back of the shop.

I smacked Evan in the arm. "Don't call me that in public, you dingus."

"Why not?"

"It's embarrassing for me."

"But, Spencer, every couple needs cute pet names for each other," Evan stated. "I don't make the rules."

"Well, you don't have to follow them either."

"I do. It's the code."

"What code?"

"The boyfriend code."

"That's not a real thing," I said.

"It's a thing."

"It's not."

"Spencer, please," he said, glaring at me. "It's a thing."

"What do I see in you?" I muttered to myself.

He shrugged. "Beats me." He must have heard me. Oops.

"Did you hear that?" I said, awkwardly laughing it off. "Anyway, what are we gonna do after this? I think you said something about lunch. How about pizza?"

"Let's see what you think in a little bit," Evan said.

"Why?"

"Because I want burgers, so I want you to just mull it over for a little while."

"Oh, now I want burgers," I groaned. "You're an asshole."

"My plans usually work, eh?"

"Shut up. You know I'm hungry, so anything you say is gonna sound like a great idea to me," I whined.

"Are you ready?" the lady asked, walking back out.

I let out a low groaning noise and stood up. "Yeah. I'm as ready as I'm ever gonna be."

And then we went into the back and I signed some forms and they made sure I was eighteen. God knows I only looked like I was twelve at this height. The lady then passed me along to another girl, a much more heavily tattooed and pierced girl sitting in a little cubicle thing in the back. I looked around at the pictures and things on her desk. It was kinda cool how this was her own personalized workspace.

Evan pulled up a chair next to the one I was sat down in and he kept his word. He held my hand the entire time I was in there. I could live a thousand lifetimes and still not deserve someone as amazing as Evan.

After it was all said and done, there was a new little feature to my face. I nice little silvery-gold ring in my nostril. I wonder how my parents are gonna react. I really didn't think about that.

I turned around in my chair to face Evan. "So how do I look?"

He smiled and squeezed my hand lightly. "Beautiful."

{Chapter: **Five**}

I walked over to the couch and sighed at Evan for waking me up before nine in the morning. He should know that I hate waking up before noon most of the time. I sat down next to him in a begrudging silence as I put my socks onto my feet. I was still half asleep and still very grumpy about it.

"You have the tiniest feet ever for an eighteen-year-old girl," Evan said jokingly as I put my second sock on.

"It makes it easier to stick my foot up your ass when you piss me off," I grumbled.

"God, you are one cranky little gingerbread girl in the morning," he said, trying to provoke me a little more.

I let out an almost animalistic groan. "I will kill you. Shut up."

"Do you want me to buy you a coffee?"

"Now you're talking my kind of language," I said, turning to him. "You're also gonna need to get me a bagel. I'm starving."

"Anything for my girl," he said, standing up from the couch. "Now, can we get a move on? I've never been late to a treatment before and I don't wanna start now."

"Why the hell did I volunteer myself for this?" I whined as I stood up.

"Because you're the best kind of person," Evan said, cupping my cheeks and pinching them slightly. "You're just too good, too pure for this world."

"Honestly, if you wanna keep *your* face looking as cute as it does, I'd suggest you remove your hands from *my* face."

"A temper as fiery as her hair, aww," Evan said with a smirk.

I scowled at him as he let go of my face. "I will end you."

"End me later," he said. "We've got things to do."

I followed Evan to the door and we got our shoes and coats on. I followed him out to his SUV and we drove to the closet coffee shop so I could get some caffeine into my system. If I didn't get coffee, I'd have been so cranky. And thank God for the bagel. If I had to go on an empty stomach, I think I might have lost my mind. We eventually arrived at the hospital where he bought me an iced lemonade to, and I quote, "Keep you quiet." I was okay with that. I feel bad that he has to deal with me most of the time, but at least sometimes I'm cool.

"This is cold," I groaned, getting a wave of brain freeze. "Ugh, why did I let you buy me this?"

"Because a Spencer with something to drink is a happy Spencer," Evan replied.

"I should put some of this in your IV needle things," I said with a pout.

"That wouldn't be very lame nerd of you."

"You're a lame nerd," I whined. "Why did you have to schedule your treatment so early for?"

"I don't like being here in the evenings," he replied. "The evening is when all the adults come in for treatments and it's when the hospital is creepy because it's dark outside."

"You don't drive yourself home, do you?" I asked.

He went to speak, but he instantly shut his mouth.

"Oh, my God, you do!" I shouted. "You're not supposed to drive anything when you've taken any of these drugs, you idiot. Have you never heard of safety precautions?"

"They don't affect me… much."

I slapped his chest. "No driving on drugs, mister."

"Jeez, fine," he said, rubbing his chest where I had hit him. "You're a little party pooper sometimes."

"I'm a party pooper because I care about your safety?" I asked. "Man, I'd sure make a terrible mother."

He gave me a blank stare. "Okay, moving on."

I pouted. "Whatever."

"How's your day been?"

I groaned. "You've been with me since I woke up. *You* woke me up, remember? It happened, like, an hour ago."

"Yeah, but I don't know what you think about stuff. I'm not a mind reader, Spencer."

"I'm still cranky and I still have sleep in my eyes," I muttered. "Does that answer your question?" I started rubbing at my eyes to get rid of the remaining sandy eye boogers.

"Just wait till that caffeine kicks in fully."

"That's not gonna be a good thing for you," I said.

"Why's that?"

"Because then I'll be full of energy to kick your ass with," I told him. "Duh."

"Pfft, even if you were fully charged, I could still kick your ass," Evan said with a slight scoff and air of arrogance in his voice. "Let's be real here."

"Shut up."

"You can't make me."

I scowled at him and tried to stare him down, but he just stared blankly back at me. I wasn't very scary. I should go to the gym every day for a year and bulk myself up and then beat him up. Yeah! I'd be scary then.

"You're the cutest girl ever," Evan said, smiling softly.

I lessened my scowl and blushed slightly. "Thanks?"

"You're welcome."

"Pretty random time to compliment me."

He shrugged. "You were scowling at me."

"Yeah, so?" I asked. "That's what I do. I scowl at you."

"Well, I figured you could use some red in your cheeks."

I sighed and rested back in my chair. "You're a dork, you know that?"

He kicked my leg lightly a few times until I glanced over at him. "You're the dork, dork."

"Real original," I said, pushing his leg down.

"Well, I thought so," he said. "Anyway, my birthday is coming up and I was wondering where I should take you for it."

"Um, I don't think that's how birthdays work," I said. "It should be me taking you somewhere, you know, since it's *your* birthday and all."

"Right, but you're my gift, so where do you think we should go?"

I blushed a little more. I was a gift, and a damn good one at that. "I don't know," I shrugged. "Somewhere nice."

"Wow, that helps. Thanks."

"I seriously don't know. You can surprise me, okay?" I told him. "Also, what do you want for your birthday?"

"I don't know. I have you already, so I think I'm good."

"Shut up. What do you want?"

"You," he said flatly.

"You have me," I groaned. "Pick something else. Pick a material object that I have to go out and buy for you."

"A clone of you?"

I leaned in and started shaking him. "What do you want for your birthday, you stupid idiot?"

He grabbed my wrists and pulled my hands from him. "I don't really want anything."

"Why not?" I whined, sitting back down in my chair.

"I dunno."

"Ugh. You're so difficult," I said with a soft sigh. "Also, I have a birthday coming up as well."

"Oh, yeah? When's yours?"

"February," I replied. "You?"

"Same."

"Day?" I asked.

"The sixth, you?"

I paused for a moment to take in this weird coincidence. "The sixth," I replied slowly.

"Seriously?" he asked.

I nodded. "Seriously."

"We share a birthday? That's the coolest shit. Wow."

"I knew there was a reason I hated my birthday," I muttered.

"Hey, I heard that, you asshole," Evan barked.

I smirked at him. "Good, you were supposed to."

"You're a jerk," he said. "So what should do on *our* birthday, then?"

"You can think of something now," I told him. "Since *you're* taking *me* out for *my* birthday."

"I'm sure I'll think of something cool to do."

"You could do me," I said, winking at him playfully.

He looked me over and shook his head. "Nah."

I sighed. "You're an asshole."

"Yeah, I know," he said, resting in his chair.

"Are you almost done? I'm hungry," I whined.

"Take a nap," Evan suggested. "That'll help you pass the time. I can wake you up when I'm done."

"That would be nice of you," I said, starting to curl up halfway in the chair so I could fall asleep. "Just, like, don't do anything to my face when I'm asleep. I don't draw my eyebrows on and I don't want you to do it either."

"But you'd look good with some Sharpie eyebrows, babe," he joked. "You don't have *that* much time to nap, so if you're gonna, get to it."

"Piss off, I'm napping," I barked at him as I closed my eyes and drifted to sleep.

It's amazing how fast I can fall asleep sometimes. I'm just awake and conscious one second and then, bang, I'm sound asleep the next. What sucks about napping is that I never dream. And I mean, come on, dreaming is half the fun of sleeping, right? Right?

I eventually felt Evan poking at my face and stomach as I opened my eyes and seen him leaning over me. I let out a yawn and rubbed my eyes as I sat upright in the chair.

"Oh, she lives," Evan said, smiling softly. "It's time to go check up with my doctor. You can come in if you want or you can stay here and get yourself awake. The choice is yours."

"I'll come with you," I said, standing up.

"I'm the one who's drugged up and yet you're acting all wonky," Evan said, helping me stand straight. "Let's go, gingersnap."

Evan grabbed my hand and we started walking after a doctor. I guess this was his doctor. Weird. I didn't picture him having a young blond doctor. I thought he would have some wise, old, balding doctor. It could have maybe even been a balding woman doctor. Can women even bald? Whatever, that's not the point of this story.

We walked into an office. It was a typical boring office. There were degrees on the wall and certifications and pictures and motivational quotes and shit. This was the exact same as every other doctor's office I've ever been to. Try to tell me it's a lie. I dare you.

"Mr. Fuller," the doctor said as she sat down at her desk.

"It's Evan," he said, pulling a second chair out for me.

I took my seat as he took his and I kept my mouth shushed and my eyes trained on him. This wasn't my appointment. This wasn't my doctor. Come to think of it, I don't know why I bothered to come in.

"You tell me that every time, but I'm so used to just calling people by their last name like that," she replied. "Anyway, we got the results from your last scan."

"And?"

"Well, they're not good per se," the doctor replied, her face dropping the air of joy it had. She glanced over to me and then back at Evan.

Evan sighed. "You can just tell us. I'll end up telling her regardless."

And to save you from all the medical talk and the beating around the bush and the next steps of treatment and whatnot, I'll sum things up for you. The cancer was more aggressive than they thought and it was looking like it had spread pretty quickly. When I heard that, I zoned out and my hands got all clammy and I felt like I couldn't breath. It felt like there were ants under my skin trying to dig themselves out. It just was not a pleasant feeling. And that's only what I felt. I couldn't even begin to imagine what Evan was thinking or feeling. He was getting more confident about beating it by the day, and I think this hit him as a major setback for his morale.

After the appointment with his doctor, Evan rushed me to his car without saying a word. He had just taken my hand and led me back to the parking lot. We got in the car and he just sat with his arms crossed on the steering wheel and resting his head on them.

"Hey," I said after a few seconds of silence. "You, uh, you okay?"

Evan stayed silent and put the key in the ignition and turned on the car. "Let's just go get something to eat, okay?"

"Yeah, sure," I said. I guess he didn't wanna talk about it right now. I think I know Evan good enough by this point to know that he'll talk about whatever's bothering him when he's ready.

"What did you wanna get to eat?" Evan asked as we pulled up to the exit of the parking lot.

"I don't know, up to you."

"Don't give me that shit. Just tell me what you want."

"I really don't care."

"Let's go for Italian," he said as we turned out of the parking lot.

I looked out the window and watched the buildings slowly turn into streaks of grey as we drove by them. Evan clicked the radio on and I just zoned out again. I think we both sort of just zoned out. I mean, Evan just got hit with the worst kind of news, and it shook the both of us. We stayed quiet the entire drive to the restaurant. He parked and we got out of the car and walked up to the doors. He held the door open as I walked in and then we went to take our seats. I love restaurants that don't require reservations. We ordered some root beer and then sat in silence as we read the menu and waited for the waiter to come back around. It's weird, huh? We wait for the waiter, like, wouldn't that make us the waiters? Whatever.

"I think I want the manicotti," I said, putting the menu down.

"I think I'll have the same," Evan said, putting down his menu as well.

I took a quick sip of my root beer. "Why's that?"

"It makes it easier." He shrugged. "And manicotti is pretty good."

"Are you okay?" I asked. I couldn't take his passive sadness anymore. It was clearly bothering him.

"No, I'm okay."

"What?"

"I'm fine," he said.

"But you said no?" I questioned.

"I don't think I really wanna talk about this, Spencer," Evan stated. "And that's saying a lot, because you're still the only person who knows about the cancer thing. I just want some time to think about it first."

I nodded. "Okay. I understand. Just know that I'm here for you, dork."

"I know. And when I'm ready to talk about stuff, I have your number in my speed dial."

"Pfft, liar," I said with a scoff. "Nobody uses speed dial anymore."

"You know what I meant, dumbass."

"Don't get sassy with me," I said. "I'm just trying to be real with you. It's 2016, not the '90s. Nobody uses speed dial."

"Well, now I should start using it just to spite you."

"You probably would too."

He nodded. "Well, it's a minor thing that'll annoy your postmodernist ass, so yeah, you better believe I would."

"Pretend to be nice to me, the waitress is coming," I said in a hushed tone as the waitress walked over.

She smiled at the two of us and got her pen ready. "Can I take your order?"

{Chapter: **Six**}

Evan stopped the car in front of the back entrance to my wing of the college. It was time to go back to school, not like I really wanted to, but also, not like I had a choice in the matter. I paid my tuition, god-dammit. I have to go.

"Here we are," Evan said, turning his car off.

"Yeah," I sighed. "I can just wait with you until your class starts."

Evan shook his head. "That would make you an hour late to your new class. And we can't have that, now can we?"

"You'll be done when I am, right?"

Evan shrugged. "Probably. I can't see why I wouldn't be done quickly. It's the first day. We're just gonna go over what to expect in the next coming weeks and stuff like that. Kinda stupid because if you're gonna allot us three hours of class time, you should use it," he rambled. "I don't care if it's only the first day. I paid my tuition, god-dammit."

"You'll be waiting here with a coffee for me, right?"

Evan sighed. "Probably not."

"Why not?"

"I have to rush over from class to pick your ass up. I don't think I have time to stop to get you a coffee," he stated. "We can get you a coffee before we go back to your place later."

"Sounds like a plan." I rested my hand on the car door's handle. "I must go. My prison awaits me."

"Ah, come on. Smile," Evan said, smiling softly at me. "You get to see all your classmates and stuff again."

I shot him a deadpanned look and sighed. "Mm, just the pep talk I need."

"I thought it would pep you up." Evan's smile widened a little. "Now go in there and learn some stuff."

"You're starting to sound like a daddy and not like a *daddy*," I deadpanned as I opened the door to get out.

Evan scoffed. "You killed the mood. Come here." He pulled my face over and kissed me softly. "I'll see you after class. You be good now."

"Yeah, yeah," I said, rolling my eyes and stepping out of the SUV. I grabbed my bag from the floor of the passenger seat and slung it around my shoulder as I shut the car door. I turned and looked up at the college as I heard Evan driving away. Man, I didn't really miss this place as much as I thought I did. I guess it was kind of cool to be back, like Evan said, I get to see my classmates again. Some of them were cool and some of them were lame. But generally, it's an arts program, so the schooling isn't that hard. It's just the coming-to-school thing that really gets your girl right in the chest.

I walked through the set of double doors near where Evan had dropped me off. I wandered through the halls a little. It was pretty crowded in here today. It made me feel even smaller than I usually do. There are way too many tall people here. Stop being so tall, damn you. I did eventually make my way to my class of the day. I liked college for this reason: We only had one or two classes a day. And today, I had only had this one. And Evan only had one class too, which just so happened to be an hour after mine. And lucky little Charlotte gets the day off today, so she'll be at my house waiting for Evan and I to return back there in a few hours.

I went to my class and sat bored as hell for the next two hours or so. To be honest, I just couldn't stop thinking about hanging out with Evan later. I think I was developing into a very clingy girlfriend, but I doubt he would care. He's pretty clingy too.

I waited outside after my class and sat down on a bench, reading one of the books that I kept in my backpack for just such an occasion. I waited for a half an hour or so for Evan's SUV to pull up. He honked a few times so I would look up and notice that it was him. I quickly put the bookmark in the book and put it back into my backpack and then I walked over and got in his car.

"Have a good first class back?" Evan asked as I buckled myself into the seat.

I shrugged. "I guess it was okay. How about yours?"

"It was just dandy," he replied with a small smile.

"I have a question, actually," I said.

"Hmm?" Evan asked as we started driving. "What is it?"

"You remember how you told me you had that Christmas Eve date or whatever? Yeah, you said you had it with my friend Charlotte. What gives? Shouldn't you two have some lingering hatred or bitterness or something?"

Evan laughed softly. "Right. I hit her up after we got out. I just explained to her what happened and we kinda laughed it off. It's no hard feelings. I told her it was a good thing she did what she did, because if she didn't, I might never have met you," he explained. "The universe works in strange ways, Spencer."

"So it's just done with? Just like that? No bitterness?"

He shook his head. "Why would there be? We both agree that the way things worked out was the way that was best for all of us."

"But she still stood you up," I reminded him.

"Yeah, and I called her a bitch and then thanked her for doing what she did. Like I said, if she didn't do that to me, then you and I would never have met. And that would be a sad, sad world to live in," Evan stated.

"So there's really no harsh feelings between you two?"

He shook his head. "Not even a little. We're beyond that."

"So everything can go on as normal?"

He nodded. "Yeah. Just don't bring it up around the two of us. That'd just be making things awkward for the sake of making things awkward."

"I like being awkward sometimes."

"Yeah, you usually are. Now, how about we get a coffee and get home?"

I smiled. "Yes. Just, yes."

"How much coffee do you need?"

"I don't know," I said, pausing to think for a minute. "A lot."

"I'll get you an extra large, okay?"

I smiled, leaned over, and kissed his cheek. "You da best, babe."

"Right," Evan said as we pulled to a stop at a red light. "So, what should we go do later though? Are we just gonna sit around your place or do you wanna actually go and do something worthwhile?"

"You can let me nap on you," I suggested. "That'd be worth-while."

"It would be for you, yeah. What about for me? Hmm?"

I cocked an eyebrow at him. "Um, hello? You get to be slept on by me, your cute little girlfriend, your adorable petite gingersnap."

"Hey, you're referencing yourself using my nickname," Evan said with a small smile stretching along his face. "This is such a monu-mental step forward for the two of us."

"Oh, shut up."

He smirked back at me as we started driving off again. "Oh, hey, I got you something earlier. I needed something to do when I was waiting to go to class."

"What'd you get me?"

"Well, I ordered something for you," he said, reaching over and opening the glove compartment. He pulled out a little slip of paper and handed it to me.

"What's this for?" I asked, looking at it.

"It's an order for a custom sweater."

"From the Bookstore?"

Evan nodded. "I went in and ordered one with your nickname written on the back of it."

"Does it say *Design & Arts* on the front?"

He nodded. "Yeah. It's custom school sweater. Be happy. It cost, like, 55 bucks."

"You spent 55 bucks to get a sweater for me that has *Gingersnap* on the back of it?" I asked. "Why?"

"'Cause you're my girl," he said with a dorky smile on his face.

My stomach did a bunch of flips and stuff. I was *his* girl. Damn,

45

what a good feeling that was to hear though. Even though I already knew I was, it still gives me a rush of endorphins to hear him say it, especially like that.

"It should come in at some point in the next month. They didn't really give me any firm date, just that it would be here in two to four weeks."

I smiled and looked at the order slip. "Can't wait to wear it all the time, to be honest."

"I hope I get the call to pick it up before your birthday though," he said, taking the slip back from me and putting it back in his glove compartment.

"You mean *our* birthday?"

"Yeah, but you're important to me, so your birthday succeeds my birthday in terms of calendar space."

I scoffed. "Nah."

He mockingly scoffed back. "Yeah."

"Shut up."

He rested his hand on my thigh and smirked. He didn't say anything. He just smirked. At least he listened to me though.

"Okay, you can talk again," I told him.

"Okay, good. I've got some important news for you." I cocked an eyebrow and tilted my head a little as he said, "I want a hazelnut coffee."

"Oh, shit, yes, get me one of those," I said, noticing that we were turning into the drive-thru of a Tim Hortons.

"You want a double-double with hazelnut, then?"

I nodded and smiled. "Yes. Please. Yes." I probably resembled a puppy at times. I get too excited for coffee, like a puppy does for their favourite toy or for going on a walk.

"I can tell I'm gonna need a coffee to deal with you all day," he said with a soft sigh.

"Oh, hush up." I sat back in my seat and stayed quiet while he ordered us our coffees. And he even got one for that bitch Charlotte that stood him up. How nice of him, right? After that, we went over to my house. Charlotte had already made it here 'cause, like I said, she had the day off today. I led the way to the house since Evan was carrying the tray of coffees for me. I opened the door and stepped inside. After Evan got in, I shut the door behind him and took my coffee from the tray as I slipped my shoes off.

"Charlotte," I called out. "I'm hella home."

"Hella go away," her voice shouted back.

"Basement," I said to Evan as he slipped his shoes off.

I walked off towards the basement and went down the stairs to see Charlotte lounging on the couch down there. "Way to make yourself at home here."

"This *is* my home, Dill Pickle," she said with a smile, sitting up so I could sit next to her. "So anyway, how was your first day of the new semester?"

"It was aight."

"Aight?" Evan asked, walking down the stairs. "It was more than aight. She was the happiest little gingerbread girl in the world, yes, she was."

"I hate both of you so much," I groaned.

"Why?" Evan asked, sitting down one the recliner next to the couch. He reached over and handed Charlotte her coffee and then set the tray down on the table.

"I don't know," I said with a small sigh.

"Anyway," Charlotte said with a slight huff, "how was your first class back, Evan?"

"It was alright," he replied. "Kinda boring, but that's to be expected either way with business stuff."

"Amen. I took a business class in high school once," Charlotte stated, stopping to take a sip from her coffee. "And needless to say, but it was the worst experience of my life. Almost as bad as the rock climbing in freshman year gym class."

"Yeah, I don't recommend business if you're someone that gets bored easily. I just tend to zone out half of the time."

"That's bad," I chimed in.

"Oh, hush it," Evan said. "You little art kids get to do all your fun stuff while all the rest of us are out there learning and studying and working our asses off with boring and monotonous essays and studies and textbooks. All you art kids get to paint and sculpt things. Like, when you guys are finished, you get a masterpiece to look at. When we're finished, we get to stare at a computer screen waiting to see if we managed to do enough writing and research to warrant us anything above a B."

"Wow, sounds rough, bro," I teased, taking a sip of my coffee. "But us art kids don't have it so easy either. We have to spend days and nights working on things that never feel like they're good enough. We're constantly worried about being judged by our peers and having them internally laugh at us if our work isn't as good as other people's. We stay up all night trying to get lines just right in some painting that's only worth five percent of our mark. I think I get where you're coming from, especially since we *barely* have any marking criteria, so we never know if we're doing what we're actually supposed to be doing."

"And I'm Charlotte!" Charlotte butted in.

"You ruined the mood," I barked at her.

She shrugged. "You guys were getting all preachy about school. I don't wanna think about school in off-school hours."

"Get her, gingersnap," Evan said, as if he were prodding a dog to attack. "Get her, girl. Don't take that from no backwater blond."

"Hey!" Charlotte shouted. "You're a backwater blond."

"I'm not even blond," Evan said, pointing to his head. "Got dark hair, mate. You lose."

"From the amount of stupidity that you both have, I'd say that you two are the blond ones."

"Hey, what?" I asked.

"Well," Charlotte said, "you guys would have to be pretty ditzy to not just open up a phone charger and get your rescue done a little quicker."

Evan scoffed. "Oh, please. We forgot."

"He didn't forget. He was just blinded by my beauty," I chimed in.

Charlotte snorted slightly. "Paleness."

"Whatever," I said with a sigh.

"I'm just saying," Charlotte said, raising her hands in surrender. "I just think y'all coulda gotten out of the mall a little quicker if you just charged your phone and called someone."

"Yeah, we would have, but we were busy having hella fun," I stated. "*Without* you." I stuck my tongue out at her to further prove my point.

"You are such a little baby," Charlotte said jokingly. "I guess I would have done the same thing in your situation though. It's not like you get an entire mall to yourself every day."

"Exactly!" Evan and I shouted at the same time.

{Chapter: **Seven**}

As the days snuck into weeks, everything seemed to be going swimmingly for Evan and I. He had dropped me off at my house from school earlier and didn't say much else, which was weird, because he's usually pretty talkative. He's probably just going to prep things for tomorrow. Because in, I looked over to my clock, less than ten minutes it would be our birthdays.

I let out a soft sigh as I fell down onto my bed. At least I didn't have school tomorrow, so I guess I could stay up and wait for Evan to call me at midnight like the dork he is. I watched the clock as the last few minutes slowly ticked by. I was almost doing a countdown in my own head in the tiniest bit of excitement for my birthday. As the clock clicked over to 00:00, I started hearing some small clicks on my window. I cocked an eyebrow as I sat up and looked over to my bedroom window. "The shit?" I muttered as the clicking on the window kept on going. It sounded like single hailstones or something. I walked over turned on the lamp that was on my desk near my window. I pulled open the window. Yes, I had one of those old-school windows that had the thick wooden frames and, yes, they were painted white. I peered out into the backyard and seen Evan standing in the dim light supplied from the back windows of my house.

"Get down here," he whispered up at me.

"Evan!" I murmured. "It is midnight! What the hell are you doing?"

"We're going on an adventure," he replied. "Come on." He turned around and then lifted something up to my window. It was a ladder. This guy actually brought a ladder with him to sneak me out. Wow.

"Why?" I asked, steadying the ladder to my window.

"Why?" he mocked. "Come on, Spencer. Come live a little with me. I'm not gonna get you killed. Promise."

I rolled my eyes. "Jesus." I ran my fingers through my hair and sighed. "Okay, fine. Give me a minute to put pants and socks on."

He smirked up at me in his victory, but I figured that I shouldn't fight it. He would probably just climb in my window and snatch me up.

I quietly started grabbing clothes from my closet to change. It was pretty cold out tonight, so I obviously needed a coat. Thankfully, I had an old winter jacket in my closet. I slipped into some jeans and a long-sleeve shirt. I pulled two socks onto my feet, not like they matched. My socks rarely match anymore. I slipped the coat on and then pulled my hair into a small, messy bun. I grabbed a beanie and covered it. I needed to dress warm. I'm a soft and sleepy creature this February eve.

I walked back over to the window and shut the lamp off as I pocketed my phone and keys, just in case. "Okay, hold the ladder," I told Evan.

He nodded and held the ladder firmly to the wall of my house as I reached my one leg over the window ledge. I pushed the window all the way up and ducked under it so I could get out. I gained my balance on the ladder and then softly closed the window before heading down to meet Evan on the ground.

He smiled at me as he moved away from the ladder. "You're a bona fide badass now."

"Nah, I've snuck out before," I said, fixing my beanie.

Evan handed me a pair of boots. "I know you don't have boots in your room." He looked down to my feet. "And socks aren't enough to keep you warm."

"See," I said, taking the boots from him, "this is why we're a good team. I consistently mess up and forget things, and then you always got my back." I pulled the boots onto my feet and it already started to make a huge difference for the temperature of my leg hands.

"Yeah. I have a brain. I know that feet get cold in the snow and on cold concrete, but you didn't think of that, did you?"

I scoffed. "You didn't tell me that you were going to make me sneak out with you tonight."

"You should have guessed that," he said, grabbing me and hugging me. "Happy birthday, gingersnap."

I groaned a little as he picked me up. "Happy birthday to you too, Evansnap."

"You look very pretty tonight," he said, kissing my forehead as he put me down.

"I do?" I asked. "I mean... I, *I do*," I said, straightening my posture and trying to sound a little bit more confident in myself.

Evan smirked at me. "You're cute."

"So, you're the big one-nine," I said, nudging his ribs.

He nodded. "And so are you."

"Eww," I said. "I'm still a little princess. I don't know what the hell you're talking about, bubs."

"Despite what fairy tales tell you, princesses have to grow up at some point too, and that starts tonight for you," Evan said, grabbing the ladder. "Now help me pull this down without making a giant bang."

"Fine," I grumbled, grabbing and holding on to the bottom part of the ladder as he worked his way up to the lowering top part of the ladder.

He rested the ladder down on the ground and let out a loud sigh of relief. "That's one chore down."

"Rescuing me is not a chore."

"I didn't mean that part," Evan snapped. "Now let's get going. I assume that the *princess* wants her coffee."

"You would be assuming right," I said, smirking slightly at him. "Lead the way, my knight in shining armour."

"I'm in a coat," Evan muttered back at me as we walked to the back of my backyard.

"Where are we going?" I asked, following him rather sceptically.

Evan turned to me as we reached the back fence. "Well, I couldn't very well just park in front of your house. I mean, I could, but clichés and something."

"I'm too short to hop this fence."

He smiled and got down on one knee, cupping his hands. "I'll help you. I got you. Remember?"

"If I fall and get hurt, you have to kiss my booboos better."

"I hope you fall on your crotch, then," he said with a wink. "Now up and over. Come on."

"I'm trying," I whined, jumping from Evan's hands and grabbing the top part of the fence. "Push me over."

"I'll try," he said sarcastically. He lifted me up and then I swung myself over the fence and landed on my feet with a soft plop on the other side. It was just an empty side street on this side, no houses other than the backyards of the ones from my street. I looked up and down as Evan hopped over the fence. I saw his SUV parked a few dozen feet down the street from where we were now.

"See, you're fine," Evan said, hugging my from behind. "Now, let's go get into some trouble."

"No, babe, no, I need coffee."

"I'll get you a coffee," he said, walking towards his car and pulling out his keys from his pocket. "And then we're gonna go get into some trouble."

"No, babe, no, I'm a soft and sleepy creature. I cannot go to jail. I cannot be arrested. I would be made a prison bitch."

"Right, yeah. We'll go get into some minor trouble punishable by community service and/or parental scolding," Evan stated. "Is that better?"

"Not a whole lot better, but I guess that beats 25-to-life."

"That's the attitude I'm looking for," Evan said as he unlocked his car with the key fob.

I walked over and hopped into the passenger seat. I'm really glad that I'm the only person who he drives around. I never have to fix the passenger seat of his car to my liking because I'm usually the only one in it anyway. "So, why did you wanna sneak me out of my house?"

"Aesthetic," he shrugged, turning the key in the ignition.

I sighed. "You're a dingus."

"We're going to that little coffee shop on the outside of town, okay?"

"Why all the way out there?"

"It's on the way," Evan replied.

I sighed as Evan turned the car around and started driving off. "Tonight's gonna be a long night, isn't it?"

Evan chuckled softly. "Yeah, probably."

***

We pulled into the parking lot of the coffee shop and Evan shut the SUV off. We sat for a moment as he rifled through the glove compartment, looking for something.

"Whatcha looking for?" I asked.

He glanced and smirked at me. "Wallet."

"Here," I said, grabbing it from right beside where his hand was and giving it to him. "Are you blind?"

He took it and gave me a dirty look. "Don't get sassy with me."

"Whatever," I said, rolling my eyes as I unbuckled my seat belt.

"Let's go." Evan opened his door and putting his wallet in his coat pocket. He walked to the back door of the SUV and opened it as I got out.

"What's that?" I asked as I seen him pulling out a small box from the back seat. "What's in the box?"

"It's a secret. You'll find out in less than five minutes," Evan replied, closing the back door. "Let's go inside and get a coffee, okay?"

"Yes," I said, leading the way to the coffee shop. I opened the door for Evan and he walked in.

Evan put the box down on a table in a booth seat and then went up to order. I sat down and stared at the box. It wasn't a very big box, but it was a decent size. I think this was my birthday present. Why was it in a bland brown box though?

After a few moments, Evan walked back over with a tray that had two coffees in it and a plate with two pieces of toast on it. He sat down in front of me and pushed the box over on the table so it wouldn't be in the way of the two of us.

"So why'd you get toast?" I asked, looking at the golden bread.

Evan smiled. "You remember how I owed you a jar of homemade raspberry jam, right?"

"Oh, you didn't!"

He reached over and pulled the box open and then pulled out a small glass jar with dark red jam inside it. He cocked an eyebrow at me as he slid the jar over to me. "Oh, but didn't I?"

"Is this seriously raspberry jam?"

"Yes," he said. "And I seriously made it myself. It took a few tries, but I think I finally got it edible enough for you."

I smiled as I looked over the glass. It had a whole bunch of little diamonds engraved into the jar and a brass lid. "I don't know what to say."

"Tell me it's good," he said with a slight laugh as he pushed the plate of toast towards me. He laid down a butter knife on the plate and waited.

I cracked open the lid and buttered a piece of toast with the jam. "Okay, you eat this one." I handed it to him and grabbed the other piece of toast and spread the jam on it. I held it up to him and we tapped toasts. "Cheers."

I took a bite and let out an audible moan. "This is actually so damn good. Kudos on your jam, bud."

Evan smiled. "You like it, then?"

I nodded.

"Okay, good," he said, taking another bite. "I still have a bunch of jars at home. I went a little overboard with it."

"So? That's a good thing," I stated. "Raspberry jam makes Spencer a, um, something that rhymes with raspberry jam."

"All I'm getting is ham," Evan said.

"Me too. But I'm not a pig. I'm a princess," I said with a sigh. "But how good is bacon and jam though. Mm."

"You are a pig," Evan stated.

I shook my head. "No. I just eat messily. I'm a human girl. I'm a princess. I promise."

Evan scoffed and pushed the plate off to the side now that we had finished eating our toast. "Anyway, I got you something else."

"Ooh, what is it? Is it a puppy?" I asked.

He gave me a deadpanned look. "Yes. I'm gonna keep a puppy in a box all night. That seems like a good idea."

"Maybe you're hiding him back at your house or something. Maybe you can let me come over. That can be my other gift."

"I actually got you two other gifts, so hush," he said, putting the jar of jam back into the box. "This is number two." He pulled out a big piece of navy fabric.

"The sweater you ordered for me!" I shouted, grabbing it from him.

"That would be this, yes."

I opened it up and looked at the back, and sure enough, in big bold letters. "Gingersnap," I read aloud. "I love it."

"Now everyone will know your name is Gingersnap," Evan teased.

"I don't care. This is such a cute sweater."

"You can't wear it every single day, y'know."

I scoffed. "I'll alternate between this one and my Creeper hoodie. It's fine. I got this. I know how to laundry."

"Do you?" he asked, cocking his eyebrow at my getup.

"Well, shut up. I didn't think I would be getting whisked away to go on an *adventure* at midnight," I snapped back. "I just figured you would call me and then come over really early tomorrow because you like being a clingy little shit."

"Yeah, but you like me being a clingy little shit," Evan stated. "It's part of my charm."

"Yeah. So what else is in the box?" I asked. I guess I was letting my curiosity get the best of me now.

"Hmm. It's pretty useless inside," Evan stated as he put the sweater back in the box for me. He pulled out another box that was actually wrapped, surprisingly well wrapped too.

"What is it?" I asked.

"Open it and find out," he said, pushing it across the table to me.

"It's a little heavy for its size," I said, picking it up and peeling at some of the wrapping paper. "I don't know if I can accept this. I didn't get you anything yet."

"I don't want anything, Spencer. I have you. That's enough in and of itself," Evan stated. "Now open it. Your reactions can be my birthday present."

I sighed and ripped back the wrapping paper. On the box was some art of space and stars and stuff. "What is it?" I asked, furrowing my brows as I looked over the box.

"Flip it over, you dunce."

I scoffed and turned the box over, removing the rest of the paper as I did. "It's a frickin' telemascope!" I shouted. "How'd you know?"

"You told me you wanted one but never got one before," he said. "So now you have one. You're welcome."

I got out of my side of the booth and went over to his and latched him into a big hug. "You're the best. Thank you, thank you, thank you, you giant nerd."

"I thought you'd like it."

"I love it, man."

"Do I win the boyfriend prize?"

I nodded and rested my head on his chest. "You betcha."

Evan pulled my coffee over and put it to my lips. "Drink up. I need you to stay awake for the next few hours. The night's not over yet."

{Chapter: **Eight**}

I followed Evan out of the coffee shop after we had finished our coffees. He carried the box of my goodies to the back seat of the SUV. He said he brought them in so I could enjoy them in proper lighting. I guess that means the rest of our night would be in the somewhat dark.

"I have chips and pop in the back too," Evan said, pointing to a second box in the back seat.

I turned as he started the SUV. "Why? Are we going for a hike or something?"

He scoffed. "Ha! Me? Hike? You're on crack. No, we're going for a midnight picnic of sorts."

"Where we going?"

"It's a secret," he replied.

"Ooh, mystery. Am I gonna get murdered? Are we gonna discover the ruins of an ancient Greek temple? Are we gonna solve the mystery of the body that was found at the old train station?" I rambled. "I don't know, but stay tuned for the thrilling conclusion on the next *Dragon Ball Z*."

"You're such a friggin' dork," Evan groaned as we backed out of the parking spot.

I smiled widely at him. "Yes, but I am *your* dork. And that means you have to care for me." He smiled as he looked up and down the empty road and turned out of the parking lot. "You didn't have to look both ways," I noted.

"Yeah, but it's an old habit that you should be glad I have," he stated. "You never know, man. All it takes is one mistake and you could be dead or injured."

"Well, we can't be having any of that."

"Exactly."

"So, uh, why are we driving away from the city?"

"Because why would my secret spot be in the middle of a city?" Evan asked. "Come on, gingersnap, use your head."

I watched the signs and bushes pass by beside us. Everything was still covered in snow though, so it was a pretty white sight. After a few moments, we turned up a winding two-lane road with no street-lights on it. I watched carefully as Evan glided the SUV up and around all of the slight curves of the road. We eventually reached a fairly long stretch of road that was straight. Up ahead, there was another road. He turned down that road and drove for another minute or two and then pulled up to an old building. From the coffee shop to here, I hadn't seen another car on the road. It felt like we were completely alone in the world right now. Just like how we were at the mall.

"Here we are," Evan said, shutting his car off.

"What the hell is *here*?" I asked. I looked around at the building. It was a long, flat type of building. It was rotted and old and concrete and pretty damn sketchy if I do say so myself.

"It's an old bowling alley called 41 Lanes. I used to come here as a kid, but it closed a few years back. Last year, my friend and I busted in and, well, nobody uses it or even comes up this way anymore," Evan explained. "It's just our little hideaway from the rest of the world."

"And?"

"And I brought you here because you're becoming such a huge and important part of my life that it only felt right to share my secret place with you," Evan said, pulling the keys from the ignition. "Come on. Let's go inside."

"I don't wanna," I said with a pouty face. "It's a scary-looking place."

"Oh, my God." Evan got out and shut the door. He walked around the car to my side and opened my door and pulled me out of the car and held me bridal style.

"I hate you," I said as he put me down onto the gravel parking lot.

"Yeah, I know." He opened the back door of the car and pulled a box out. "Hold this."

I took the box from him and then followed him over to a door a dozen feet away or so. He slipped a key inside and opened it.

"You have a key?" I asked.

"Yeah," he replied, turning to me. "My friend and I, we replaced the locks we broke so we could have keys for the place."

"That's actually kind of smart," I said, following him inside the building.

"Now, you just wait here," Evan said, picking something up from the counter at the entrance of the bowling lanes.

I heard a button click and then a beam of light shot out from Evan's hand. I guess he had a flashlight stashed away here. He's pretty smart sometimes, I can give him that. I watched as the light from his flashlight disappeared behind a wall or two. I waited in the darkness for him to come back. After a minute or so, a bunch of the lights shuttered to life and turned on.

I walked over to see some of the lanes of the bowling alley all lit up and polished. I guess Evan and his friend did a little restructuring to this place to make some of the lanes work again. I walked over and set the box down at the little table in the fourth lane. I looked at the screen and it lit up with Evan's name and mine. I guess he wanted to have a bowling match. I turned around and walked over to the rack of bowling shoes. They were all clean and polished. I grabbed a pair in my size and put them on and left my boots underneath the table. I took my coat off as it had started to get pretty hot in here. Evan must have talented friends if they can resurrect a bowling alley. Like, what the hell? He has heating and lighting and a working bowling lane? How?

"So?" Evan's voice echoed from down the building. "Pretty cool, right?"

I turned to see him walking over to me from where we had entered the building. I nodded. "Yeah. I'm impressed."

"It's mostly just basic upkeep."

"Nah, I mean, you own a bowling alley, dude."

"Meh, kind of. Did you get your shoes on?" he asked as he walked over and grabbed a pair of bowling shoes for himself.

I nodded and lifted my foot up. "Nice red and blue ones."

Evan smiled. "I just wanna let you know that I don't lose very often."

"Why's everything a competition with us?" I asked.

He shrugged. "Dunno."

I scoffed. "I'm still gonna win though."

"Nah," he replied, sitting down next to me.

"Yeah," I said, pushing him. "Dorks can't beat nerds."

Evan smirked. "Mm-hmm." He leaned over and kissed me. "Nerds can't beat dorks, babe. Everyone knows that."

I shrugged him off and opened the box of goodies up. I grabbed a can of root beer and cracked it open. "This is the good in the world." I took a long and satisfying drink and then let out a loud belch. It echoed through the empty bowling lanes next to us.

"You're gross," Evan said, cocking his eyebrow and giving me a one-sided smile. "In a cute way though."

"How can gross be cute?" I asked. "When it's me." I smiled at myself. I'm funny.

"So, it's your birthday, right?" Evan asked. "Tell me about your biggest material want. That's what birthdays seem to be associated with, so hit me."

"Um, I don't know. I have a telescope and a boyfriend. I guess I'm pretty good."

"Okay, no, shut up. Think bigger. What kind of house do you wanna live in?"

"I don't know. I never really gave any thought to that. I guess I'd be cool with a regular house."

"Car?"

"Oh, okay, actually, yeah, I do have a big car want."

"Okay, so tell me. I'm interested.

"I have a thing for old muscle cars, man," I told him. "I really like the old Barracudas, the hemis."

"They are pretty nice," Evan agreed.

"Actually, no, scratch that. I think I'd want a Dodge Challenger over anything else in the world," I told him. "They're such nice cars. And I mean the old ones, not the new models, but them old '70s Challengers with the huge-ass motors and rumbling for miles and the burning rubber of the tires. Mmm."

"You went from bookworm to gearhead in 3.5 seconds," Evan said with a small laugh. "Maybe someday we can work out a way to get you a Challenger."

"I doubt that'll happen. Old cars are so hard to come by these days," I stated. "And I'm no millionaire, so I don't have the cash to throw down on some collector car that's only been driven for 100 miles or less."

"So what if you built your own?" Evan asked.

I shrugged. "I don't think I have the time, money, or knowhow to do that. And don't offer to help. I don't think you have the time, money, or knowhow either."

"You're saying this to a guy who made a rundown bowling alley work," Evan stated. "And might I remind you, I did it at seventeen years of age."

"Yeah, but cars are different. I don't know."

"Let me help. If it's your dream car, lemme at least help."

"You do too much as it is," I said, turning to him and furrowing my brows a little. "Why are you always trying to outdo yourself and go bigger and better and keep doing these things?"

He shrugged. "I wanna keep doing things and making people happy. I know you don't like thinking about it, but if I die soon, what else will I have lived for, y'know? What is a life if not a tool to make other lives better?"

"That's a really good way to live and all, but why me? It makes me feel kind of guilty to be accepting so much from you."

"Sorry, I just like making you happy. And these are all memories and things that will remind you of me in case, you know, I'm not here anymore."

I wrapped an arm around him and rested my head down on his

shoulder. "You're not gonna go anywhere anytime soon. I promise you that."

"No, but you don't know that."

"I do."

Evan shook his head. "You don't."

"I know you're scared of dying, but you don't have to let go yet. You don't have to let go ever. Dying doesn't have to be some grand poetic clock, ticking down its seconds until you have to say a final goodbye. It comes and it happens when it does, but you can't live your entire life based on the fact that you're gonna die someday," I stated. "You're living like you're scared to die, and I know that's not how *you* should live."

"It's not just that, Spencer," he barked back. "You know it's gotten worse. How can you still be so hopeful about all of this?"

"Because you're a fighter," I told him. "I can see that in you. You're a man of your word. You said you'd make me raspberry jam and you made me some. It's something as stupid and meaningless as that that makes me realize that you're not just gonna give up. That's not you. If you make a promise, you're gonna see it through. Most people would shove aside something as small as raspberry jam, okay, but you, you didn't do that. So now I need you to make me a promise for me right now."

"What is it?" he asked, wiping his eyes. I guess he had teared up a little, I hadn't even noticed.

"I need you to promise me that you're gonna fight this cancer like hell. I need you to fight it like how you would want me to fight it if I had it," I said, looking him dead in the eyes. "Promise me you'll fight."

He nodded. "Okay." He sniffled. "I promise."

"No more acting like you're giving up. No more acting like you're on your deathbed. No more acting like this is your final wish from a genie," I stated. "You're gonna fight, you're gonna win, and you're gonna live for a long time to come."

"I love you, Spencer," he whispered, leaning over and hugging me tightly.

"You what?"

"I love you."

63

I smiled and wrapped my arms around him tightly. "I love you too, Evan."

"I mean it, asshole. You're the best thing in my life and I think some part of me knew from the moment I met you that you were special and perfect and that I just needed you in my life, and look how right you proved that part of me to be."

"I meant it too, asshole." He took a deep breath and kept on holding me. I didn't mind. He was warm and he smelt good and he was mine and I loved him. "Hey, Evan?" I asked.

"Mm?"

"Why did you wait to tell me?"

"What do you mean?" he asked.

"Like, to tell me that you loved me like this. Why wait till now? Why not tell me this on New Year's Eve when you first said it?"

He shrugged. "It didn't feel right. This does. But I guess it doesn't matter in the end. Really, any moment spent with you is the right moment, right?"

"I'm sorry," I whispered.

"For?"

"Me."

"What?" he asked.

"Like, I just... I dunno," I said with a small sigh. I gave up on trying to speak and just let myself melt into Evan's warmth. I just wanted to lose myself inside of him right now. I couldn't let go of him even if I wanted to. I just wanted to stitch myself into this moment of time and never leave it ever again. I wanted to just feel this pure emotion for the rest of my life. There could be a storm raging outside, but as long as I stayed in here and in Evan's arms, I don't think anything else could ever matter. There could be a flood and I would stay anchored to this seat with him. There could be a tornado and I would let the wind pick us up and throw us around, but I sure as hell wouldn't let go. This boy was worth walking through Hell for. This boy was worth taking a bullet for. This boy was worth dying for. And I would gladly do it over and over and over again if it meant he could exist in this world.

I gripped Evan a little tighter and started to sob softly into his sweater for no real reason other than the fact that my body had just lost control of itself. I was gone. Head over heels, face to the ground, spiralling down an abyss—I was falling for this boy. I had zoned out for a long time as I sobbed on Evan's sweater. He eventually cupped my cheeks and kissed my clammy and tear-coated face. "I'm still here, Spencer. I promised."

I sniffled and buried my face back into his chest.

God, don't let me leave this moment. Please.

{Chapter: **Nine**}

Evan had dropped me off at five in the morning after we had a round of bowling and went for hot chocolate. But after that night, I just felt different, and I don't know if it was in a good way. I had the box of his presents sitting in the corner of my room, untouched from that night, as if I were scared to relive that deep, emotional tsunami we had entrenched ourselves from.

But my birthday was exactly a week ago. A week ago, I was asleep from a night out, and now I'm lying here in my bed, doing nothing productive for the world or myself.

"Knock, knock," Charlotte said from my door.

I rolled over in my bed and looked at her. "Hey, buddy."

"You look like hammered shit," Charlotte said, walking over and sitting on my bed.

I shrugged. "Hungover shit."

"Evan's been calling me because you won't pick up your phone, reply to texts, or answer the door. What's going on?"

"I just don't feel it," I replied.

"You tell me you confess undying love for each other, but now you're just not feeling it?" Charlotte asked rhetorically. "Right, okay. What's going on, Spencer? This guy is an amazing guy and you're gonna just let it waste and rot away because of something in the past?"

I nodded and mumbled, "That's pretty much the sum of all its parts. Yeah."

"Okay, look, I get that you hate getting close and you're scared of things that are real, but come on!" Charlotte groaned. "Evan is worth that risk."

"Shut up," I groaned, rubbing my forehead. "I'm hungover and not in a very understanding or listening mood right now."

"I don't give a shit," she barked back.

"I do," I said. "I wish I were single still. Being single makes things a lot easier for me to deal with."

"Of course you think that. Everything's easier when it's just you that you have to think about."

"Exactly. So let me live an easy life."

"Do you love Evan?"

I sighed. "Yes. I love him a lot."

"An unhealthy amount?" she asked. I nodded, and so Charlotte smacked my arm. "So stop talking like this and go talk to him! God-dammit, Spencer!"

"I just don't see how I can manage to get any closer to him," I said.

"You'll find ways."

I sighed. "Look, dude, I get it. You want me to be happy, and yes, he makes me happy, but you know what else makes me happy? Not being broken up with or cheated on or used."

"Dude," Charlotte whined, "Evan is a grade-A boyfriend to you. There's no way he'd cheat on you or use you or break up with you, barring that you don't go and do something majorly douchey or slutty."

"Do I do douchey and slutty things often?" I asked, raising an eyebrow at her.

"That's not what I meant to imply," she grumbled. "I just don't want you to throw him away, okay?"

"You can't throw away a human being," I said. "Not even if their personality is full of dead maggots."

"Don't change the subject to Katy from senior English."

"Sorry." I pushed myself to a sitting position against my headboard. "I just don't see me and Evan working out in the long run."

"That's not a very good explanation as to why though."

"I don't have a better one. I just don't see it."

Charlotte sighed. "Okay, let's go get you some glasses, then."

I groaned loudly and glared at her. "Why can't I just live my life, man? Why are you so adept at making me feel like shit for not wanting to be with a boy?"

"Because this boy is very good for you and he is like Polysporin and he will try to fix you."

"I don't need to be fixed," I stated. "I need to be left to me and just me."

Charlotte groaned. I could tell she was getting pretty annoyed at me, but this is one thing I'm always gonna be stubborn about. I hate making the wrong choices, and as far as I know, Evan isn't a wrong choice, but he could be. Y' know?

"Stop worrying about being wrong," she said. "Life isn't a test, Spencer. It's a great adventure and one that'll be a whole lot better if you spend some of it sleeping next to, or on top of, a cute guy that treats you the way you deserve to be treated."

"Honestly, what if I don't even want that?" I asked. "What if I'm asexual?"

"Oh, shut up, you would have told me if you were." Charlotte glanced back over to me. "You're not are you? Is this you coming out to me? Because, if so, I'm sorry for being a dick about you being with Evan if you don't wanna be for the sex thing, I get it."

"I'm not asexual," I said. "But thanks for letting me know I have your support."

"I'm your best friend. I'll support you no matter what flag you fly," Charlotte stated. "You're not scared to have sex with him though, are you?"

"Well, isn't that at least in part where this derives from? Right?"

"Yeah, I guess."

I sighed and reached over for my phone. "Look, more missed texts and calls."

"He misses you, asshole."

"Yeah, I feel bad," I said, dropping my phone to the bed.

"You probably should. I don't know how many times I have to tell you that Evan is a quality guy for you."

I shrugged. "You could say it a couple more times."

"Spencer," Charlotte whined, shaking me a few times.

"Ugh, this means I have to have a long and drawn-out talk with him about my sudden emotional distance, doesn't it?"

Charlotte nodded. "I think he at least deserves that."

"Curse him for being such a good guy. Why can't he be shitty like every other guy I've liked so that I wouldn't feel the urge to stay with him?"

Charlotte smiled at me.

"What?" I asked, cocking an eyebrow at her.

"So you *are* staying with him, yes?"

I let out a loud sigh. "Yes. You're right. He's a very nice guy and he's very good for me. I would be stupid to let that walk away from me."

"So I got through to you?"

I shook my head. "Nah. I think he did."

"I'm both impressed and sad."

"Why?"

"Because you're not gonna run away from him, but it's not because of me," she said with a pout.

"You woke me up and I'm hungover."

"Who'd you go drinking with last night?" she asked.

"No one. I drank by myself. I'm nineteen. I can do that legally now," I stated. "So you cannot be mad at me. I'm a grown— Okay, well, I'm a woman now."

"I wasn't gonna give you trouble for *drinking* alone," Charlotte said. "I was gonna give you trouble for drinking *alone*. You know I'm a phone call away."

"Yeah, pfft, and let you hog all the whiskey? No way," I muttered back to her. I had a point. She would always drink *my* booze because she felt that I was too small or something. She would do the same to Mindy too. It's kind of annoying because Mindy and me, we knew our limits.

"I wouldn't hog all of it," Charlotte mumbled back. "But either way, what do you wanna go do today? Shall we go and see the world?”

“No.”

“Oh, come on, you can’t just mope in your bedroom because you have a hangover and wanna avoid your boyfriend.”

I scoffed. “I just wanna lie here until the need for physical intimacy goes away.”

“Morning dew?”

“Oh, you,” I said with a wink.

“Get up and get dressed, you turd.”

“I am dressed,” I said, whipping my blanket off to reveal my jean-covered legs. “I didn’t get undressed from last night.”

“Is they clean though?” she asked, cocking an eyebrow and looking down at my jeans.

I shrugged. “I don’t wet the bed, so I’d assume they’re pretty clean.”

“Ha, you’re funny.”

“I don’t,” I snapped at her. “Don’t joke about wetting the bed. That shit’s nasty. Sleeping in your own pee and shit, the hell you take me for?”

“You’re getting a phone call,” Charlotte said as my phone started aggressively vibrating on the bed.

“Who is it?” I groaned, falling over to the side and lying on my bed.

“It’s Minderella.”

“Ooh, gimme,” I said, sitting back up and grabbing the phone. I checked the caller ID to be sure and then answered the call. “Hey, boo.”

“Hey, you little shit,” Mindy squeaked back.

“I was gonna call you and check up on you today,” I stated. “You beat me to it!”

“Yeah, I usually do,” she chimed. “So how’s life?”

“It’s good, it’s good. How’s life with you?”

“Monstrous. Yeah, there was a flood and a fire and a hurricane and a blizzard and then Satan knocked up my girlfriend and we had this whole legal battle for custody of the kid and shit. It was a mess.”

“Are you high?” I asked.

“No, that’s just my way of saying life here is always pretty good.

I'm happy here. You don't gotta worry about that," Mindy said. "I'd let you know if there were ever something that bothered me."

"I know."

"Yeah, but how's Evan?"

"Oh, I, uh, I haven't talked to him in a week," I stated.

"Why the hell not?" she asked. I could tell Charlotte heard because she gave me a knowing look.

I sighed. "You know why. The whole *lingering pain of a boyfriend of the past* thing."

"Right, that. I'm gonna go ahead and assume Charlotte already gave you a lecture about this, so I'm gonna save my breath."

"You're too smart for your own good," I told her. "She's sitting on my bed, actually. And she did just finish giving me that lecture."

"Well, look, I'm planning on coming back into town at some point in, like, I don't know, March. Yeah, probably then, and we should all hang out and have fun like the good ol' days."

"Those days are dead, Mindy, come on," I said with a small sigh. "Let's party and hang out like the good *new* days."

"I'm also not gonna be bringing my dorky girlfriend with me. Okay, actually, I haven't decided that. She has to be on her best behaviour for the next month and a half or so," Mindy said. It sounded like she was talking directly to Haley, her girlfriend, when she was saying that.

"Yeah, that'd be super cool if you brought her out," I said.

"Whoa," Charlotte chimed in. "Don't be telling her to bring her goddamn girlfriend out here. Who the hell am I gonna have to mack on if you have Evan and she has Haley? Not fair."

"Suck it up and go get a one-night stand," I said, glaring slightly at her.

Charlotte sighed. "Whatever."

"I'll find someone for Charlemagne," I said. "I'm sure Evan has a friend or two that's single."

"That's using your brain," Mindy joked.

"I tend to use my brain a lot, actually," I said. "Just keep me updated on when you wanna come down and we'll try to work something out so we can go to a party or do something cool together."

"Duh," Mindy replied. "But also, don't go mess up things with

71

Evan. And can you also try not to get so drunk that you send booty pics to me? I'm in a relationship now, Spencer. My booty pic days are over, bud."

"Did I do that?" I asked.

"Yes, you texted me, like, three," she replied. "And as nice as they are, I can't be your booty pic collector."

"My bad," I said. "I was having a good booty day and I needed to show someone."

"That's what Evan is for!" Mindy whined.

"Nah, he's not a good judge of form and shape."

"Oh, my God," Charlotte said with a laugh. "You sent her drunken booty pics?"

"Shut up, Charlotte. She likes girls. She lets me know if I'm looking like a queen or like a peasant."

"Yeah, Haley thinks they looked nice," Mindy said. "Keep 'em and send them to Evan someday or something."

"Much thanks," I said with a sigh. "I'm gonna turn my phone off when I drink from now on."

"Wow, only nineteen and you're saying that," Charlotte said. "Not sure if that's a good thing or a bad thing."

"Good thing. It means I'll make less mistakes," I said.

"Okay, but you were one contact away from it being a mistake," Mindy said. "Think about that."

"Ooh, yeah, sending a booty pic to my mom might have been a little weird," I said.

"Yeah, anyway, it's gonna get hectic over here because we're throwing a little gathering, so I will talk to you a little later on," Mindy stated. "Love you, butthead."

"Love you too," I said. "And Charlotte does too."

"Didn't hear it, but I know it's true," Mindy said. "Okay. Bye, bye."

I hung up my phone and put it down on the bed next to me, and then I let out a loud and very embarrassed, no pun intended, sigh. "It coulda been worse."

"It was," Charlotte said. "You sent them to me too. It was in a group chat." Charlotte pulled out her phone and showed me the messages.

"Oh, hey, I know that booty," I said, handing her the phone back. "I was having a good booty day. Sue me."

"You're like this weird little bookworm with a kinkster hiding inside her, aren't you?"

I shrugged. "Probably. I'll let you know when I unleash it."

"Feeling a little less hungover?"

I shrugged again. "I guess. Let's go get some food and maybe that'll help me feel even better."

"There's a pizza in the oven cooking for us," Charlotte said.

"How? Are you magic?"

She shrugged. "Is being psychic considered being magic? 'Cause I put it in the oven before coming to wake you up."

"Ooh, you're my hero."

She got off my bed and stretched out her back. "I thought so. Now let's get down to the kitchen before it burns."

"Burnt pizza is like a happy sadness," I said as I stood up.

"How so?"

"It's like, it's still pizza, right, but it's burnt."

Charlotte mimed an explosion coming from her head. "Mind blow, dude. Whoa."

"Shut up and lead the way down the stairs."

"Aye, aye, captain," she said, walking out of my bedroom and heading for the stairs.

{Chapter: **Ten**}

I dropped my plate into the kitchen sink and walked back over to the table and sat down. Charlotte looked over and sighed very loudly and quite aggressively at me. "I'm not cleaning your fucking dishes."

"I don't want you to," I said. "I'll just wait for Jordan to do them."

Charlotte groaned. "Man, you're just the laziest kind of person today, aren't you?"

"I'm hungover, shut up," I whined. "I'll just get Evan to come over and do them. Y'know, since we have to have *the talk* or whatever."

"Yes, but try not to make it obvious that you're just using him as a dishwasher if you do get him to come over here," Charlotte stated. "I don't think he would appreciate that very much."

"He's my bitch."

"Okay, but you gotta entice him a little. Give him something in return for him doing your dishes, like, damn, woman."

I scoffed. "It's fine. But I probably shouldn't ask him to do them right away after not talking to him for a week."

"I'll cut you a deal," Charlotte stated. "I'll do ya dishes if you go have *the talk* with Evan."

"Go for it," I said, pulling my phone out of my pocket. "I'm gonna shoot Evan a quick texty text."

"Never say that again." Charlotte walked over to the sink and started running some hot water.

"Why not?" I asked, typing out my message to Evan.

"It's lame as hell," Charlotte said, squirting dish soap into the sink. "But then again, you are pretty lame."

"I'm the lamest," I said, sending the message and pocketing my phone. "I bet he's in the neighbourhood already."

"Why's that?"

"You're making me talk to him, right?" I said. "That means you had him on standby, didn't you?"

Charlotte winked. "Maybe."

I groaned. "Why?"

"Oh, shush. He's at a coffee shop somewhere. He'll bring you a coffee and you can shut the hell up and talk to him."

"Okay, so I can't do both of those things at the same time though. I can't shut up and talk at the same time," I stated. "You dumb."

"Shut up, you know what I meant," Charlotte snapped. "Now go wait for Evan, you're making me salty."

I scoffed at her as I walked out of the kitchen and into the living room. I waited for a few moments until I heard a knocking at the door. I got up and went over and swung the door open.

"You don't talk to me for a week and then you tell me to come over like it's nothing? You don't answer my calls or texts? What the hell, Spencer?" Evan shouted, stepping inside. Okay, so seeing him irritated was a first for me.

"That's what I wanted to talk to you about," I said, closing the door.

He grabbed me and hugged my tightly. "God, I fucking missed you so much."

I hugged him back and smiled softly. "I missed you too."

"Never stop talking to me like that ever again, you fucking asshole," he barked, still hugging me tightly.

"I can't make any promises."

"Yes, you can."

"What if you flirt with my best friend?"

"I already have," he joked.

"I mean after this moment in time, dingus," I snapped back.

He set me down and frowned a little. "So, you wanna tell me what's been going on with you?"

I nodded. "Just not here."

"Thought you might say that," Evan said, opening the door. "Let's go get a coffee."

I grabbed my coat from the closet next to the door and smiled. "You just get me," I said. I slipped my shoes and coat on and then I followed him out the door, closing it behind us.

"Shouldn't you tell Charlotte you're leaving?" Evan asked as he pulled out his keys and unlocked his SUV from a distance.

"Nah, she'll figure it out," I said, walking to the other side of the driveway and getting in the passenger side.

He chuckled softly to himself as he got in. "Whatever you say."

***

We pulled up to the parking lot of the coffee shop that we always go to. I looked up and noticed the sign. "Has the sign always said Lattedale?" I asked, unbuckling my seat belt.

"Well, that's the name of the coffee shop, so I sure would hope so," Evan deadpanned. "Okay, get out."

I got out and walked up to the front door with him. "I just mean, like, that's a clever name, don't you think?"

"It sure is," Evan said, opening the door. "It's a pun on latte and Lauderdale."

"Why Lauderdale?"

"That's where the guy who made it is from."

"Like, Fort Lauderdale in Florida?"

Evan shook his head. "It's a neighbourhood in Edmonton."

"I did not know that," I said. "Look at me, learning new things all the time."

"Anyway, you want a bagel or anything?" Evan asked as we walked up to the register.

I shook my head. "I ate before I left."

"You sure?" he asked. "I know how much you love food."

"Fine, get me some doughnut holes for later."

"Chocolate and sour cream glazed?"

"Duh."

"Go sit down," Evan said as he pulled out his debit card.

"Aye, aye," I said, turning and walking off to our usual seat in the corner of the shop. I liked this seat because of the windows and the view of everything outside. It was quite a nifty seat. After a couple minutes, Evan walked over with a box of doughnuts in one hand and a tray with our two coffees in his other hand.

"They were all out of your doughnuts, so I got you sadness and plain."

"You better be lying to me," I said with a small pout.

"Nah, they had your shits, don't worry," Evan sat down across from me and slid the box of doughnut holes to me. "I got you decaf though."

"Stop," I whined, taking my coffee from the tray. "Thank you, by the way."

"Anytime," he replied with a small smile. "You can just go ahead and open up about the thing now."

"The thing?"

"The not-talking-to-your-boyfriend-for-a-week thing," he replied.

I sighed. "Right, yeah, gotta get all emotional and crap."

"So tell me what's going on."

I took a deep breath. "Okay, so it's like this, there was this guy I did the do with that once, you know this, I told you, and so I was pretty much in love with the dude after that because he was my friend and he said such sweet nothings to me and it made me think that he really wanted me forever, and so after we done did the do, well, take a wild guess."

"They were really sweet *nothings*."

"Bingo," I said. "He left me and he hasn't spoken to me since. He was my best friend and I thought that maybe he still cared about me, but he apparently didn't at all. He was just using me for that one time so he could say that he got me. He wanted to stop talking to me a few months before that, but he figured he could use us being friends as leverage to get in my pants before he threw me away."

"Kinda wanna punch this guy," Evan said flatly.

"Get in line." I smirked a little. "Anyway, you can imagine the kind of resonating effects that kind of thing has on a teenage girl's psyche. I've just looked for reasons not to date or meet anyone or let anyone new get close to me. You're the first person other than him to get this close to me and it scared me, so I tried to distance myself from you, and it was really goddamn stupid of me, I know."

"I get it."

I let out a sigh. "I'm really sorry, Evan."

"It's okay. I'm not mad. I just wanted an explanation is all. I get it," he replied. "It's not that hard to understand, you were hurt and human nature dictates that we try to avoid things that will get us hurt. It's the same reason you don't put your hand down on a hot stovetop."

"But you're the most amazing guy I've ever met and you didn't deserve that cold shoulder."

He scoffed. "It was more like the entire arm."

"Oh, hush," I barked. "You know what I mean. You just... you deserve so much better than what I can offer you."

"Hey, regardless of what I do or do not deserve, I chose to be with you," Evan stated. "There's nothing holding me back from leaving you. I'm not obligated to be with you in any means, but I *choose* to be with you because I *want* to be with you."

"You're really lame, you know that?" I said, wiping a little bit of tears from my eyes.

"Yeah, you tell me that a lot."

"Do I also tell you that I love you? 'Cause I do."

"You may have mentioned it before."

I winked at him. "Slip of the tongue."

"Just try not to leave me for a week again, okay?"

"I'll do my best," I said, sighing softly. I really am such an asshole though. I don't have any real reason to have not at least told him what's up earlier or something, or why I even felt the need to suddenly not talk to him. I'm dumb.

"How've you been though?" Evan asked. "It's been a week. I miss knowing about your days."

"School and stuff."

"Work?"

"Nah, I'm getting a new job at a diner by the school and I haven't started there yet. I still have some money saved up, so we good," I replied.

"Masturbating and watching Netflix?"

I smirked. "You just *get* me."

"Coulda called me to do it for you, just saying," Evan said with a little wink as he took a sip of his coffee.

I scoffed. "You ain't got the skills. Anyways, how was your week? What did you do?"

"Work and school," he replied.

"Where do you work?" I asked.

"I don't wanna tell you. I don't want you coming in and bugging me all the time."

"Oh, please, you'd love to have me at work with you."

"No, it'd be distracting," he stated.

I opened my mouth wide in shock. "How dare you!"

"Well, I'd literally just wanna sit there and talk to you the whole goddamn time, and that'd be a sure-fire way to get, well, surely fired."

"Nice wordplay," I said. "But I still wanna know. C'mon, tell me. I promise not to come and bug you… too often."

"Here," he replied.

"You work where?"

"Here," he repeated.

"Is that a bar or something?"

"No, like, I work here. I work in the place we are currently sitting in," he explained. "I got a job here a while back because, well, I'm usually here anyway."

"What the hell? Why didn't you weasel me into a job here?" I asked, furrowing my eyebrows at him.

"I didn't think you needed a job," he replied. "And I don't think us working together would be a good idea. And we're not taking different shifts because then with school and work schedules, we'd never see each other."

"You could just move in," I suggested. "I'm sure my parents wouldn't care. We would be able to see each other every night that way. Aww, look at me, I'm a little problem solver."

79

"How does that solve any problems if we don't have any problems to start with?" he asked. "And if I were to move in, where would I put all my stuff? I've seen your room, it's not big enough for two people's personal effects."

"You can store the nonessentials in the attic?" I suggested.

He shook his head. "If we end up still being together a year from now, we'll just go out and get out own apartment."

"Promise?" I asked, holding my hand out and offering him my pinkie finger. I haven't done a pinkie promise in so long.

"Promise," he said as he begrudgingly wrapped his pinkie finger around mine. "Haven't done a pinkie swear since, like, grade seven."

"Well, you're gonna start doing them again, nerd."

He scoffed. "Rude."

I took a sip of my coffee and let out a sigh. "So good."

"You sure do like your coffee."

"Yeah, dude, I run on caffeine. I'm pretty sure half of me is just caffeine and the other half of me is made up of sass and sleep."

"I believe it," Evan stated.

"You should."

"I said I believed it, relax."

"So, what should we do for the rest of the day?"

Evan shrugged. "Beats me. What do you wanna do?"

"Dude, I don't know, that's why I was asking you," I stated. "I'm cool with going to my house and laying in bed all day and watching Netflix."

"Okay, but you're cool with doing that any day and every day," Evan stated. "I don't know. I kinda wanna do things."

"My butthole is off limits," I stated flatly.

"Not that. It's never that."

"What if one time it is though? I gotta cover my bases, ya know?"

"Shut up," Evan barked. "I meant, like, let's go buy some stuff and then bake cookies and brownies or something."

"I feel like that'd be a bad idea."

"What? Why?"

"Because they'd either be burnt to shit, or I'd end up eating them all," I told him. "And if I eat them all, I might lose my figure, and we don't want that."

"You wouldn't lose your figure," Evan stated.

"Oh, yeah? And how do you know that?"

"I don't know." He shrugged. "I'm just assuming based on how much you eat on any other day."

"I don't eat that much," I argued.

"Well, you do sometimes."

"That's not what we should be talking about right now," I barked. "We should be talking about what kind of cookies we wanna make."

"I thought you said it was a bad idea?"

"I said that, but I didn't mean it," I said with a wink. "I'm feeling like we should do sugar cookies. I'm sure the store has the packs of dough with the hearts in the middle. And then we can also get the stuff to make chocolate chip cookie dough. That's something I know how to cook from scratch."

"It's Valentine's Day tomorrow, isn't it?"

I nodded. "Yeah."

"Shit, I totally forgot. I didn't plan anything."

"Just get chocolates and come over and cuddle with me all day while we watch lame movies, 'kay?" I told him.

"That sounds like a good time. I vote in favour of that."

"Good," I said, standing up and grabbing my box of doughnut holes. "Now let's go get some cookie stuff."

"Right away, madam," Evan said, standing up.

{Chapter: **Eleven**}

Valentine's Day was pretty boring, so I'll save you the 2500-word story and just sum it up and say that it was a really nice and calming day. Evan and I ate the leftover cookies and brownies that we had made from the day before and the chocolates he had bought, which he bought a lot of, by the by. We spent a good eight hours in my bed, so that was pretty nice.

And now it was Monday, and Monday means school, and that means I wanna die. Even though class was done, waiting for Evan to come around and pick me up was complete hell. Like, I don't get it. He's usually on time. I pulled my phone out and went to my contacts and called him. It rang a couple times and then he answered.

"Hello?" his voice said.

"Where the hell are you?" I asked angrily.

"I'm running late with doing things today. If you would prefer to not take the bus, you can come meet me down by the drug store up the road, I have to go over that way anyway. I can grab you on the way back home."

"You better not take forever to come get me," I whined. "I'll just buy a Snapple and a bag of chips or something. I'll see you soon, dork."

"Yep, see ya soon. Love you."

"Love ya too," I replied. I hung up my phone and let out a quiet groan. Why does he have to do this to me? He could have texted me earlier to let me know so I wasn't just standing around like a doofus for the past half hour.

I popped my earphones in and started walking toward the drug store. It was only a ten-minute walk, so it's not the end of the world. And it gives me an excuse to buy a snack. I've been hungry all day anyway. I turned down the small street that led to the drug store and looked around. It's always so eerily empty on this street, even though it's between a college and a pretty busy plaza of stores. It's always so creepy. And then I felt someone grab me from behind. They covered my mouth quickly and threw a bag or something over my head to keep me from seeing anything. Before I could even scream, they had stuffed something in my mouth to keep me quiet.

This is it. This is how I die.

I was quickly thrown into a vehicle, I assume. I could feel my heart beating in my throat. My palms were all clammy. I tried to stay calm and keep my breathing nice and slow. Why was I being kidnapped? In broad daylight of all times? In a nice suburban neighbourhood of all places?

I tried to get the gag out of my mouth, but no luck. I tried to wiggle my head out of the cloth bag over my head, but no luck with that either. I gave up on trying to wiggle out of my restraints when I heard the car we were in pull to a stop and shut off. Someone opened the back door and pulled me up to a sitting position. They pulled on me and I stepped myself outside of the car. I heard the door close as I took some steps away from the car. I felt the crunch of gravel and twigs under my feet. Where the hell did they take me? Oh, man, I'm definitely murdered. Tell my mom I love her. Tell Evan I regret not taking us to the next step. I repent, I repent.

I was walked over a few more feet and then sat down on a bench or stump or something. I heard things being crumpled. It sounded like chips bags and stuff. Weird. After a few moments, I heard footsteps come over to me and stand me up. I felt someone hug me tightly then. The hell is going on? After the person put me down, the bag was ripped from my head and the light of the world swamped back to my eyes.

I looked around quickly, not even noticing the people. I was just trying to get a sense of where the hell I was. And that would be a forest somewhere, implied by all the trees surrounding us. When I finally turned to see who had hugged me, it was Evan, with a smirk on his face.

"You!" I shouted. "That was *not* funny!"

"I know," he said. "It was her idea." He nodded behind me.

I turned and seen Charlotte standing there with a smirk on her face. "You pile of shit!" I shouted at her. "Why did you think that was a good idea?"

"Because Evan wanted this to be a surprise," she replied.

"Wanted what to be?" I asked.

"Taking you here," Evan chimed in. "This is the wee bear hideaway, don't cha know?"

"Do you have food with you at least?" I groaned. "I haven't eaten all day and I'm hungry and this kidnapping thing just made me waste valuable energy on being scared for my life."

"We got you doughnut holes, a coffee, a pack of juice boxes, and some chips and crackers," Charlotte said, pointing to a backpack on the ground. "Now let's go exploring!"

"I seriously hate both of you," I said, walking over and pulling an orange juice from the backpack.

"We know," Evan said, hugging me from behind as I stood back up. "But we love you very much and we know you'll forgive us."

"Lick me," I barked, poking the straw into the juice box.

"Just tell me where," Evan whispered into my ear. He chuckled and picked up the backpack, swinging it onto his back as he walked over to Charlotte. "Shall we get on with it, then?"

"Why are we going into a cave?" I asked, looking at the direction Evan started walking.

"It's a childhood thing," Evan said. "I think you'll like it."

"Is there a bear? Because I want it to maul the two of you."

"Now that's just uncalled for."

"You kidnapped me!" I shouted.

"You make some good points," Evan quipped back. "Come on. It'll be fun."

"Fine, but I'm not gonna enjoy this," I said, pouting as I took a sip of my orange juice. I had all rights to act like a pissy five-year-old right now. They kidnapped me. That is goddamn illegal. I should seriously just report them to the authorities. But alas, I followed Evan and Charlotte into the cave. It got pretty dark in the cave after we rounded the first slight corner.

"Do you have a flashlight?" Charlotte asked.

"Duh," Evan said. "Check the small pocket of the bag."

"Right." Charlotte unzipped a pouch on the backpack and pulled out three small flashlights. They were the kind you would put on a keychain, just little LED ones.

"Gimme one," Evan said, holding his hand back.

"I just took them out, damn, chill," Charlotte barked, handing him a flashlight. She handed one to me too. "Just in case you get lost in the big spooky cave."

"That won't happen," I said with a small scoff. "Wait, that won't happen, right, Evan?"

"This cave is small. It's just dark," Evan replied. "You're not gonna get lost down here with the blind cannibals."

"Don't even joke about that shit," I snapped. "That movie is terrifying."

He smirked at me. "Shush." We walked for a minute until we came across the ending of the cave. There was a small pond in the opening and a small fire pit near the shore of said lake. There was a stack of firewood in the corner too. Did Evan already come to prepare this place for us? Well, it *is* Evan, so he probably did.

"Charlotte, can you go and get the cooler?" Evan asked as he started to light up a fire.

"Sure thing," she said, walking back out.

"This is where I'd bang you," Evan said once she was out of earshot.

"What? No," I said. "I'm not having sex in a cave."

"I was kidding," he stated. "I don't wanna lug a mattress in here. It's bad enough I had to carry this firewood in. I would be lying if I said I didn't wanna bang you in here though."

I sighed. "Yeah, yeah. But I knew you would have brought the firewood."

"Well, yeah. I'm not gonna use it if it wasn't mine."

"Fair point," I said, grabbing a stumpy log to use as a stool. I set it beside the fire pit and sat down as the fire caught on some of the twigs. The cave lit up and the light danced on the rocky walls.

"There we go," he said, pulling over another stumpy log for him to sit on. He set the backpack against his log and sighed.

"So, how big and how deep is this little pond?" I asked, looking at the dark water next to us.

"It's, like 20 feet wide and goes 50 feet back and at the back it's 20 feet down and right by us it's only five feet or so. There's a drop at the back is pretty steep though, so it's pretty shallow up till that point and then BAM. It just drops," he said. "I had to put up a little rope so I would know when the drop off was."

"Oh, okay, good."

"Why?"

"I like shallow water," I stated. "It's nice. No energy required."

"Well, good."

"Good."

"So what makes this place so special?" I asked, taking off my coat. It was getting pretty hot in here now that there was a fire going.

"I used to come here a lot as a kid. That's what makes it special," he said. He turned and pointed to the large wall behind us. "All those drawings were made by me and my friends growing up."

"Childhood memories." I sighed. "Simpler times."

"Things have changed so much since back then," Evan said softly. "Like, I didn't have cancer back then. I didn't know you back then. I didn't think I would ever go to college back then. You know, things seem like they change so fast when you're looking back on them, but as every day ticks by, nothing ever feels all that much different."

"Yeah, 'tis the perpetual spiral of life."

He smiled and laughed softly. "Yeah. I guess when I say that we all die at different speeds, I always forget to mention the part about slowing down and enjoying the scenery. What's a life without making memories, right?"

"Boring," I replied.

He laughed softly and leaned over and kissed me. "I love you."

"Yeah, you too," I said. "So did you bring s'mores materials? I wanna get the taste of dork off my lips."

"Rude," he said with a small pout. "But I did bring stuff for s'mores."

"You're the best."

"I know."

I got up and pushed my log closer to his and then sat back on it. I rested my head over on his shoulder. "I could get used to a simple existence like this."

"There's nothing simple about *you* though."

"Hmm?"

"You're this complex enigma of wonderful and beautiful. You're smart and funny and kind, well, you are sometimes, and you're just so calming to be around. Even when all we're doing is sitting in empty silence, I would still choose those moments over any other moment without you. You're complex because it baffles me how you can do next to nothing and yet I still feel so at home with you," Evan stated. "Oh, and because you're a giant nerdy dork."

"You're a dork," I said, smiling up at him.

He smirked back. "Yeah, but I'm *your* dork." He leaned over and kissed my forehead.

"Don't you ever forget it."

"Okay," Charlotte's voice said. "I got us the thing."

"Why did we need a cooler?" I asked.

"To keep the drinks cold," Evan replied, turning around on the stool and taking out some of the juice boxes and cans of pop.

"Also, where's my coffee at?" I asked.

"Here," Evan said, quickly handing me a silver thermos as if to shut me up right away. Actually, that was a smart move on his part.

"So, what should we do first?" Charlotte asked as she pulled a log over to sit on.

"I 'unno," Evan replied. "Gingersnap, what do you wanna do?"

I mumbled something, but I was busy with trying to open the thermos. The lid was twisted on so goddamn tight. "Babe!" I whined, handing the thermos to Evan.

He took it from me and smiled as he twisted the lid open. "At least I'm useful for something."

"You're useful for a whole lot more than that," I said, taking the thermos back from him.

"Oh, yeah?"

"Yeah," I said, taking a sip from the thermos. "You're also a very good cuddler. You're very warm and soft and comforting."

"Aww, you."

"Too much," I said, pushing him back. "Let me enjoy my coffee."

"Yeah, I'd hate to see what would happen if Spencer didn't get enough caffeine throughout the day," Charlotte chimed in.

"I'd die," I replied flatly.

"I don't doubt it."

"Anyway," Evan said, "let's have us a swim."

"We didn't bring any swimsuits though," Charlotte stated.

"So strip down to your underoos," Evan replied. "It's basically the same damn thing."

"Fair point," Charlotte said.

"Yeah, okay, let's do it. We can make s'mores while we dry off."

I sighed. "Goddammit."

"What?" Evan asked.

"I was enjoying my coffee."

"Just put it beside the fire with the lid on and it'll stay nice and toasty for you," he replied.

"Okay, fine, whatever, let's go swimming," I said, standing up and stretching out. I put the lid back on the thermos as Charlotte and Evan started to disrobe themselves. I took my shoes and socks off and then bunch up my shirt into a ball and stuffed it into my one shoe as best I could. I stuffed my socks into the other shoe. I slipped out of my pants and put them on top of my shoes so they weren't on the cold rock floor of the cave.

"Are you ready yet?" Evan asked as I turned around.

"Shut up," I snapped. "I don't want cold jeans when we get out."

"Okay, okay," Evan said. "Ladies first."

Charlotte sighed. "This better not be freezing cold."

"It's usually not," Evan said as Charlotte took a slight running start and jumped in.

Charlotte popped back up from the water. "Ah. It's not even that deep. Lame."

"No shit." He smirked and looked over at me. "It's just deep enough for Spencer to be able to stand with her head above the water though."

I went to go and punch his arm, but he dodged and jumped backwards into the water. I sighed and followed the two of them and dived into the water, curling into a small ball and letting all the water just penetrate my skin. I may as well get the shock of the slightly cold water over with right away. I stayed at the bottom of the water for a little while longer. I stared up at the shimmering water line and the light on the walls of the cave. Everything was so distorted in the most beautiful kind of way. I turned and saw Charlotte and Evan splashing water at each other. I smiled to myself a little.

Things aren't so bad here.

{Chapter: **Twelve**}

Today was pretty hella. We got home pretty late, so by the time I was done showering and finishing up homework, it was already almost three in the morning. Spencer no likey. I plopped onto my bed on my stomach and let out a soft groan as my damp hair covered my face. I directionally exhaled as hard as I could to get it off my face.

I closed my eyes and tried to force myself to sleep, but I just couldn't. So instead of sleeping, I lied there with my eyes open, staring at the wall and wondering about space and stuff. Like, space is a pretty wild place. There's burning balls of gas that are hundreds of times bigger than our planet and there are giant clusters of galaxies. And we haven't even explored our galaxy, let alone any of the other ones. We've only been to the moon. That means we've been to two planetary bodies out of a possible quadrillion, or however many there actually are. Space is too big, man. Also, there are quasars and black holes and pulsars and nebulas and supernovas. Space is so cool.

But enough of that. I need to sleep. I closed my eyes again and tried to get tired. I felt myself getting pretty sleepy and then I started to hear a tapping sound on my window. They were kinda far apart, only a tap every few seconds or so. I sat up in my bed and looked around. I heard it again and figured that it was coming from my window. I swear to God if this is Evan doing this shit to me again, I will lose it.

I pulled the window open and looked down. "What the hell is wrong with you?"

"Oh, good, you're awake," Evan said with a small smile on his face.

"Of course I'm awake, asshole, you're throwing pebbles at my window again," I said loudly but in a hushed tone.

"Come down."

"What for?"

"A coffee and a talk with your very loveable boyfriend."

I groaned. "Fine. Put the ladder up."

Evan smirked. "Already is."

"What?" I asked, looking down and seeing the ladder. I don't know how I missed it. It's a big silvery pile of shit leaning against my house, but I was more focused on Evan. "Alright, hold it in place."

"On it," Evan said, leaning against the ladder to make sure it didn't shift as I climbed down it.

I grabbed the boots from last time I snuck out (they were still in my closet) and slipped them on. I slipped on the custom sweater that Evan got for me. It wasn't really cold enough for a coat tonight, so yeah. I grabbed my phone and keys and stuffed them in my jean pockets. I pushed the window wide open and scooted over the ledge. I made my way down the ladder nice and slowly. And remember, it's better to take it slow than to take it dead.

"Any slower and I would have had to just let you fall so you'd get down here already," Evan sassed as I reached the bottom of the ladder.

"Honestly, shut up. I'm half asleep and the ladder is cold and slippery, and you need to just shh," I snapped at him as he laid the ladder back down on the ground. He put it behind my shed the other time. Eh, I guess he'll do that after he helps me climb back up.

"Okay, let's just get going. Come on, I'll boost you over the fence again," Evan said as he started walking towards the fence in my backyard.

I followed him over and waited for him to kneel down and cup his hands. I used his hands as a platform and jumped up to the top of the fence, grabbing it and then pulling myself over. This fence climbing should be enough of a workout for me, right?

"So, where we going?" I asked as Evan dropped to the ground.

"Where do you think?" he said, dusting off his knees. "To our favourite coffee shop in the world."

"Yeah, I figured."

"Why'd you even ask?"

"I thought you might take me somewhere nice after kidnapping me."

"You stopped talking to me for a week," Evan barked back. "I think we can call it even now.

"Okay, okay," I said as we started walking towards his SUV. "You make a fair point with that one. We're even."

***

"So, what do you want this time, princess?" he asked.

"Stop that," I snapped. "I just want coffee. I ate when I got home and I'm not that hungry. If I get hungry, I reserve the right to order food at that time instead."

"Okay, so you're taking a rain check on the food." He unbuckled his seat belt and opened his door. "Alright, let's get inside. I'm in need of caffeine."

"I'll go sit in our seat," I muttered I got out of the car.

"Good girl," he said. "And I'll go order our coffees."

"Good boy," I mocked.

We walked up and he held the door open for me. In turn, I held open the next door for him. We walked in and I went to the seat and he went to order, as per our routine. I sat down and looked out at the land around the coffee shop. It's always so weird to be here at night. Everything was so dark out there and it was so bright in here. It's just such a crazy contrast.

"Two coffees, coming right up," Evan said as he walked over with a coffee in each of his hands. Now this is a sight I like seeing.

"Gimme, gimme," I said, taking the cup of coffee from Evan. I peeled the tab back and started sipping it. I winced a little as the liquid burnt my lip, but the scold of the liquid cannot hold me back. I need my coffee.

"It's hot, Spencer," Evan said with a small smirk on his face.

"I know," I said, fanning my tongue. "But I didn't care."

"Idiot," he muttered.

"Hey, I heard that."

"You were meant to."

I scoffed at him. "Rude." I took a sip of my coffee now that my tongue was already burnt. "So what did you wanna talk about?"

"Life and stuff."

I sighed. "You could have just called me or something."

"I wanted to see your pretty face," he replied.

"You coulda Skyped me, then."

"I wanted to see your pretty face in full HD."

"Shh."

He took a sip of his coffee and sighed. "Okay, so maybe I also just wanted to talk to you about me."

"About you?" I asked. "Well, me, oh, my, that's just a little self-centred and egotistical and narcissistic of you, isn't it?"

"It's about my health though."

"Is it good news?" I asked. "Are you gonna tell me good things about your health? Because I really don't wanna be sadder about it than I already am."

"Spencer," he said softly, "when is it ever good news with me?"

I sighed softly. "Right. What's going on, then?"

"I feel so goddamn weak, Spencer. I feel so tired. All the fucking time, I *feel* like I'm dying," Evan said softly. "I'm just… so tired."

"Hey, you're gonna fight through this," I said, resting my hand on his. "Don't talk like you're going to sleep or giving up the fight. That's not you."

"I know, but it's just so hard to be hopeful when you feel so tired all the time."

"You don't need to be strong to win, Evan, you just need to be hopeful and keep fighting," I said as he lowered his head down to the table. I got up and walked to the seat beside him and hugged him. "I'm here for you, okay? I know that I can't really help or anything, but I'm here."

"I don't wanna die, Spencer," he said, his voice shaky and low.

93

"You're not gonna die," I stated, rubbing his back a little. "Well, okay, you're going to die eventually, duh, but you're not gonna die anytime soon. You're gonna die as an old, old man who has a cute ginger wife named Spencer."

"And if I don't?"

"Don't marry me? Pfft, that's your loss, buddy."

"I meant, like, what if I don't live to be an old, old man?"

I shrugged. "Then I guess you pissed me off and I killed you. But I'll think about you every day when I'm in jail. But the main point I want you to learn is that you're not gonna die anytime soon. I refuse to let you die."

"Spencer, you know you don't have a choice in the matter."

"Yeah, you right, but I'm also right."

He sniffled and let out a loud sigh. He didn't say anything back, so I didn't say anything else. I just sat and used my one hand to slowly rub his back as he lied on the table. I had my other hand free to drink my coffee with. After a while, I heard some snoring coming from Evan. Little shit fell asleep on the table. Now I'm all alone. Well, I could talk to the cashier lady, but I don't wanna bother her. She probably likes the quiet of the night shift. I sighed and pulled out my phone. It was at full charge, so I guess I could just scroll through Twitter and Tumblr and other sites to help pass the time. I probably sat for a good two hours or so next to Evan as he slept. I ended up drinking his coffee so it wouldn't go to waste, and so I could have a free coffee.

Evan stirred awake and sat up and let out a yawn. He rubbed his eyes and looked around and then turned to me. "You let me fall asleep?" he asked, rubbing his eyes again.

"I did, yes," I replied as I put my phone away.

"Why?"

"You got sad and then I was rubbing your back and you didn't reply to me and then I kept rubbing your back and I guess it put you to sleep."

"You want another coffee?" he asked.

I shook my head. "No, I drank yours on top of mine, but if you got me a hot cocoa, I'd love you forever."

"I can do that," Evan said as he got up and stretched. He turned and looked out the window. "Hmm, the sun's rising."

I looked past him and out the window to the slowly lightening sky outside. It was actually pretty bright now, but the sun wasn't peeking over the horizon just yet.

"We should go out and watch the sunrise on the beach," he suggested, walking off to get his coffee and my hot cocoa. I waited patiently for Evan to get back, which didn't take very long, only a minute or less. He handed me my hot cocoa and then we went outside into the brisk and nippy February air, like the Lights song. "Get in the car, nerd," Evan said as he walked out the door after me.

"Why?"

"Just get in," he replied, opening the door to his SUV.

I groaned and walked to the passenger door and got in. "Where are you taking me now?"

"To watch the sunrise."

"I can see it right now," I said. "The ocean is right there, nothing is blocking my view." I guess I should have mentioned that the coffee was shop was just by the coast on the outskirts of town. All well, now you know.

Evan sighed as he started the car. "You're annoying."

I smiled at him as he started to back out of the parking spot. And then we were off, although not very far. He drove two minutes up the road from the coffee shop and then pulled off and parked on a large flat section of beach.

"See, this is a better place to watch a sunrise," Evan said as he turned the car off.

"Where are we gonna sit?" I asked.

Evan chuckled. "Do you think I go anywhere without being prepared?" He got out of the car and went around the back and opened the trunk.

I got out and walked around to see what he was doing.

"Here you are, my love, a seat that isn't my face," he said as he handed me a foldable chair. You know the ones, those camping chairs with the netted cup holders.

I took it from him and put my hot cocoa in his trunk as I popped open the chair. "I guess a nasty green camping chair is better than getting sand all up in my cracks."

"Cracks? You only have a— Never mind," Evan said, taking the second chair from his trunk.

"Did you forget I had a vagina?" I asked. "Evan, goddammit, man."

"I'm still basically asleep. Cut me some slack."

"If you're still asleep, why didn't you just let me drive?"

"Do you even have your licence?"

I sighed. "Did you ever ask? I just don't have my own car. I coulda drove us here."

"Nah, there weren't any cars," he replied. "It's fine. We're fine."

"Stop driving when you're not in your right mind," I barked as he closed his trunk. "It's not safe to drive after your chemo and it's not safe to drive if you're still half asleep."

"Have I gotten into a car accident yet?"

"Not yet," I grumbled at him.

"Then quit your worrying."

"You just said back in the coffee shop that you didn't wanna die and now you're okay with that possibility because you're irresponsible at driving?"

"No," he replied as we set our chairs in the sand in front of his SUV. "I just think that dying in a car wreck is a quicker way to go than dying by cancer. At least if I get my head smashed into my engine block, I won't have to constantly have the thought of it looming over me every minute like a leech."

I turned to the sunrise and closed my eyes for a minute. I took a few deep breaths to try to rid myself of Evan's bullshit. I turned back to him and he smiled at me.

"I know what I'm doing, Spencer," Evan said. "I'm not trying to kill myself. I'm not trying to get hurt. I just know that I can manage for myself even if I'm half asleep or whatever. Once I get in a car, all I see is the road."

"I just want you to be more responsible," I stated. "Let me drive you once and a while, honestly, it's not gonna hurt your manhood to let me drive."

"Shush," Evan said. "We can talk logistics later. For now, let's just enjoy the sunrise."

I turned back to the horizon and watched as the waves rolled over each other and crashed onto the beach. The sky above was turning a bright pale blue and pale pink mixture. It was pretty analogous to a lazy winter morning. But I haven't slept in a while, so excuse the lack of poeticism.

{Chapter: **Thirteen**}

I jumped back out of the way of a pot of boiling water being dropped right in front of me. I jumped further back than I thought I ever possibly could in such a situation. I jumped further back than I thought *I* was even possible for me.

"I'll clean it," Charlotte said as she had hopped onto the countertop to avoid being burned by the boiling water.

"Yeah, you better," I snapped.

"I'm not cleaning it up. I know that," Evan chimed from his seat over at my kitchen table.

"Can you fill the pot with more water, Spencer?" Charlotte asked as she reached for a dish towel.

"You're gonna need more than that," I said as I leaned over and picked up the pot we were using. I put it on the counter and then took off my socks. I walked over to the sink as Charlotte went off to get a bigger towel. I stood and filled the pot with water and then put it back on the stove. You know, at least the water on the floor wasn't cold, so my feet got a little bath. Even thought I was clean already. I'm always clean. Being clean is good form.

"I guess the KD is gonna take even longer to make now," Evan whined as I sat next to him at the table.

"Oh, boohoo, you're still gonna get food," I said, looking down at my bare foot. "I need to paint my nails, bruh. You should do it for me."

"I could never colour in the lines," he replied. "So you'd have better luck just putting your foot in a bucket of paint."

"A simple no would have sufficed."

He smirked at me a little. "I don't like a simple no though."

"Shut up."

"Okay," Charlotte said, walking into the room with three big towels. "This better soak up the water."

"I don't know if you needed three. This was more of a two-towel water alarm," I joked to her.

"Hey, look at this, nerd," Evan said, tapping my leg with his foot.

I turned and looked at his phone to see a cute little Yoshi drawing. "Aww, that's cute though."

"Yeah. I know you like Yoshi," he said, continuing to scroll through whatever app he was on. Evan's such a dork. He'll just occasionally show me things like that whenever he sees something he thinks I'd like. So cute.

"So I wanna drop out of school," I said into the empty silence that had settled into the room.

"You what?" they both said, snapping their gazes to me. It was almost creepy how in tune they were with each other right now.

"I want to leave school," I repeated.

"Why the hell would you do that?" Evan asked.

I shrugged. "I wanna make the most out of life, and I don't think going to school is how I'm gonna do it. I'm just not looking forward to the next three years after this shitty one."

"You have to stay in school," Charlotte stated.

"I don't *have* to do shit," I replied. "But I wanna just spend the most time that I can with all my friends before we all grow apart and die off."

"Oh, I see what this is about," Evan said flatly. "I know what you mean, and that's a dumb idea, Spencer. You can't just do that because of the thing."

"What thing?" Charlotte asked. "Why am I being kept out of the loop here? Tell me. I'm trustworthy."

"No," Evan said sternly to her before turning back to me. "Listen to your own words that you always say and then think about how dumb it would be for you to make a choice based on the opposite of your words."

"Seriously, what the hell are you guys talking about?" Charlotte asked.

"Charlotte, not now. You don't need to know," Evan barked.

"Evan, you know good and well what, uh, what he told me was a possibility, and I just want to take that into account, you know, make every moment last and stuff like that," I explained.

"You're not dropping out of school," Evan stated.

"You're not my dad."

"No, I'm your boyfriend, and as your boyfriend, I have to look out for you and help you to make good choice, not bad ones."

I sighed. "Okay, shit, you got me on that one, but what if I was wrong?"

"Then so be it," Evan said. "Enjoy what you have now and not what you have not."

"I'm literally so beyond confused right now," Charlotte said with a sigh as she hopped onto the counter.

"Good," I said.

"You're staying in school," Charlotte stated. "I might not know what the hell you two are talking about, but I do know that I'm on Evan's side with this one. You're staying in school. You can't just throw that away for more time with friends. None of us are going anywhere anytime soon."

"Whatever, fine," I muttered. "It was just an idea, okay?"

"It wasn't a very good one," Evan stated. "You're more than smart enough to know that, Spencer."

"Shut up. I'm acting out of duress."

Evan sighed. "No, you're really not though."

"Guys, it was just an idea," I told them. "I just wanted your opinions and you both have overwhelmingly opposite opinions. This time, and this time only, I'll let the majority rule. I'll stay my in soul-sucking college."

"Good," Charlotte chimed. "You'll thank us when you get a good job and have a nice house to live in."

"I'll be thanking you too, then," Evan said.

"Why would you thank you?" I asked.

"Because if we stay together, I'd be living in that nice house with you, you idiot," Evan replied.

"Man makes a point," Charlotte said, turning to check the water.

"Just shut up and make the mac and cheese," I barked.

"I'm trying to," Charlotte snapped back. "I can't make the water boil any faster or the food cook any faster."

"Well, sure you can, if you try hard enough."

"You're an idiot."

"No, you."

Evan sighed. "Why did I let you drag me over here?"

"I don't know, 'cause you love me or some shit," I told him. "Really, it's your fault, not mine."

"I never said it was your fault," Evan said. "If you used your ears for anything other than pretending to be an elf, you'd know that I let you drag me over here. I know I coulda said no."

"Did you just make fun of my ears?"

"They're kinda pointy," Evan said. "But it's cute, okay? Don't be sad about it."

"No, I just, I never noticed that," I said, running a finger along my ear. "They don't feel pointy."

"They don't have to feel pointy to look pointier than average ears."

"But I would be able to feel the sharper angle, you idiot."

Evan sighed. "Just look in a mirror sometime."

"I'll do it later, I'm lazy," I said, turning and taking a sip from the coffee I had left on the table.

"Whatever you say, gingersnap."

"Stop," I grumbled. "It's too early in the day for you to be sassing me."

"It's past noon," Evan replied.

"What's your goddamn point?"

"Be nice to each other," Charlotte chimed in. "I don't wanna be your marriage counsellor just yet."

"Yet?" I asked.

"Ever," she corrected herself.

"Ever," Evan chimed, glaring at me.

"We won't need marriage counselling, babe. We're the best couple ever," I said, winking at Evan.

"That's what makes you two such perfect candidates for my first ever appointment," Charlotte stated as she dumped a heap of pasta into the boiling water in the pot.

"I don't ever wanna get counselling for my marriage," Evan said. "Marriage counselling is where marriages go to die."

"Sometimes," I added.

"Well, if you need counselling, odds are, you shouldn't be with that person anyway. I don't think relationships should require counselling for it to work out. It's just kinda lame is all. I don't know."

"Shh," I hushed him. "How's the mac and cheese coming along?"

"It's coming along," Charlotte replied.

"Make it come faster," I snapped.

"You nasty," Evan said, shaking his head at me.

"I'm gonna go outside," I said, standing up and grabbing my coffee cup. "I need some air."

"I'll come with you," Evan said, getting up.

"No screwing on the porch, buds," Charlotte said as Evan and I started to walk out of the room.

I headed outside and sat down on the front step as Evan closed the door behind us. He took a seat next to me on the cold, cold concrete.

"So, what's on your mind?" he asked me as he rested his arm around me and pulled me over to him.

I sighed and rested my head on his shoulder. "I don't know. Life and stuff, I guess."

"Can you be a little more specific?"

I let out a guttural groan. "I just feel like there's never gonna be enough time. Like, no matter what we do, it's not enough. No matter how much time we give to someone, it's not enough. It's just not enough."

"It's enough because there can't be any more time."

"Not enough, Evan. There's not enough time for everything I wanna be able to do in life and there's not enough time to spend with the people I love the most," I reiterated. "There's not enough."

"Why are you so worried about time running out?" Evan asked. "Is there something you're not telling me? Are *you* dying? Are you moving away in a few months? Are you scared of growing up? What is it?"

"It's you," I replied softly. "I'm worried about being wrong. I just told you that."

"I thought there might have been something else dragging on your time so to speak."

"Nope. It's just you. I got to thinking about me being wrong and I just don't think I can cope with that, Evan."

"Spencer," he said, pulling me tightly into him as he rest his head down on mine, "I know it's a shitty thought to think that I might be gone someday soon, but like you said, the odds of that are low. I promised I would fight it, and now I'm gonna do it one better, I promise I'll beat this. You're gonna be stuck with me for a long time, okay, nerd?"

"I just wanna spend all day with you all the time," I whined.

"Nah, I can't let you do that," Evan replied. "Schooling is important. I'm gonna be here for your when you're done schooling. You know, provided you want me for that long."

"Of course I will. You're my nerd."

"Then listen to your nerd and don't make any rash decisions. Live your life normally, like you never even met me in some respects."

"So I should go get loaded and take as many guys as I can in one night?" I asked jokingly.

"Is that what you did before me?"

I shook my head lightly. "No. Never."

"Then don't go off and do that, ya dumbass."

"But, baby," I whined. "I like to take seven guys in one night."

"Shut up," Evan said, turning and kissing my forehead. "Your ears really do have a little point to them though."

"Leave my pointy ears alone," I whined. "I still don't even believe that they're that pointy."

"They're not insanely pointy in an instantly obvious way, they're subtly pointy in a natural way."

I scoffed. "Whatever you say, loser."

"Just for that, you're not getting your back massage later."

"No, wait, I'm sorry," I said quickly. "You're not a loser. Please rub my back and bum later. I need it."

"Get me some sunglasses first. You're too pale."

"I am not!" I protested. "Yeah, no, you actually do have a point there though. I like being pale though. It's more fun to draw on my skin, but I also don't look as good in a bikini. Upsides and downsides, I guess."

"If I might add my professional opinion, I think you look really good in a bikini. Just saying."

"Professional opinion?"

"I'm a straight dude. We spend half of our formative lives looking at pretty girls in bikinis."

I scoffed. "Thanks, nerd. You always know *just* what to say to make me hold you to a high standard and still humanize you at the same time."

"I try not to be a poetic teen douchebag, but sometimes it happens, and then I have to humanize myself in some way."

I smiled at him. "You're just nailing this whole spiel right now."

"I can nail more than a convoluted speech," he said, winking at me and clicking his tongue.

I winked back. "Maybe someday."

"Someday can wait," he said. "I'm not in any rush to have sex with you. I mean, okay, that's a lie, I would do it right now, but I just mean that I'm waiting for you to be ready. And this is a conversation we can have another day."

"Why's that?"

"I feel like Charlotte'll bust down the door and tell use that our lunch is ready any minute now."

I sighed. "Yep, you're probably right. And thanks for being so understanding with the sex thing. I know it's usually a really big part of a relationship, but I kind of like building the building before adding the elevators."

"Odd metaphor," Evan said.

I shrugged. "Odd metaphors are kinda my life."

"In a way, are you an odd metaphor?"

"Nope, don't be trying to inception me or get me all up in my head. It's too early for that shit," I told him.

He smirked at me. "Shh, just let it happen."

"No, I refuse to have another existential crisis."

"I'm sorry."

The door opened up behind us and we turned around to see Charlotte standing there looking down at us.

"Food's almost done," she said. "You should come back inside."

"I guess we should," Evan said.

"Yeah, you go in," I said as he stood up. "I'll be in in a second. I just need a moment to myself."

"Alright, you do you, honey booboo," Evan joked as he went inside and closed the door.

I sat and watched the empty street. There was never any traffic on my street. I guess that's a perk of living on a side street. I took a sip of my coffee and closed my eyes and took a few deep breaths. I don't know why, but I just felt like something bad was looming. It's almost like the feeling you get when you see dark storm clouds rolling in. You know it's coming, but you don't know exactly when or how bad it'll really be, but it's coming. I stood up and opened my eyes. Nothing seemed any different, but it sure as hell felt like it.

{Chapter: **Fourteen**}

March Break is always such a great time of year for me. It's a week off of school, although we're supposed to be studying and stuff and working on projects, but I think they know good and well that none of us are gonna be doing anything school related for a good few days.

Yeah, but anyway, I woke up to a banging at my bedroom door. I bolted upright and went over and opened the door. "Who the f—" I began to shout before being tackled to the ground in a tight embrace.

"I missed you!" Mindy's voiced yelled out.

"I tried to stop her," Charlotte said from the doorway.

I wrapped my arms around Mindy and hugged her back as I stared daggers at Charlotte. "She's five feet tall. You did nothing."

Charlotte shrugged. "You needed a good Mindy hug."

"Not like this," I whined.

"I missed you so much," Mindy yelped as she rolled off of me and sat upright.

"I missed you too, Mindy. Although I might have missed a few breaths right there too," I groaned, sitting up and grabbing a pair of pants from the floor. I stood up and slipped into them. I don't wanna risk getting a carpet burn on my poor little tushy.

"What do you guys wanna do today? We can all go drinking or

something," Mindy said, her eyes full of light and happiness. "I haven't seen Spencer get drunk in a while, so let's go do that."

"Yeah, I'm game for drinks," I said, walking over and grabbing a sweater from my closet.

"It's noon though," Charlotte said.

"Don't be a buzzkill, Charlotte," I groaned, slipping the sweater over my drool-stained shirt. "Let's go get some coffee and then some lunch and then we'll go for drinks."

"I could go for a coffee, actually," Mindy stated, standing up.

"Let's do coffee," Charlotte said as she turned and headed out the door.

"It feels so good to be back. I missed you so much," Mindy said, hugging me again.

"I missed you too, you little shit," I said, tightly squeezing her back. This time, I could actually hug her properly.

"Ooh, we should go pick up Haley," Mindy said as we let go of each other, turned, and walked out of my room.

"Haley?"

"My girlfriend?" Mindy said, sounding surprised that it didn't come to me right away. "She's in town too. I left her at Charlotte's house while we came over here."

"You're staying at Charlotte's?" I whined as we walked down the stairs. "That's so not fair. You know I need my Mindy."

"Sorry, bruh. She needed an extra room with a proper bed so she could sleep with Haley," Charlotte stated.

"Well, I have an extra bed in the basement!"

"Do you?" Mindy asked.

"Yes!"

"Hmm. Maybe we can split the stay or something," Mindy said. "Either way, you can still come hang out every day with us."

"Yeah, yeah, at least we know who your favourite is," I grumbled as we slipped our shoes on at the door.

"*You* are my favourite," Mindy groaned.

"Thanks," Charlotte said, pushing Mindy with one hand as she opened the front door with the other.

"Well, Spencer's my height. She gets me."

"Just for that, Spencer gets shotgun," Charlotte said as she pulled her keys from her pocket.

Mindy smirked. "Well, I was gonna sit in the back anyway."

"Oh, right, okay, never mind. Mindy, you get shotgun," Charlotte said. "I'm trying to punish you a little, so this is how we're gonna do that."

After the two of them bickered a little, we were off to Charlotte's house to pick up Haley. And for pretty much the entire ride over, Mindy and Charlotte bickered about nothing. I missed it though. Their bickering was what made me feel like a sane person.

"Whoa," I said, looking at the car in her driveway. "Who's BMW?"

"Haley's," Mindy replied. "She's got *money*."

"You sure did hit the jackpot, huh?" I said jokingly.

Mindy nodded. "Mm-hmm. Now you two stay here, I'll run in and get her."

"Take your time," Charlotte said, shutting the car off. We watched Mindy run inside and disappear for a few minutes. She really was taking her time though. After a few minutes, she came back outside with a purpled-haired girl in tow. And this wasn't, like, *purple*, it was more of a lavender. Periwinkle, if you would.

Mindy hopped back in the front as Haley got into the back. "This is Haley," Mindy said to me.

I shot her a flat look. "Couldn't tell."

"Haley, this is a little bitch named Spencer," Mindy said, turning to Haley. "You can beat her up if you want."

"I'm gonna beat *you* up," Haley barked back at Mindy.

"And I'm gonna help," I said.

"And I'm gonna film it," Charlotte chimed in as she started the car.

Mindy sighed. "I hate all of you."

"Yeah, we're used to that," I said. "I don't think you've ever really liked us. I mean, we're pretty mean to each other sometimes."

"That's just what friends do," Mindy replied.

"If we weren't friends, I would beat you up for real."

"Why?" she whined.

"Because, I dunno, you're a little dork."

"That's true," Haley said.

"Don't encourage her," Mindy snapped.

"Encourage me," I whispered. I don't know why, but picking on Mindy is always so fun. She gets so agitated with us, but we love each other. I kinda feel bad sometimes, because two-on-one isn't fair, but now we have three people that'll rag on her. Poor girl.

"So, what do we want for lunch?" Charlotte asked as we backed out of the driveway.

"We can figure that out over a coffee," I whined. "I'm still so tired. I only just woke up, like, fifteen minutes ago or whatever."

"And you look that good?" Haley asked. "Lucky you."

"You have A1 sleepy look too," Mindy chimed.

"Not really. I still have to at least put some effort into it to look good," Haley stated.

"Wait, so did you guys get in this morning?" I asked.

"No…" Mindy said quietly. "We got in last night."

"And you didn't tell me?" I shouted. "What the hell, man? I could have come to hang out last night with you!"

"I sorta figured you and Evan woulda been off doing whatever it is you two do together," Charlotte stated.

"Which is generally just watching Netflix and eating food," I said. "Not a lot of fun, really."

"Yeah, but he can give you the D?" Charlotte questioned. "That's fun, isn't it?"

"Oh, loads of fun, yeah."

"Please tell me you guys have done the nasty by this point."

I stayed quiet and looked out the window. I could hear Charlotte let out a soft sigh and Mindy snicker slightly.

***

We got to the coffee place and Charlotte made Mindy and Haley order our coffees. And then Charlotte dragged me off to a booth right away, probably to lecture me about something. "Alright, why ain't you two banging?" she asked as she tossed me into a booth. Called it.

"Because," I said, shrugging, "I dunno."

"Bullshit. There has to be a reason," she said. "You guys have been together a few months now, you both love each other already because you both fall way too hard and way too fast, but it's super cute that you two love each other anyway because you two are really good together."

"We just haven't done it because I'm not really ready for that."

"If it's because *him*, then you need to let go of that," Charlotte said. "Not every guy is gonna do that same bullshit to you. Especially not Evan. He's such a world-class guy. I don't think I should have stood him up. My fault on that one, I guess."

"Well, it's not like I haven't done anything for him," I grumbled.

"Okay, but hand jobs are only acceptable if you're in high school."

"Shut the hell up," I snapped. "I'm not ready for anything too serious right now. It's just… It's too much anxiety for me. This is what happens when you get hurt though. You start trying to avoid the thing that caused the hurt in the first place. Which is smart, might I add. If you burn yourself on a stove, you don't put your hand back down on the stove. You learn."

"Okay, but boys are not stoves, they're not gonna burn you," Charlotte stated. "Well, I at least hope they aren't gonna burn us."

"No, they'll just use us for sex or worse," I said. "Namely, make us fall in love with them and then leave without reason or warning. Y'know, just boy things."

"That was one guy. You got your heartbreak out of the way early, so now you can focus on this one, your first true love," Charlotte told me. "Who knows, this could be the guy you marry."

I smiled a little at the idea of living with Evan until we grew old. But I mean, beyond my issues and his cancer, what are the odds of living happy ever after?

"Spencer."

I looked up at her and raised an eyebrow slightly. "Yeah?"

"Do you love him?"

I exhaled slowly and nodded. "Yeah, I'd be dumb not to. He's perfect."

"You know, in the two years I've known you, I don't think I've ever heard you say such a truthful thing."

"What?"

"Well, like, I can hear it in your voice that you actually mean that," she said. "I haven't heard you say something with such sincerity since I asked you the same thing about You-Know-Who."

"Stop," I said. "You're gonna make me throw up. I don't wanna think about him anymore and I just don't think I'm ready for sex. I'm a born-again virgin."

"Oh, shut the hell up. I was just curious why it hadn't happened yet," Charlotte stated. "And you told me your reason why, and I completely understand it. If you're not ready, you're not ready. I think if he loves you, it's not gonna matter either way."

"Okay, thank you wise Sensei Charlotte."

She smirked at me and then moved to the next seat over as Mindy and Haley came over with our coffees.

"Hope it didn't take as long as it felt," Haley said as she sat down.

"It always feels longer than it is," I said, taking my coffee from the tray.

"Dick joke?" Mindy asked.

I winked at her as I peeled back the tab of my coffee lid.

"Anyway," Charlotte said, "what do you guys wanna do tonight? Are we gonna do drinks and stuff?"

"Yeah. Didn't we agree to doing drinks later?" I asked.

"I was hoping Haley would help me out and not want to go get drunk," she replied.

"Meh, you don't need to be our DD or anything," I told her. "I can just call Evan and he'd make sure we got home in one piece."

"That's cruel and unusual punishment," Mindy said as she started playing with a straw wrapper. "What did that poor boor ever do to you to deserve that?"

"Deserve what?" I asked.

"Driving the four of us home."

I blinked a couple times and raised an eyebrow. "What's so bad about that? I don't get it?"

"Four girls," Charlotte said as she sipped her coffee.

"Four *drunk* girls," Haley corrected.

"Yeah, but he can sleep with one of them, so that's, like, a consolation prize," Mindy joked, still fondling the straw wrapper.

"Yeah, but we're not doing that," I said. "We'll just go to a bar near Charlotte's house so we can walk home afterwards." And let me tell you right now, that didn't go well.

"Yeah, smart idea," Charlotte said, pulling her phone out.

"Drinks on me, then?" Haley offered.

I smirked and glanced over at Mindy. "This one's a keeper."

"Yeah, she is," Mindy said with a big, proud smile on her face. "My little shit-disturber."

"I'm taller and heavier than you," Haley said, wrapping an arm around Mindy and pulling her into a hug. Haley kissed her on the face and Mindy jokingly made a disgusted face.

"You two are disgustingly cute," I groaned. "Goddammit."

"You're that disgusting with Evan sometimes," Charlotte chimed.

I shrugged. "Yeah, but he's not a cute girl. It's not the same."

"He's got a floof in his hair and he wears beanies and baseball shirts and he does that thing with his face."

"He smiles?" I questioned.

Charlotte nodded. "That's the thing."

"You're an idiot," I said with a sigh, sipping some of my coffee. Man, this shit was really good. I could drink coffee forever, but that's definitely not healthy. My heart would have a resting pulse of a thousand BPM, minimum.

"I'm feeling doughnuts," Haley said. "Should I get a dozen?"

"A dozen?" Mindy asked. "That's three doughnuts each?"

"Aww, you taught it math," Charlotte joked.

"Piss off. Math is for nerds," Mindy snapped back.

I laughed a little. "Hey, at least you're breaking the stereotype of all Asians being good at math."

"Exactly," Mindy said, raising her hand for a high five. "Fuck the system!"

I smacked her hand. "You said a mouthful."

"Speaking of a mouthful." Haley stood up from the table. "I'm gonna go get us a dozen doughnuts. Is assorted good? Or do any of you want a specific doughnut?"

"I want a sour cream glazed," I told her. "At least one sour cream glazed."

"I'm good with assorted," Mindy said.

"Me too," Charlotte chimed in.

"Alright, I'ma go get them doughnuts, then," Haley said, turning and walking off to go order the doughnuts. I feel like doughnuts are quickly becoming the primary focus of this *chapter* of my life. But do I care? Not really. Doughnuts are so damn good.

After the doughnut meal, we weren't very hungry for lunch. We ended up just going back to Charlotte's and dicking around. Then around dinner, we had dinner. I know, shocking, right? We went to the bar down the road from Charlotte's and the four of us got absolutely plastered. I mean wasted. I mean hammered. The four of us were just absolutely rangle-flangled.

I'm actually really surprised we were able to make it back to Charlotte's house in one piece. I'm even more surprised that none of us threw up at all. Haley and Mindy went off and, assumingly, they had some drunken sex in the guest room. Charlotte barely made it to her bed, which was pretty funny to watch her try to get up the stairs. And what happened to me, little ol' Spencer? Well, I passed out on the countertop in the kitchen because, and I quote myself, "It's nice and cold." Not good for the back, but hey, it was refreshing on my drunken skin. And then I let the slow spinning of the world around me put me to sleep.

{Chapter: **Fifteen**}

I groaned as I sat up on the countertop I had fallen asleep on. Who the hell let me sleep on a counter? I'm the smallest human bean in the house and yet nobody moved me to the couch. I swung my legs over the edge and hopped down from the counter and landed with a soft little thud, which was the exact opposite of the thudding in my brain right now. Seriously, why do hangovers have to be a thing? God, I feel like such shit right now. I stumbled over to Charlotte's living room and I pulled out my phone. Figures. It's bright and early and nobody else would be up at eight in the morning, but I sure am.

I let out a sigh and called Evan.

His sleepy voice answered, "It's way too early for you to be up. What do you need, gingersnap?"

"Come pick me up from Charlotte's and bring me to get coffee?"

"For you and her?"

"No, for me and you," I mumbled back. "And hush, you're being too loud, jeez."

"Hungover, huh?"

I grumbled something that I thought meant yes.

"I'll be right over. Drink some water while you wait," he said. I heard some shuffling and a bed creaking as he hung up.

"Love you," I muttered to the dial tone as I hung up my end and put the phone back into my pocket.

I got up and wandered off to the kitchen and grabbed a couple of Tylenol pills from the medicine cupboard they had and then a bottle of water. I popped the pills into my mouth and washed them down with the water. I yawned as I walked over to the front door. I debated on leaving a note for the girls, but nah, they'll just text me when they wake up and then I'll tell them I left. I put my shoes on and fixed my sweater. I grabbed a hair tie from next to the door and put my hair into a messy bun. I don't think Evan's expecting me to look good right now anyway. I straightened my sweater out as I stepped outside. I sat down on the steps of Charlotte's front porch as I waited for Evan. By the time he got here, I was already done sipping my water. I stood up, tossed the bottle in the blue bin, and walked down to the street.

"Hola," I said, opening the door to the SUV and getting inside.

"You look so beautiful," he said, leaning over and turning my face with his thumb to kiss me.

I smiled a little at that. "Thanks. I look like shit, but thank you."

"I don't think I've ever seen you look bad, ever," he stated. "Pretty sure you might be an IRL goddess."

"Nah," I said, blushing a little. "Let's just go get coffees, dork."

"Also," he said, reaching over to the glove compartment, "drink this." He handed me a bottle of something. "It's aloe vera drink. It should help detoxify you and crap."

"Well, it's worth a shot." I cracked it open and took a big drink of it. "Okay, so this is actually good, but what's with the chunks of pulp? Chunks, Evan. There are *chunks* of plant in my drink. Why?"

"That's what makes it good for you, so shut up and eat-drink it," he said as we started driving.

"Rude," I muttered as I took another drink. "Try to avoid potholes and stuff. My head is throbbing."

"I thought hitting every bump might be a nice thing to do."

"No sassing me either. I'm not in a good mood."

"Okay. What can I do, then?"

"You can kiss me, get me coffee, and then take me home and cuddle me until I feel better," I told him. "Especially that last thing, do that one for sure."

"Can we nap?"

"This why I love you."

"Well, I mean, you woke me up at eight during our week off. I wanna go back to sleep," he said with a small laugh. "I mean, I don't mind that you did, I'm just still a little tired."

"I'll nap with you any day at any time of it," I said. "You're warm and you smell good and you're comfortable to lay on."

"You should get me a shirt that has 'World's Best Body Pillow' written on it or something. I'd wear the shit out of it."

"Maybe I will," I stated. "And it wouldn't even be a lie."

"And I can get you one that says something about being the world's best body warmer or something. I don't know."

"My toes are always cold though. I'm not a very warm-bodied body," I told him.

He shrugged. "Other than your toes and fingers, you're pretty warm."

"You already got me a custom sweater, so chill," I said, rubbing my temples. "Man, why do we think it's ever a good idea to get drunk? I throb, Evan. Throb. I can feel my brain throbbing in my skull. Why did you let me do this to myself?"

"Well, in my defence, I wasn't with you last night."

"You should have been." I let out a groan and then took a long drink of the aloe vera drink.

"You could have called me up. I would have made sure you didn't get completely hammered."

"Yeah, but being drunk is fun. So instead of stopping me from getting drunk, you should invent a perfect hangover remedy," I stated. "That'd be so much more helpful."

"I would if I could, but hangovers are your payment for getting drunk," Evan stated.

"Payment?" I asked. "Isn't it bad enough that I had to pay for my own drinks to get drunk in the first place?"

"No, but getting drunk is like borrowing happiness from the morning after," he stated. "You're paying back that borrowed happiness by suffering through some pain."

"That's stupid," I whined. "I just wanted to have a fun night and then wake up feeling all good and shit, but nope. Why can't we have nice things, Evan? Why?"

"Because good things come at a price. I dunno."

"Yeah, but why does the price have to be my sanity?" I groaned. "My head is going to explode. That's a thing that is going to happen."

"Oh, shut up and keep drinking stuff. You need fluids. Fluids always help."

"Then why do I still feel like trash?"

"Because you're hungover," Evan said with a small smirk on his face. I'd hit him if he weren't driving and if I weren't dying.

I let out a low, guttural animal noise and rested my head back on the headrest of the seat. "I'm gonna die, Evan. I'm not gonna make it."

"Oh, would you shut the hell up."

"Babe. Please. Kill me now. Release me from my suffering. I cannot go on any longer. I am weak. I grow tired of living. Set me free into the great beyond."

"Dude, it's just a hangover, relax," he said with a small laugh.

"I know, but my head is throbbing and my back hurts so much."

"Why does your back hurt?" he asked as we pulled into a drive-thru.

I hesitated a minute. "I, uh, I sorta might have slept on a counter."

He turned to me and gave me a perplexed look. "You did what?"

"I slept on a counter."

"Why?" he asked as we reached the drive-thru speaker. "Hold that thought."

I nodded and then he turned and ordered our coffees and then pulled up to the window. He paid and then handed me my coffee after they gave it to him. He put his coffee in the cup holder.

"Okay, so why did you sleep on a counter last night?" he asked as we pulled out of the drive-thru.

"I don't know, it seemed like a good idea at the time," I said, trying to drink a little bit of coffee, but since we were in a moving car, I ended up spilling it down my shirt. "Fucking dammit."

"You're like a goddamn child," Evan said, grabbing napkins from the glove department as he waited for the street to clear so we could

117

turn out. "Here." He handed me the napkins and took my coffee from me and put it in the other cup holder. "Don't friggin' touch the coffee until we get to your house. I don't need you spilling it again."

"It's kinda hot when you're bossy," I said, dabbing my shirt and legs dry with a wad of napkins.

"No, I'm kinda annoyed."

"Why?" I whined. "Oh, my God, Evan, did you just say you were annoyed with me? And you sound agitated. Did I just, for the first time, frustrate you?"

"Yeah," he said. "You just spilt coffee on my seat and you're being a little whiny turd, *but* I love you, so it's okay."

"Sorry, I'll pay for you to clean it or whatever," I said, balling up the napkins and putting them in the side of the door.

"It's fine, just don't spill anything else," he said. "Let's just get you home and safe in your bed so you can't mess anything else up, okay?"

"Yes, please," I said, taking another drink of the aloe vera drink.

"See, you don't spill that."

"It's in a bottle," I replied. "I'm actually just a toddler."

Evan sighed. "Yeah, you're acting like one now."

"I'm just hungover because I went out with friends."

"I know."

"Hey, how come you don't go out with friends?" I asked.

He scoffed. "I do. I just don't bring you out with me when I do. I don't think you'd like hanging out with dudes."

"Well, you've met my friends, you dork. I wanna meet yours."

"Why would you want to meet any of my friends?" he asked.

"Just your best friend. You've met Charlotte and she's my best friend, which actually reminds me that you have to come meet Mindy," I told him. "She's the reason we went out last night."

"Fine, hold the wheel," Evan said, grabbing my hand and putting it on the steering wheel.

I watched as he pulled out his phone. "I don't think this is any safer, dude."

"Shut up and keep your eyes on the road and tell me if I need to brake," he said as he quickly started typing away a message to, assumingly, his best friend. After a few seconds he took the wheel back and then we got to my house. We drank our coffee and then we took a nap in my bed so I could try to get over this hangover.

When we woke up, well, when I woke up, I texted Mindy and Charlotte to let them know I had jetted off because of the hangover. I went downstairs and got myself a big glass of water and chugged it back. Evan came down the stairs as I was gonna go back up them and he hurried me out the door.

We went off and got some more coffee, this time though, we got three coffees. And then we drove all the way up to the bowling alley. In the parking lot, there was another car, an old muscle car.

"Nice car," I said as we pulled up.

"It's okay," Evan said, turning the key and shutting the SUV off.

I opened the door and stepped outside with the tray of coffees in my hands. I followed Evan over to the doorway and we went inside. I heard the distant sounds of clattering bowling pins.

"I guess he's started the party without us," Evan said as he shut the door behind us.

I stayed behind Evan a little as we walked over to the brightly lit bowling lane that his friend was at.

"Oi!" Evan shouted.

His friend looked over to us and scoffed. "Well, it's about time you showed up."

"Sorry, we slept in," Evan said.

"It's five."

"What's your point?"

"So, this must be the lovely Spencer," his friend said, looking directly to me now. "I've heard quite a bit about you. This guy doesn't really shut up about you."

Evan smiled a little. "He's got a point there."

"I'm Collin, Evan's partner in crime," he said.

"And I'm Spencer, Evan's partner," I said, putting the tray of coffees down on the table. As Collin moved over to grab a coffee, I managed to get a good look at him. The dude was tall, let's start there, he must have been a foot taller than me, maybe even a little more. He had a nose ring and a messy pompadour hairstyle. Speaking of his hair, it was a light brown colour, which sort of matched his hazel-coloured eyes.

119

"Where's Kenzie?" Evan asked, pulling a box of pizza from seemingly nowhere. I guess Collin had bought it and put it on the other side seat thing.

"Oh, yeah, me and her aren't really a thing anymore," he replied.

"Lame," Evan said, putting pizza down on a paper plate and handing it to me. "Eat up, nerd."

"Thanks," I said as I took the plate.

"It's not lame," Collin said, walking over and taking a piece of pizza. "I just outgrew her."

"Makes sense," Evan said with a small shrug. He walked over and took a seat and then pulled me down to sit next to him. He kissed my cheek and then my forehead and smiled at me "I won't outgrow *you.*"

"You're already too big," I said with a wink as I clicked my tongue.

Collin cracked up a little as he tried to take a sip of coffee, which he ended up spilling because I made him laugh.

"Both of you: toddlers," Evan deadpanned.

"Oh, come on, that was kinda funny," Collin said, putting his coffee down and taking off his sweater. At least he had a shirt underneath, proper planning.

"Well, yeah, she's not wrong, but still, you both spat up coffee on yourselves today," Evan told him. "*Toddlers.*"

"I was hungover," I snapped.

"And I was laughing," Collin stated.

Evan shrugged. "Learn how to drink things, guys."

"I'm revoking your cottage privileges," Collin said to him.

"Oh, shit, okay, you're not a toddler. I'm sorry. Please don't revoke my cottage privileges."

"Speaking of, are we going up sometime soon?" Collin asked.

Evan shrugged. "I mean, yeah, I want to." He turned to me. "Do you wanna come to the cottage with us?"

"I like cottages," I said with my mouth full of pizza.

"You like catfish?" Evan teased.

I smacked his arm and gave him an angry face as I swallowed my food. "Cottages, asshole. I like cottages. I wanna go to a cottage."

"It's settled, she gets your room. In two minutes, she's proved to

120

be funnier and feistier than you," Collin said. "Where ever did you find her?"

"The mall. You know the story," Evan said back, grabbing his coffee from the table.

"I was on the clearance rack," I said, shrugging. "Kind of an unpassable bargain."

"Oh, you sure the story didn't involve you and a dressing room?" Collin asked with a wink. "Yeah, he told me."

I smacked Evan a few times. "Dammit, Evan. You just talked yourself out of a fun time later."

"I'm on my period anyway," he joked back, grabbing my arms and stopping me from smacking him anymore. "I'm sure if you were me, you'd have told your best friend the same things."

"You make some good points," I said, pushing his arms off me.

Collin picked up a bowling ball and sighed. "You two are just *so* cute together."

{Chapter: **Sixteen**}

After spending a few days together, the bunch of us headed to Collin's cottage. And by bunch, I mean that it was Evan, Collin, Charlotte, Mindy, Haley, and I. We all hung out a few times and now we were heading up to the cottage for a few days to enjoy the last little bit of our week off.

We pulled into the cottage's driveway after Collin. He had led the way for us, even though Evan knew the way. We had all piled into the SUV because carpool. When we got there, I got out and looked up at the cottage. It was a pretty big cottage that looked like a log cottage, but I'm sure that was only for decorative purpose. I peered down into the backyard and saw a fire pit way down by the water. Of course the cottage was also beachfront property.

"So how bad are the bugs?" Haley asked as we walked to the back of the SUV to get our bags.

"Not very bad. And if they do get bad, we have bug spray here," Evan replied, opening the back of the SUV.

"Okay, good. I don't do bugs," Haley said, grabbing her bag and swinging it over her back. She took a second bag, Mindy's probably, and then headed over to Collin.

Evan swung my bag over his shoulder and then grabbed his bag and carried them off to meet up with Collin as well. Charlotte took her bag from the trunk and I closed it for her, which made no sense, because I'm too short to reach the top of the thing to pull it down and close it.

"So, um, the rooming situation should be pretty obvious," Collin stated as I walked up to the group that had formed around his trunk.

"It's not," Mindy said. "Can you explain it?"

"Spencer with Evan, Haley with Mindy, Charlotte in the other bedroom, me on the couch," Collin said as he pulled his bag out of the trunk of his car. "Understood?"

"Can you go over that again?" I asked jokingly.

"Shush," Collin said to me as he closed his trunk. "Okay, so Evan's getting his usual room, duh, and Haley and Mindy can have the other basement room. Charlotte, you get the master bedroom, since you're the odd one out and all. The other rooms are all off limits right now because they're being used for storage until the summer, so there's no room switching available."

"Ooh, alright, let's go see the rooms, then," Mindy said.

Collin nodded for us to walk up to the house. We followed Evan up to the front door and then Collin cut through the group of us with a key out. He unlocked the door and let us into the cottage.

The door led us into a wide, open living room area. The big room was covered in hardwood floors, had some white couches and a TV set up on the wall. There was a fireplace opposite to that on the other wall. There were two hallways on either side of us that led down. I could see the way on our left led into a kitchen. The right hallway led to rooms. I guess that the bathroom was probably directly behind the wall on our right and that there was some closets or something behind the wall to our left. I noticed that the one wall in front of us was all glass, so it overlooked the backyard and lake. There also seemed to be a railing just past the couches and stuff before that large glass wall. Why would there be a railing by the window?

"So this is the top floor," Collin said as he shut the door behind us. "Evan's room is up to the right because he's a whiny baby and needs a nice view over the backyard and the lake."

"Oh, hush it. I just like nice views," Evan barked.

"Whatever," Collin said. "Anyway, the bathroom's to the right, kitchen's to the left. The stairs to the *basement* are just up here." Collin headed through the living room and to the railing. "Just down here, follow me."

"I'll show Spencer around later," Evan said as we walked over to the railing.

I peered down and saw a large room with a pool table and a foosball table. There were at least two or three TVs down there as well. Lots of couches too.

"Yeah, that's fine. I'm gonna get these three settled into their rooms and then go check the kitchen for food," Collin said as the four of them walked down the stairs.

"This place is cool," I said as Evan and I turned around.

"Yeah, it's pretty neat," he said, starting to walk towards our room.

"I kinda really enjoy this place already."

"You know, I have a transparent tent up here. If the weather is clear, we should go camp under the stars one of these nights."

I smiled a little at him. "That's so lame. We need to do it."

He stopped at the first door down the hallway and opened it. "This is our room, nerd."

I looked around at the room. The back wall was all glass. The other walls were a pale sky blue colour. The carpet was a light grey colour. The bed was at least a queen and has white sheets with silvery covers. Now that boring descriptions are done.

"I love it," I said, walking in and jumping onto the bed. "UGH! It's so comfy."

Evan walked over and plopped our bags by the end of the bed and then he plopped down next to me. "Yeah. I love this bed."

"I love you," I said, rolling over and laying my head down on him. I curled up and wrapped a leg over him and nuzzled into him a little more.

"You're a dork," he said, kissing my forehead.

"Your dork."

"I'm so glad you're my dork."

I smiled and shut my eyes to sleep. I don't know why, but being in Evan's arms made me feel so safe, like all the rest of the world just fell away and it was just the two of us, and feeling that safe makes me wanna sleep because I'm pretty much always tired anyway.

"Wake up," Evan's voice said softly in my ear.

I shot upright to him shaking me on the bed. "What? Where?"

"You fell asleep," he said, standing upright and letting go of me.

"I did," I said, wiping my eyes and yawning. "Did you fall asleep too?"

He shook his head. "I let you fall asleep and then I tucked you in and went to hang out with the others for a little while. I wanted to let you nap."

"Thank you," I said, pulling the blanket off of me. "Is there any tea here?"

"You want a tea?" he asked.

I nodded.

He kissed my cheek. "Okay, I'll make you one. You just go downstairs and hang out with those nerds."

I nodded and got out of bed. I stretched out, which caused Evan to give me a weird look. "What are you looking at, bud?"

"You," he replied as I walked past him. "Watching you stretch out is such a cute sight because you just so tiny, aww."

"Shut up and make me a tea, peasant," I said as I walked out of the room.

"I like it when you're bossy," he said, closing the door over behind us. "It's kinda of hot."

"Yeah, you are."

"No, you," he said as he smacked my bum. He walked off quickly so I couldn't do anything back to him.

I scoffed and headed down the stairs to the basement. It was a well-furnished area. Lots of stuff to do for recreation in here. A few TVs, pool table, foosball table, air hockey, darts, gaming systems, a ping pong table, and a little bar.

"Hey, there she is," Mindy said. "Did you enjoy your nap?"

I nodded. "I did."

"Who naps at a cottage? Like, come on, enjoy the cottage life," Charlotte said, offering me a seat on the couch in between her and Mindy.

"You want something to drink?" Collin asked.

I looked around and noticed that they all had a beer in their hands. "Um, no. No, thanks. Evan is off making me a tea."

"Well, if you need anything, just ask."

"Do you have any whisky?" I asked.

Collin nodded. "Lots."

"I'll want some later."

"Do we have stuff to make s'mores?" Mindy asked. "I want some."

"Of course we do," Collin replied.

***

"Do you just burn all your marshmallows?" I asked Evan as he put another near-black wad of goo onto a graham cracker.

"It's not burnt, it's cooked," he said, putting the chocolate and other graham cracker down on top.

"It's burnt. The outside is like charcoal," I said, grabbing another marshmallow from the bag beside us. We had a few bags of marshmallows, so every couple basically got their own bag. Except that Collin and Charlotte left a while ago to go to the store or something. So it was just Haley and Mindy and Evan and me.

"So, where did the other two run off to? It's been well over an hour and a half since they left," Haley asked.

We all shrugged.

"Collin probably roped her into getting McDonald's or something," Evan said, then sticking half of his s'more in his mouth.

"That's lame of them," I said. "Bitch knows I like me some burgers too."

"Maybe they're hooking up," Mindy said, sticking a marshmallow over the fire.

"I doubt that," Evan said. "Collin just went through a breakup and he doesn't generally rebound this fast. He likes to move on before finding someone else."

"It's been a few days, maybe he has moved on?" I suggested.

Evan shook his head.

"Whatever, I bet they are hooking up." I positioned my marshmallow over the fire. "Nobody takes this long to go to the store."

"Collin might if he feels like going to other stores," Evan said.

"I still think they're hooking up," I said. "Just a hunch."

"No way. See, if they were hooking up, he'd have to ask me for a condom."

"Why would he ask you?"

"Because I always have a condom in my bag," Evan replied. "It's better to have it and not need it than to need it and not have it."

"Why wouldn't he just buy some at the store?" Mindy asked.

"He's cheap. He just borrows mine because I never use them," Evan explained.

"Sorry," I whispered, pulling my marshmallow back from the fire.

"It's not your fault? The waiting makes it special," Evan said, eyeing my marshmallow.

"Oh, this? This is what a normally roasted marshmallow looks like. See how it's golden and not burnt," I said, teasing him.

"I bet needing condoms sucks, huh?" Mindy asked with a sly little smirk on her face.

"Shut up," I barked at her.

"Oh, I just got a text," Evan said, pulling out his phone. "It's from Collin." He handed me the phone. "You may do the honours, princess."

"Don't call me princess," I said, taking the phone. I cleared my throat loudly aggressive and aggressively loud. I started to read the message aloud, "Hey, bro, I borrowed a few condoms from your bag. Charlotte and I thank you for your gratitude. XOXO, gossip girl."

"Dammit," Evan groaned.

"I told you!" I shouted, handing his phone back. "I'm so good at guessing things with people."

"Collin's such a little slut," Evan groaned as he started typing back a message to Collin.

"Yeah, but I think the two of them are cute together," I said. "I only thought they would hook up because I seen them eyeballing each other the past few days when we were all hanging out."

"This is true, I saw it too," Haley said.

"I didn't wanna believe it to be true," Evan said with a sigh as he stuck another marshmallow onto the end of his stick.

"They're cute together," I said.

"I didn't say they weren't, ass clown," Evan said back. "I just don't think it's a smart idea for those two to date because now what's gonna happen if they break up? It'll be hard to get the group together."

"Stop being a baby."

He scowled slightly at me and then he looked down to his phone. "Well, at least he left me with a few condoms, how nice of him."

"How many did you have in your bag?" I asked.

"Enough," Evan replied as he put away his phone.

I sighed. "Well, I'm a little sour that they couldn't keep it in their pants until later. Like, we're all supposed to be hanging out together, man."

"Yeah, that's kind of annoying," Mindy said.

"You know, my friends Oliver and Emily do this shit sometimes," Haley stated. "They go off to bang and I'm left with Mindy and our friend Dylan just sitting there and wondering why we came to hang out at their house."

"Yeah, with couples, you need to bring them out of their house, otherwise they get horny and go banging instead of hanging," Evan said.

"Or sleep," I said. "I like to nap."

"You're so innocent sometimes," Mindy said with a small smile.

"Yeah," I said. "Innocent little angel with clean hands and a virgin smile."

"Nope," Evan said with a smirk.

"Innocent little angel with the purest of souls," I said, scowling at him.

"Nope again."

I sighed. "I guess our bedroom has no headroom now."

"Clever wordplay, bud," Haley chimed, sticking her hand in the air.

I smacked it and gave Evan a very triumphant smile. "Nerd."

"You're the nerd," he replied.

"We're gonna fight later," I threatened, staring daggers at him. "And I'm gonna *beat... you... up.*"

"You're so short, you can't even reach *up.*"

Mindy made a loud oohing sound. "I place my money on the

feisty redhead."

"Smart money's on the Gingerfightis," Haley said. "But can Oceanus turn the odds and win as the underdog. We'll have to tune in later to watch this one. You don't wanna miss this."

"This is why I love you," Mindy said, turning and kissing Haley.

"Why do you both think Spencer would beat me up?" Evan asked them.

"Have you seen her fight? She's scrappy," Mindy said. "She's tough too."

"She stubbed her toe last night and cried for five minutes."

"It really hurt," I said in my defence.

Evan gave me a small, one-sided frown.

"It did," I said. "You're the one who kissed my foot."

"You made me!" he protested.

"I did no such thing," I lied.

He sighed and shook his head. "You know what, I'm gonna make you sleep without blankets tonight."

"Whoa, that's a bit harsh, buddy."

"You're my girlfriend. I can't really do anything that's meaner," he said. "I'd have to deal with the aftermath of it."

"Yeah, you would," I said with a smirk.

He winked at me and stuck his marshmallow over the fire. I watched intently as he let it burn and catch fire for a few seconds. I really don't get how this boy likes gooey charcoal... or how he likes me for that matter.

{Chapter: **Seventeen**}

I waved a goodnight to the group as Evan led me up the stairs. Charlotte and Collin came back after three hours of being gone and the rest of us all roasted them for being gone so long. It was a good time. And yeah, I think they want to try being a couple. They're cute together.

"So, fun day?" Evan asked as we stepped into our room.

"I guess so," I said, taking my shirt off as he shut the door over. I leant down to my backpack and pulled out all of my clothes. "I don't even think I packed a shirt for sleeping in."

"Sleep topless," Evan said as he walked over to the nightstand on his side of the bed. He clicked the lamp on and then grabbed the TV remote.

"I could, but I'm a little self-conscious about my nip nops."

"I'm sure they're just cute little pink dots, right?"

I scoffed. "Shh." I gave up on finding a shirt and I walked over to the light switch and turned off the overhead lighting. I walked over to the bed and climbed up next to Evan. I lay back against the pillow so I could watch the TV. Apparently, we were watching *The Simpsons*, which I didn't mind. It's a pretty good show.

"You have such a cute belly," Evan said with a small smile on his face. He rolled over a little and traced his fingertips over my bare stomach.

"You're giving me goose bumps," I said, looking down at all the small bumps forming on my stomach and ribs.

"When you lay down and all your ribs become visible."

"Are you just stating obvious observations about my body?"

He shrugged. "Maybe."

"Nerd."

He sighed and sat up. He took his shirt off and handed it to me. "Just in case you opt to not lie topless with me, there's this you can sleep in."

"Thanks," I said, laying it next to me as he laid himself back down beside me.

"Don't want it?"

"Nope," I said, grabbing his wrist and putting his hand back onto my belly. "Keep doing the fingertip thing."

"Is this relaxing to you?"

I nodded. "Yeah." I sat up a little and undid my bra. "No gawking. The girls need to be free."

"Yeah, yeah," he said. "They're just boobs."

I tossed my bra at his face and he used his head to toss it to the floor. "This is much more comfy."

"I knew they were little pink nip nops," he said, winking at me.

"Shut the hell up," I barked. "You are here to trace your fingers along my stomach and ribs, not to look at my boobs."

"You're lucky I love you. I don't normally let people boss me around."

I smiled at him. "I love you too."

"So are we gonna go to sleep soon or are we just staying up doing this?" he asked.

I shrugged. "I kinda like this. This is a good idea. I like being gently rubbed with fingertips."

"I'll give you a different tip," he muttered.

"I heard that!"

"You were supposed to!"

I winked at him. "Maybe later."

"I can do it for myself, I have hands."

I scoffed. "You like my hand better, come on."

"I do, but that's not the point," he said with a little laugh.

I let out a loud sigh. "I'm not even friggin' tired."

"Yeah, I feel you on that one there. I'm wide awake," Evan said. "I mean, you had a nap, so at least you have a reason for being awake at—" he stretched out to check the clock behind him, "—two in the morning."

"We should go do something," I said.

"Nah, then you would have to put your shirt on, and I kinda like you better without one."

I smirked. "And I you. But if we go take a walk or something, I promise to sleep in only panties tonight. You'll have a 98% naked girl next to you."

"Sold," he said, grabbing his shirt from beside me.

"Ew, wait, have you banged any girls in this bed before?" I asked.

He cocked an eyebrow at me and scoffed. "Not this bed. This bed is brand new. Why?"

"Just curious," I said, getting up and stretching out.

"Whoa," Evan said, looking over at me.

I cocked an eyebrow. "What now?"

"You stretching while topless is so hot. Good show."

"Shut up," I said, leaning down and picking up my shirt. "Let's go." I put my shirt back on as he rifled through his nightstand drawer for something.

"Flashlight, incoming," he said.

I looked over and smacked the flashlight out of the air to the ground instead of catching it. All those months of spoogeball haven't paid off yet.

Evan looked over to me and then down to where the flashlight fell and then he looked back to me. "Right. We'll work on that."

"Yeah," I said, picking up the flashlight.

Evan walked over to the door and opened it. "Shall me and the lady get going for an evening stroll?"

"What if we get attacked by a bear?"

"Do you want me to bring his hunting rifle?"

I shook my head. "Guns are scary."

"Okay, let's get going, then," he said.

I walked past him and over to the door as he shut over our door and then followed me. "It's cold," I whined as we got outside.

"It's brisk," Evan said, sounding like he was correcting me or something. "Aww, look at that, your nipples are hard."

"Do I ever bring it to your attention when a part of your anatomy is hard?" I asked. "Y'know, like every morning we wake up together?"

"No, lately you just play with it," he said.

"I don't bring attention to it!" I barked. "That was my point!"

"I know, I was just bugging you," he said, kissing my forehead.

I pouted at him as he grabbed my hand and interlaced his fingers with mine. We headed off down the driveway and then turned down the gravel road and started walking. We clicked on our flashlights when we got to the end of the driveway because of how dark it was out here.

"So this is nice," I stated after a little bit of awkward silence.

"Yeah, fresh air is nice," Evan said.

"It can be."

"You know, I haven't used a flashlight since the mall, well, other than at the bowling alley."

"Hmm," I said. "You know, I haven't used one since the mall either. Man, I miss being locked in the mall with you."

"Me too."

"I gotta be honest with you," I said, "I was a few days more of solitary confinement with you away from jumping your bones."

"Dammit," he muttered. "Why'd I let you get us rescued, then?"

I shrugged. "You didn't want to get cabin fever? Well, I guess in our case it would have been mall fever."

"I feel like getting out of the mall and falling in love with you was worth being rescued."

I smiled and pushed him a little with my elbow. "You're so lame."

"I know I am."

"Yeah, but it's okay, I'm lame too," I admitted.

"Yeah, I know you're lame."

I scoffed and we both sort of let some empty silence fill the air as we walked along. The sound of distant crickets and soft wind in the trees around us did enough talking to keep us entertained.

"So, um, I have question," I asked after we had walked in silence for at least ten minutes.

"Yeah, fire away," Evan said.

"Why haven't you been keeping me updated on your C-word news?"

"You can say cancer," he said. "And I don't really know. I just don't like telling you anything unless it's good news. I hate seeing you get sad about things I can't change or help."

"Is the chemo working?"

"They think it's slowing the growth, but not fully stopping it. I've been on a rest period lately though. I do have to go back in for more soon though," he explained. "And when I do, they'll run me up to date on things and I'll tell you what's going on then."

"So things still aren't looking very good, then?" I asked.

He shook his head. "I can even feel myself losing this battle."

"Don't you say that!"

"Spencer, stop, I'm sick of us having this argument. We do this every time. You make me promise to fight and I tell you that I'm scared to die. There's nothing either of us can do to change the fact that I am dying," he said firmly.

"You're not dying!"

"Spencer, do you wanna know why I haven't told you anything?"

"Why?" I asked, knowing that I would dread what was about to come from his mouth.

"They've told me that I could die in as little as six months," he said softly. "*Six fucking months*, Spencer."

"No, please stop. You're not gonna die in six months, Evan. You're not."

"I could though. I could die in six months or six decades. They don't know yet, and I'm terrified because the latest scan results are gonna really tell me what my fate is," Evan said, his voice cracking. "I'm not ready to give up hope on living, but it's hard when you *know* you could die before your next birthday."

"Have you told anyone else about your cancer?"

He shook his head. "No. They can't know."

"Evan! That's selfish of you, okay? You're gonna wait until you're on a deathbed to tell them you have cancer? You need a rock, and your friends will be there for you."

"You're my rock, Spencer," he told me. "I only let you know because you're special. You made me feel more things in three days than anyone else made me feel in my entire lifetime. I knew you were more than just some girl. From the moment you opened that door and got me out of the boiler room, I knew I would end up telling you."

"How could you know that?" I asked as we stopped walking.

He sat down on a rock by the side of the road and shrugged. "I don't know how I knew, I just did."

"You should still tell your friends," I said, sitting next to him. "They'd wanna know."

"We've been over this. You're the only one who knows," he said. "There's still hope for me to fight this off, so don't give up on me just yet."

"Never," I said, kissing his cheek. "I'd never give up on you."

"I'm just so scared of dying. I have so much more life to live," he muttered. "I've got all my love to give. I will survive."

"Listen, babe, I love you and all, but if you sing another line of that song, I'm leaving you," I barked.

"What? You don't like Gloria Gaynor?"

"No, I just don't like that song."

"I will survive," Evan whispered to me.

"Stop," I whined.

"Sorry," he said. "I just like that song. It gives me hope that I might actually survive."

"You will survive. I'll make sure of it."

"Yeah, I hear sex helps."

"I'll help you in a different way. I can't spend all my days getting laid and neither can you," I said.

"It was a joke anyway," he said. "I think just being near you helps. It certainly takes my mind off of things until you bring it up. I kind of hate that you care so much about my condition and how I'm doing."

"I'm your girlfriend," I told him. "It's my job to care."

"You're probably the best girl in the world for me."

"You're probably the best guy in the world for me," I said, slightly mocking his tone of voice.

"You wanna head back to the cottage? I'm kinda hungry," he said as he stood up.

"I guess so," I said, yawning as I stood up.

"You want a piggyback ride?" he asked.

"All the way back?"

He nodded as he grabbed my flashlight. He clicked it off and put it in his pocket. "Okay, hop up," he said as he bent down a little.

I jumped onto his back and wrapped my legs around his waist and my arms over his shoulders. "Why don't I get you to do this all the time? You're big and strong and I'm small and light."

"You wanna walk in silence?" he asked.

"Do you?"

"Kind of."

I sighed a little as I rest my head down on him. "Okay, we can walk in silence."

And he walked in silence because I was on his back, so I wasn't walking at all. We made it back to the house and he let me down just outside the front door. We crept inside and noticed the lights were on.

Mindy walked out of the kitchen and yelped. "What are you doing here?"

I looked over and saw her standing there naked as she tried to cover up her lady bits.

"I'll go to our room now," Evan said, darting the other way.

"Why are you naked?" I asked her.

"Haley and I were doing fun stuff and then after that we got hungry. I came up naked because everyone was asleep and I was being lazy," Mindy said, letting her arms down after Evan closed over our door.

"I thought you usually shaved."

"I do, I was just lazy. Stop looking, you lesbo."

I gave her a deadpan look and scoffed. "There's the pot calling the kettle black, huh?"

"Yeah, for real. Anyway, where did you two run off to?" she asked.

"Oh, we went for a walk because we couldn't sleep."

Mindy turned and walked back to the kitchen. "Well, if you're hungry, I made some mac 'n' cheese, so you can take some for him."

"You're the best," I said, walking into the kitchen with her.

She walked over to the pot of pasta on the stove and slopped some into two bowls. There were already two bowls sitting on the counter that had some in them. Mindy stuck spoons into two of the bowls and then came over and handed them to me.

"Thanks," I said, turning around and heading off out of the kitchen.

"No problem," Mindy said, following me out. "Goodnight, gingersnaps."

I walked into the room and used my foot to close the door behind me. I set down the bowls on the nightstand on my side of the bed. I took my shirt off and let my boobies free again. I handed Evan a bowl of mac 'n' cheese as I sat on my side of the bed.

"How'd you make this so fast?" he asked as he took his shirt off and tossed it to the end of the bed.

"I didn't," I said, grabbing my bowl from the nightstand. "This is what Mindy was making in the kitchen."

"Why was she naked?"

"She and Haley had sex and she was too lazy to put a baggy shirt on or something," I said with a shrug. "Whatever."

"Then I guess we came home at a really good time."

I nodded as I put a spoonful of noodles in my mouth.

We ate and then put on some scary-but-not-at-all-scary movie as we cuddled in bed. I ended up falling asleep first, as I usually do, and that was because Evan was tracing his fingertips over my bare back the whole night. And because the blankets were so soft and warm on my skin. It's easy to fall asleep when you're this cozy.

{Chapter: **Eighteen**}

"Wake the fuck up, bud!" Mindy's voice shouted out. I could tell she was trying to be as loud as she possibly could be too.

I shot upright and looked over to the door and threw my pillow at her. "Shut your mouth! People are sleeping!"

She ducked the pillow and smirked at me. "Aww, I haven't seen those boobs in a long time. But get the hell awake. We're making pancakes and then going fishing."

I groaned and grabbed Evan's shirt from the end of the bed. "We'll be out in a few."

"Help," Evan mumbled.

"Yeah, I kinda figured," I said as I put on the shirt. I got up and went to the bathroom and grabbed a wad of paper towel so I could go *help* Evan with a special morning problem. But he helped with mine at the same time. So that was nice of him. I hope I cramped his wrist >:) 'cause mine sometimes get cramped too. After that, which took about fifteen minutes, I went to the bathroom and cleaned myself up, did my makeup, and uncramped my hand. Winky face. I went back into the room and then Evan and I headed to the kitchen. Mindy and Haley were cooking up some pancakes and Charlotte and Collin were sitting next to each other trading kisses.

"It's like I'm living in this weird utopian roommate situation," I said as Evan and I took a seat at the table. Since the table had one side against the wall, each couple got their own side of the table, which was kinda nice. And it was nice that each side had its own wooden bench.

"Yeah. Everyone's so happy this morning. This is the start of most horror movies that star young people on any kind of getaway," Evan said.

"Pancakes will protect us," Haley said, smacking a pancake down onto a plate. "Order up!"

"Stop yelling. I'm right beside you," Mindy said as she grabbed two plates of pancakes and brought them over to Charlotte and Collin.

"How come they get theirs first?" I asked.

"They didn't stay in their room for an extra twenty minutes after I woke them up," Mindy stated.

"Well, I am a sleepy creature," I whined. I felt Evan nudge my side a little and I smacked his arm as if to tell him to shut up.

"So we're gonna go fishing later. I have a boat and we're gonna go fishing later," Collin said as he started to cut up his pancake.

"Is that a good idea?" I asked.

"Is what a good idea?"

"Trusting you to drive the boat?"

"Oh, yeah, I've only crashed five times," he joked. At least, I hope he was joking about that.

"Oh, that makes me feel much more comfortable about going out on the lake with you," I said. "See, if you had crashed seven or more times, then we'd have a problem."

"Yeah, yeah," Collin said, brushing off my joke as he stuffed a large hunk of pancake into his mouth.

"Hurry up, Mindy," I whined. "I'm starving. You're letting me die."

Mindy grabbed a spoon from the sink and threw it at me. "Shut the hell up. You'll get your pancakes when you get them, goddammit!"

"Babe," I whined, shaking Evan, "make her give me pancakes."

"I would if I could." He smiled at me a little as he pulled me closer to him on the little wooden bench that we were sitting on. He then planted a kiss on my forehead.

"You're useless," I muttered as I rested my head on his shoulder.

"I know."

"Pancakes, coming up," Haley said, tossing two more pancakes to a plate beside her on the counter.

Mindy grabbed the plate and walked it over to Evan.

"How come he gets his first?" I whined.

"He didn't whine about it!" Mindy said as she walked back over to Haley.

Evan smirked and slid his plate to me. Mindy sighed and flipped him off as she hopped up onto the counter to sit.

"I love having a boyfriend." I grabbed the bottle of syrup from the middle of the table and slathered the pancakes with it.

***

"Just hold it straight up and then swing it over your head," Evan whined at Mindy, who didn't know how to fish for the life of her.

"I'm trying, but the waves," Mindy whined back.

"This is kind of entertaining," Haley said from behind me.

I lolled my head around from my seat of the boat and nodded. "It makes fishing a little bit more bearable."

"It really does," she said, climbing over the railing and sitting next to me.

We were watching the others fish right now because there were only four rods and the back of the boat wasn't really big enough for all six of us to be casting off our lures into the great waters of the lake anyway.

"Are we fishing for us to eat the fish?" Haley asked.

Collin turned around from his seat at the edge of the boat and nodded. "Of course. Why else would we go fishing?" He turned back and cast out his line. "But don't worry, nobody else needs to gut them. I can handle that."

"I hope you guys can handle the fishing too." I brushed my hair out of my face and put it up in a ponytail. "Mama needs to work on her tan."

"Oh, that's your stomach? I thought someone left a work light on," Collin cracked without even looking back at me.

This is why I don't wear bathing suits around people. Everybody's gotta make fun of the ginger for being pale. Haley looks pretty pale too, but I guess my red hair wins out. For some reason, Charlotte still has her California tan. And Mindy, well, she's half Asian, so naturally she's got darker skin than any of us.

"You're pretty pale too," Evan taunted.

Collin scoffed. "I'm not pale."

"You haven't been shirtless outside since at least October," Evan stated. "You gotta work your tan back up."

"Yeah, yeah," Collin mumbled. He stood up and walked over to me and handed me the fishing rod. "Can you do me a solid and hold this while I go and drive us to a new spot? There's no fish over here."

"Sure thing, captain," I said, getting up and taking the rod from him as he passed by to go to the front of the boat to steer us somewhere. I stood by the end of the boat and looked out over the lake. It was actually pretty big and we were smack in the middle of it. I looked down and wondered how deep it was. It looked deep. It got all dark and spooky down below us.

I heard the engine of the boat kick up again and figured that Collin would go slowly, since we were all standing by the back of the boat, but this little shit just gunned it. I grabbed the little railing next to me on the side of the boat and then we hit a pretty big wave and it made me let go of the railing since it was already wet and slippery, and then little Spencer went sploosh into the water behind the boat.

And the thing with that... I don't know how to swim.

I started kicking and flailing my arms, but I was already in a panic at this point. "Help me!" I screamed out to the boat, which had already made it pretty far off by now.

"She can't swim!" I heard Charlotte's voice yell out. Well, at least she has my back.

I started sinking into the water by this point, which was bad because they wouldn't know where I was if I went under the surface. And in a lake this big, that's not good. I kept kicking myself up, but I couldn't keep myself afloat any longer. I took one last breath before I felt myself slip under the water. I could see the boat become a mess

141

of wavy blurs as I sunk down a little lower. I kept flailing around, but I think it was doing more harm than good at this point.

The seconds ticked by and I just slipped lower and lower into the water. I couldn't see anyone near me yet. I called it, I knew they wouldn't be able to see me if I slipped under the water. After a while, I couldn't hold it any longer. My mouth exploded open to take in a huge breath of air, but it wasn't air, obviously, and instead, water flooded my mouth and nose. I could feel my body trying to cough it back up, but that wasn't working or helping this situation.

I looked up at the surface of the water. I watched the sunrays dance around in the water. I guess this is where my life ends. Beyond the water filling my lungs, it's not so bad. I started seeing less and less around me as blackness crept into my field of view. Blackness all around and things started to feel numb and empty. I felt my fingertips grow colder and colder. My eyelids started feeling heavier and heavier as the seconds ticked by. It got to the point that my arms and legs wouldn't even move for me anymore. They were lifeless.

I was lifeless.

At least floating here in the water like this was kinda relaxing. I felt at peace in a way, but also kinda annoyed. I'm only nineteen. I'm still a baby, I don't wanna die yet. There was so much I wanted to do before I died, so much I wanted to see, so many places I wanted to visit. I thought of Evan next. I thought about his smile and his eyes. I thought about the way he laughs and how he's always trying to look out for my best interests. I remembered the nights we snuck out and the time we went to the cave, and I couldn't help but wish the water here were as shallow as it was there.

I managed to smile a little at the thought of Evan. Somehow, thinking about him made the idea of dying a little less scary. It made the thought of dying almost comforting in a way. As long as he was my last thought, it would be okay. I would be okay. I smiled again and closed my eyes for a moment, ready to meet my maker, and then I felt something warm wrap itself around my body. And when my eyes shot open, the sky was above me. So was Evan's face. And so was Haley's.

I took in a deep breath of air and started coughing up water from my lungs. "It hurts! It hurts so bad!" I shouted through the coughs as

I rolled to my side. I could feel my lungs emptying themselves. It was not a pleasant experience. You think accidentally getting a little bit of water in your lungs is bad, try having them at least halfway filled with water.

After my coughing stopped for the most part, I realized that I was crying my eyes out. I balled myself up in the fetal position and sobbed into my knees. I could hear them all talking to each other, but I paid no attention to them because my lungs were on fire right now. My throat was hurting, my nose hurt, my hands were shaking, my legs felt like jelly, my eyes burned, my head was throbbing, and I was freezing cold.

I felt a towel get tossed over me. My ears were ringing from my head throbbing and from me crying and sobbing so hard. I could tell that we were on the boat still. I felt the cold wooden deck under my weeping body.

"Evan," I croaked, my voice hoarse and weak. I heard some shuffling and then a soft thud.

"Yeah?" his voice answered.

"Am I dead?"

"No," he said, laughing softly. "I got you out."

I raised an arm over his shoulder and pulled myself up, sniffling loudly as I did. "Hold me."

"Yeah, of course," he said, quickly following through on my request. He wrapped me up in the towel and picked me up. He then sat down and let me sit in his lap. I rested my head down on his chest and shut my eyes again, trying to focus on his heartbeat and not the throbbing in my head.

"You know," he whispered into my ear, "you make it a point for me not to die, but I think I should make it a point for you not to die either."

"Sorry," I said, kissing his neck. I would have kissed his lips, but I still feel like I just died, you know, 'cause I did.

"Why didn't you tell us that you couldn't swim?"

"I didn't exactly think I would fall in."

Evan kissed my forehead and hugged me tightly. "Well, you're okay now. Just focus on breathing air, not water."

"Mm," I mumbled. I could feel myself getting sleepy. I figured he wouldn't mind if I napped on him.

When I opened my eyes next, I was back in bed at the cottage. I was wearing a baggy T-shirt and my bikini bottoms. I rubbed my eyes and looked over at the clock. It was around four. So today really did just happen. Jesus Christ, man, I drowned today, but yet I still fit in time for a nap.

I stretched out a little and saw a glass of water on my nightstand. I lunged for it and guzzled it down. The irony in that, huh? I noticed a little note on the table next to where the glass had been. I picked it up and read it. All it told me was that they would be outside on the back porch area so Collin could barbeque us some ribs for dinner.

I sighed and swapped my bikini bottoms for a pair of cotton panties because much warmer and much more comfy. I slipped into a pair of jeans and threw my messy hair into an even messier bun. I went to the bathroom, peed, and then looked in the mirror as I washed my hands. My face was a total wreck. I *literally* looked like a zombie. My eyes looked sunken, my cheeks looked paler than usual, and my lips were pale and chapped for some reason.

I sighed and walked off to the kitchen to grab a bottle of water from the fridge. For some reason, the cold hardwood felt just *so god-damn good* on my bare feet. I walked down to the basement and then opened the glass sliding door to the porch and walked over to the group of nerds sitting at the outside dining table.

"She lives!" Mindy yelled, running over and hugging me.

"Hola," I said, still sounding raspy as shit. It was probably from all that coughing.

"I'm sorry for almost killing you," Collin said as Mindy let go of me.

"I'm sorry for almost letting you kill me," I said jokingly as I walked over and took a seat next to Evan. "Thanks for the water, by the way."

"I kinda figured you'd be thirsty." Evan leaned over and kissed me on the lips. "Coughing does work on the throat."

"Why'd you leave me in my bottoms though?" I asked, whispering to him.

He shrugged. "I didn't think you'd want me to see your lady bits."

"I don't really think I would have cared at the moment."

"Next time."

I scoffed softly. "I never wanna drown again. It hurt and it was scary."

"You wanna learn to swim?" he asked.

"Aren't we gonna eat soon?"

He shook his head. "We thought you'd be out longer than you were. Go change back into your swimsuit and I'll go give you a basic lesson. It's really easy. Trust me."

{Chapter: **Nineteen**}

I floated on my back in the water, waves softly lapping over my stomach as Evan held his hand on my neck to make sure I kept my head above the water.

"See?" he said. "Floating isn't that hard. You just have to stay calm and let your body do the work for you. And it helps that you have boobs, they add buoyancy."

"I know they do, dumbass," I sassed. "This is actually kind of relaxing, just letting the water hold me up like this."

"Yeah, they have these chambers of extra salty water, 'cause salt makes you float better or something, and they get you to go in and they shut the door and you float in the dark and it makes you hallucinate or something," Evan rambled. "I actually really wanna try it out sometime."

"Maybe we can go together, nerd."

"Maybe."

I let out a small sigh. "Man, forget swimming, floating is where it is at."

"I know, but floating isn't gonna help you if you're stuck in the middle of the lake."

"Sure it can. I can let the waves carry me or—" I started doing snow angel movements in the water to propel myself, "—I could do this."

"So, water you thinking about?"

I sighed loudly. "I hate you so much."

Evan smiled over at me. "I know you do." He grabbed my leg and pulled me back over to him. "So what did you think about when you were drowning? If you don't mind my asking?"

"Not at all," I said. "First off, it was this realization that I was actually dying, then it was a kind of resentment that I haven't done all I want to do, and then the last thing I remember thinking about was you."

"You thought about me? Why?"

I shrugged. "I 'unno."

"You love me," he said with a small smirk.

"I do." I stood myself up in the water. Thankfully it was shallow enough here for me to stand upright. "But you already knew that I did."

"I can see it in your nerdy green eyes," he stated.

"Okay, hold up, how the hell can eyes be nerdy?"

He shrugged as he walked out to the deeper water. "Yours are just nerdy. Don't ask questions, Spencer. I don't even understand these things myself."

"Your eyes are nerdy," I barked back at him as I followed him to the deeper waters. I felt the waters creeping up to my neck and then I froze and just looked at Evan.

"Come on." He walked back over to me. "You have to come out to where your toes can't touch the ground so that you can learn to swim. You can't tread water if you can still touch the bottom."

"Dude, I drowned today. That was traumatic, give me a moment." I took a few deep breaths as the water lapped at my neck. "Hold my waist and don't let me go under."

He nodded. "Aye, aye, ma'am." He went behind me and grabbed my hips with his hands and then stepped me forward. "The key is to stay calm, okay? Just kick nice and fluidly and use your arms in the same kind of way."

"Like this?" I asked, kicking my legs calmly.

"I would assume that you're doing a pretty good job," he replied.

147

"I'm barely holding you up right now."

"Hey," I said, turning myself around slowly in the water. "This is kinda easy." I smiled triumphantly once I was fully facing him. "I did it. I turned around in the water! I'm Michelle Phelps."

"Michael?"

"Michael is a boy name, and I am a girl," I stated smugly.

"Sorry, sorry," he said, smiling at me. "You're actually swimming right now."

"I know. I can feel myself kicking the water. And I have a reason to kick it. It tried to suffocate me earlier," I said, pouting slightly. "Take that water."

Evan smiled and pulled me over and kissed me right on the lips. "I'm so proud of you."

"For?"

"Not drowning this time," he said with a small smirk tugging at his lips.

I sighed. "I would hit you, but I need to learn how to tread water better first."

"You'll be able to do it like a second nature after a while." He pushed me out into the water a little. "Just remember to stay calm. Calmness will help you stay afloat."

"I am calm, asshole," I barked back as I floated away from him.

"Don't sound it," he teased. "But at least your voice is almost back to normal.

"Yeah, but I kinda liked my raspy voice. It made me sound like a badass."

"Nah, it made you sound like a smoker."

"Badass," I barked, furrowing my brows a little.

"Smoker," he said, floating himself over to me. "Anyway, are you ready to learn how to do the actual swimming thing?"

"I know how to do the thing," I said. I felt his eyes watching me intently, waiting for me to do the thing, but I didn't do the thing. "Okay, so I could probably use some help."

"Yeah, I thought so," he said. "Latch on to my back and I'll walk us back over to the shallow area so it's easier for you to get a hang of the motions and whatnot."

I wrapped my arms around him and he waddled us back over to

near the shore where the dock was. I let go and let my feet sink into the wet sand at the bottom. It's nice feeling ground beneath you.

"So the basic swimming move is pretty—"

"I know what it looks like. Tell me what to do to help my breathing while doing it," I barked.

He shot me a scowl. "Anyway, you rude little nerd, you have to just kinda turn your body and breathe when you lift your arm up."

"Sounds simple."

"It is," he said as he walked over to the dock. "I'll swim out, like, fifty feet and then you do the same."

"Okay," I said, following him over to the dock. I stood next to him and then he took off swimming.

He stopped and then turned to me. "Okay, now you try. Remember to stay calm and focus on when you should be breathing."

I nodded and then did as he did. I kicked little flutters and pretended my arms were windmills. I managed to get my breathing down pretty quickly, because, as you should know, breathing is something we do all the time, so it's only natural to find a breathing rhythm.

"You're a quick learner," Evan said, grabbing me as I swam by him.

I let his hands guide me to a stop and then I stood up in front of him. "Thanks. I tried to actually listen to what you said and then copy what you did. Works wonders when you pay attention, huh?"

"Are you trying to throw shade at me? I usually listen to what people tell me," Evan said. "For example, if you had told me that you couldn't swim, I would have known to dive in right away instead of thinking that you could swim."

I frowned a little. "I probably should have told you."

"I don't know. I feel like it was kinda our bad for not asking if everyone knew how to swim or not." Evan shrugged. "It's just one of those things that we expect everyone knows how to do. Swimming is generally something that people learn as a kid."

"Like riding a bike."

"Can you ride a bike?"

I smacked his arm. "Of course I can ride a bike, you idiot."

"Without training wheels?"

I stared daggers at him and then walked past him. "I'm just gonna keep swimming, just keep swimming." I dived into the water and started swimming back toward the dock.

"Just keep swimming," he called after me.

I swam back and forth from the dock to Evan a few times. And then I did it a few more times just to be sure. After that, I made him come back out to the deep water with me to teach me how to swim underwater properly. It was a little frightening to be fully underwater again, y'know, since last time I had been underwater I *died*. But he put up with my nervousness and me whining at him and he helped me get my underwater swimming up to par. And then we treaded water together for a little bit.

"I'm all wrinkly," I said, looking at my hands as we walked up the shore to the backyard of the cottage.

"Me too," Evan said. He stuck his hand over on my face. "Feel the wrinkles?"

I smacked his hand away. "I feel them. I have some of my own."

"Why do humans gotta wrinkle up after being in water?"

I shrugged. "Beats me, dude. I thought it was either because we absorb too much water or because we get the wrinkles for added grip underwater. Those are the only two explanations I've ever seen."

"They both sound a little fake," he said smugly. "I'd like to think it's because we're undergoing the same process that makes a grape turn into a raisin or something. Nature is cool."

"Just in time," Collin said to us. "The barbeque is on and the ribs are about to be Q'd."

"Spencer and I were having a lovely talk about our pruning fingers," Evan stated as him and I walked to the dining table.

"My toes are all wrinkly too," I said, pulling my foot up onto my lap. "Look."

"I can see that."

"I need to repaint my nails," I mumbled, looking at my fingers and toes and their shedding colour. "Wanna do it for me when we get back? That'd be nice of you."

"Spencer, we've been through this."

"Goddammit, Evan."

"Stop bickering," Collin barked. "I'll make one of you go inside with the other three so I don't have to listen to you."

"Sorry," Evan and I said in unison.

"It's okay, just try not to be annoying," Collin told us. "If one of you wanted to go and help make potato salad with the other three, that would actually be nice of you, because I'll be honest, I don't think any of them know what they're doing other than Haley."

"Yep. I'll go help," Evan said, standing up.

"You're gonna leave me with Collin?" I asked.

Evan nodded. "Is there a reason that I shouldn't?"

"He's weird," I said, shooting Collin a sly smirk.

"Maybe go get changed and then come help carry stuff from the kitchen," Evan suggested.

I nodded and got up from my seat. "I like that plan. This bikini makes me feel *exposed*, and I'm not sure I like feeling like that for extended periods of time."

"Who does?" Collin asked. "You guys go do whatever. I'll yell in if I get finished before you guys come out with the sides and salads."

"Sounds fair." I walked past them and over the sliding glass door. "Okay, so don't burn yourself and don't eat all the food."

"I won't," Collin replied.

Evan walked over to me and then I turned and followed Evan inside. I followed him up the stairs and then we split up. He went to the kitchen and I went to the bedroom. I nakified myself and then plopped into bed, wrapping myself in the blanket. I let out a loud, guttural, animalistic groan of pleasure. These blankets were so soft and so perfect for a soft and sleepy creature like me.

After a few moments, I got out of the bed, begrudgingly of course, and I got dressed in what I had been wearing before getting into the bikini again. I went to the bathroom and tossed my hair up in a messy bun and then I fixed my makeup real quick. I didn't wanna look like death all night. It's not a very flattering look.

I waddled my way to the kitchen and slinked over to the table. I took a seat and watched the group of four losers try to whip up sides for dinner. I don't even think they noticed me, to be honest. None of them bothered to ask me for any help, so I just assumed that I had somehow turned into a ghost for the time being. And I didn't mind. I'd end up eating all the food before I could get it in the big-ass bowls they had anyway.

"Spencer," Evan said, walking over to me with a bowl of potato salad, "take this down to Collin while we clean up and finish with the macaroni salad and fries."

"Ooh, fries," I moaned, standing up and taking the bowl from him.

"Yeah, calm down, I know you're always a slut for fries," Evan said as he walked back over to the counter.

I scoffed. "I just really like them." I walked out of the kitchen and back outside. I set the bowl on the table and then took a seat at the table.

"Looks good," Collin said, peering over at the bowl.

"I could say the same." I nodded to the barbeque and the ribs that were cooking on it.

"Yeah, if only it would cook faster," he whined. "I'm so hungry, man." He walked over and took a seat across from me at the table. "How's your throat feeling?"

I shrugged. "Better. My throat's not messed up anymore and my voice isn't as hoarse from the coughing."

"That was actually pretty terrifying earlier."

"I bet."

"It was," he said. His usually amused expression was replaced with a softer and more sincere one. "We all dove in and looked, well, except for Mindy because she was too small to be able to pull you out and we needed someone to still be on the boat."

"You all dove in?"

Collin nodded. "We had to. We had no idea where you were. Haley was the one who found you though."

"Haley got me out?"

Collin nodded again. "Her and Evan took turns giving your CPR until your eyes just shot open and then, well, you know what happened after that."

"Yeah, I just realized that I didn't ask who pulled me out, I just sorta assumed it was Evan who did because he was the one right over me when I woke up."

Collin smirked. "Probably doesn't help his ego."

"Probably not."

"So, how scary was it?"

"Dying? You're asking how scary dying was?"

Collin awkwardly looked down at the table. "Yeah, that's about it."

"It wasn't horrible," I stated. "I mean, it was totally horrifying, but once it's happening, it was just a peaceful emptiness. It's weird. Your body knows what's happening to it and I think it just keeps you from panicking more about it."

"That sounds terrifying."

"It wasn't so bad after the lungs filling with water thing."

Collin sighed. "You know, we should really take you to a hospital or something. Like, you were probably clinically dead for a minute there."

"Nah, I feel fine. It was just the water in your lungs. If you get the water out and get the person breathing, they're fine. Shaken up and horrified, maybe, but they're okay," I said. "Well, I at least feel okay."

"You're sure?" He stood up and walked over to check the ribs. "You know you don't have to lie and try to act okay if you're not."

"No, I know. I feel fine. My throat's a little bit sore and my lungs still feel wheezy, but I'm fine. There's no reason to rush me to the hospital," I told him. "If there was something wrong with me, I would have told Evan and I would already be at the nearest hospital."

Collin laughed a little. "Evan did want to take you regardless of if you felt okay or not. I told him to lay off and let you decide."

"Yeah, he's always thinking of me. He's a pretty awesome guy."

"Yeah. He is."

{Chapter: **Twenty**}

After dinner, I helped gather some dry leaves and twigs with Mindy so we could have a fire later on. We ended up with a fairly large pile of the stuff sitting a few feet from the fire pit. Once it started to get dark, Collin fired up the fire. Get it? And then we all took our seats on little benches around the pit.

"This is kinda nice," Mindy said, cracking open a bottle of beer.

"It is," Charlotte said, resting her head on Collin. "It's really relaxing."

"I wish we had hot chocolate," I mumbled.

Without saying anything, Evan stood up and walked off. Was he really gonna go make me a hot cocoa right now? Like, was that something that he was actually going to do?

"Where's he off to?" Collin asked.

I shrugged. "Beats me. Maybe he's going to get more marshmallows since we didn't get any to roast."

"Somehow, I doubt that, bud."

"Me too," I said with a sigh as I pulled out my phone.

"You're texting him to get marshmallows right now, aren't you?" Collin asked.

I nodded. "I want some now." I typed away and sent the message as fast as I could so Evan would get it before he came back.

"Predictable."

"Shut up," I barked, putting my phone back in my pocket.

"The sky is so filled with stars," Haley noted, looking up. "You never see this many in Toronto."

"There's not a lot of light pollution here," Collin stated. "It's one of the best parts about having a cottage, to be honest. I love looking up at the sky and seeing so many stars."

"You guys are nerds," Mindy teased. "The only stars I need are the ones in my bae's eyes."

"You guys are all so lame. Y'all need to stop being so lame," I muttered to them.

"I'll push you into the fire. Shush," Mindy snapped back.

"Mm-hmm." I listened to the crackling of the logs in the fire. It's so weird that things on fire make a crackling sound. Like, what's the science behind that? Why does burning make such weird but calming noises? Anyway, we sat in a silence for a little while. Mindy and Haley were cuddling together. Charlotte was all snuggled up on Collin. But me? I was left all alone because Evan just ran off somewhere and has been gone for the past five minutes.

A few moments later, Evan came back and sat next to me. "Here." He handed me a thermos.

"Did you actually?" I asked.

He nodded and then reached over to a plastic baggy. He pulled out a bag of marshmallows and handed them to me. "Got us marshmallows too." He tossed a bag over to Collin and then a bag over to Mindy.

"Beautiful," Mindy said, picking up the bag.

"I'll go get the roasting sticks," Collin said, setting his bag down next to his bench. "Evan always forgets at least one thing."

"Yeah, not true. I just didn't have enough hands to carry six metal rods with sharp points on the end," Evan argued.

"Fair point," Collin said, walking off and then coming back a few seconds later with the metal rods that we used to skewer and roast the marshmallows. He handed one to each of us and then took his seat next to Charlotte.

"The night sky is so pretty," I said, looking straight up into the vast, inscrutable chasm of outer space above us. "Look at all those stars and shit."

"Yep. It's beautiful," Evan said, pulling my face down by chin with his finger. "But the view's still better down here." He winked and smirked a little at me.

I scoffed. "Yeah, you're cute and all, but *space*." I looked back up at the stars. "It makes me feel so small."

"That's because you are," Charlotte teased.

"Pfft, piss off." I grabbed a marshmallow from the bag and stabbed it with the metal rod. I stuck it over the fire and let it roast a little.

"Your marshmallow caught on fire," Collin noted.

"What?" I looked at the end of my stick and groaned. "Evan." I pulled the rod over to his mouth and he blew the fiery goop out. "Now eat it. I don't like burnt marshmallow."

He sighed. "Fine." He grabbed the rod and ate the marshmallow off of it.

"Do you think it's gonna rain tonight?" I asked.

"No?" Collin replied. "Why would it rain? It's the clearest night we've had in a long time."

"Why do you ask, little gingersnap?" Evan asked, putting a marshmallow on his metal stick.

I shrugged. "I dunno. I was gonna see if I could convince you to spend the night out here on the lawn with me. Y'know? Like, let's sleep under the stars. That kind of thing."

"I like the way you think." He moved the end of his rod over to my face. "I roasted this one for you." I smiled at him and bit the marshmallow off of the end of the rod. It was perfectly roasted to my liking.

And then we sat there for an hour and a half longer with our friends. We had some good laughs and roasted some good marshmallows. After that, they all went inside and Evan got us blankets and stuff so we could sleep on the grass and not get grass stains all over our clothes.

"Here." He tossed me a pillow as he walked by me with a heap of blankets. He set the biggest blanket down on the ground and then put the other blankets on top. He basically made the bed, literally.

I dropped my pillow down beside where he put his. "It looks cozy."

"Don't patronize me." He straightened out the blanket to make it look a little nicer. "No shoes on in the bed."

I raised my leg and showed him my bare foot. "I wasn't wearing any to begin with. You should know that I hate shoes by now. I'm all about that free-foot life."

"More like that three-foot life," he muttered.

"Was that a shot at my height?"

He shrugged. "Maybe."

"Come here."

"No, you're just gonna hit me," he said as he took off his shoes.

"Come. Here," I demanded, pouting at him.

He groaned and walked around the bed to me. "Yes?"

"I'm not short." I smacked his arm. "You're just too tall."

"See! I knew you were gonna hit me."

"No, come back." I pulled his head down and kissed him. "You're a dork and I love you a little."

"Why not a lot?"

"Because I'm a little little."

He cocked an eyebrow. "What?"

"Just... Let's lay down, okay?" I whined, pushing him back to his side of the bed. I crouched down and crawled under the blankets and then rested my head on the pillow and looked up at the sky as Evan got into the "bed" next to me.

"The stars really are pretty," he said as he wrapped his arm under my head and pulled me into him.

"Yeah," I said, resting my head on his shoulder. "They really are."

"You're prettier though."

"Don't make a lame reference to how my freckles are like stars trapped underneath my skin and how it proves that galaxies are born in the hearts of goddesses or anything like that."

He laughed a little. "I can safely say I was not gonna say that. I was just saying that you're prettier."

"And I was using reverse psychology."

"Your freckles are like stars trapped underneath your skin, and I guess it just proves that galaxies are born in the hearts of goddesses,"

157

he said, clearly trying to sound poetic about it. "That better?"

"Little bit." I pointed to the sky. "I birthed those."

"Stars are pretty big, Spencer. I don't know how you managed to get even one of those out of your tiny body, but okay."

"They're made of gas."

"Ate a lot of burritos, then?"

I nodded.

"And you didn't share?"

"It was billions of years ago. I didn't know you then."

He sighed. "Fair enough. But you owe me."

"I'll make you some burritos," I said, smiling softly. Evan's such a dork, to be honest, but he's my dork, and I was really, *really* glad that he was *my* dork.

"I wonder if we get to explore space and stuff when we die. Do you think we get to float around and visit other planets and stuff? That'd be cool."

"We're not talking about death again." I let out a small sigh. "I'm sick of thinking about you passing away."

"I'm just trying to ease you into reality," Evan said. "Sorry. What do you wanna talk about?"

"Let's hear you talk about me some more," I replied. "You know, 'cause I'm a narcissist and whatnot."

"You're a nerd," he said, kissing my forehead.

"I wasn't suggesting it. I was demanding it."

"Yeah, but you know I don't listen to you if you're being demanding."

"What are you talking about?"

He shrugged. "I dunno. I'm kinda tired."

"Do you wanna sleep?"

"With you?" he asked. "Every day since I met you."

"No, I meant sleep sleep, not *sleep* sleep."

"Ohhh. I knew that."

"We can do the adult thing some other day," I said. "After I get over my irrational fear of getting boned."

"Yeah. Well, I'm just gonna rush you into something, Spencer. Come on. You know me better than that."

"I also don't want this decision to be all on me," I told him. "It makes me feel kinda shitty if you're all raring to do the freaky and I'm still over here hiding from the fact that I have to move on from my past."

"First step to moving on is admitting you have to," he said as he rolled over and laid his arm over me. "Now, can we sleep?"

"I guess so," I muttered, rolling over and letting him spoon me. "Maybe I can be the big spoon sometime?"

He kissed my neck. "Keep dreaming, bud."

***

I woke up in the middle of the lawn by myself. Why does Evan always run off in the mornings? I don't care if he makes me food and crap. I like it when I wake up in his arms. Whatever, he's an ass.

I sat up and stretched out. I looked around and noticed a lack of anybody outside. The sun was up and the air smelt of morning. Yes, the air can smell of morning, shut up. I stood up and wrapped the blanket over me. I walked up to the house, enjoying each step in the slightly wet grass. It was cold and refreshing in a natural way, not like when you step on cold tiles with bare feet.

I walked inside and wiped my wet feet on the rug and walked upstairs. I heard a lot of commotion in the kitchen. I walked into the kitchen with my blanket still wrapped around me. "Hola, bitches. I have awoken from my eternal slumber."

"Look who decided to show up," Mindy sassed.

"What do you mean? Nobody woke me up!"

Everyone turned to look at Evan.

Evan shrugged. "She looks so cute when she's sleeping. Sorry that I don't like ruining that."

I could feel myself blush a little. "Well, I still would have liked to be woken up." I tossed my blanket at Evan. I walked over to the counter and grabbed the coffee pot and poured myself some coffee. At least they left some for me.

"Well, you know how your people get," Mindy said.

"What do you mean '*your people*'?" I asked, pouring a little sugar into my cup and mixing it around with a spoon.

"Gingers," she replied. "You guys have shorter tempers."

"What the hell? My hair has nothing to do with that!" I barked back, grabbing the cream and pouring a little into my coffee.

"You're a mutant, Spencer. Red hair is caused by a gene mutation. Come on, this is basic biology."

I turned to her and cocked an eyebrow at her. "Then I would know it. I'm smart, you dingus. I get good grades."

"Maybe you missed that day of class," Mindy said, shrugging.

"Okay, knock it off," Charlotte said. "I don't want poor little Evan to be stuck with a cranky Spencer on the ride home."

Evan smiled at me. "I know how to calm her down though."

"No, you don't," I said, walking over to him with a big smile on my face. I kissed him and sat down next to him.

"I do so," he argued.

"Okay. I'll entertain the thought that you know how to get me in a better mood. How would you go about that?"

Evan scoffed. "Hot chocolate and forehead kisses."

I groaned. "Okay, you got me."

Evan smiled. "Did you, uh, did you bring up the blankets?"

"Oh, shit, no. Was I supposed to?"

He kissed me and stood up. "I wasn't expecting you to, but they do need to be picked up. I'll go do that."

I smacked his butt as he walked off. I turned back to the others in the kitchen. "Okay," I said, "so now what?"

"Well, I was gonna make pancakes, but Haley wants hash browns," Mindy stated.

"Dude, sue me, I like hash browns," Haley barked. "I saw a little diner on the way up here that we should stop at on the way down. We could get breakfast there."

"Deal," I said.

"See," Haley said, "I have good ideas. The smartest person in the room agrees with me, so it's obviously the *best* idea."

"Fine, we'll go get hash browns for breakfast," Mindy whined.

"It's settled," Collin said. "Now everybody go pack up their stuff and wait by the front door."

I watched as the gaggle of my pals walked out of the kitchen. I didn't though. I wanted to wait for Evan to come back. I pulled my feet up and sat cross-legged on the bench. The bottoms of my feet were kinda green and earthy. I guess I'm no longer just an elf princess. I'm an elf princess of the forest, the guardian of the swamps and valleys.

Well, a girl can dream anyway.

{Chapter: **Twenty-One**}

I dropped a spoon into my sink and rinsed the bowl with insanely hot water from the tap. I hate eating any kind of canned soups for this reason. The sauce is so hard to get outta the bowl. I gave up after getting most of it rinsed. I'll just clean all the dishes later anyway, so whatever.

"Hello," Jordan said as she walked into the kitchen.

"Hey," I said, turning to her.

"It's pretty early. Why are you up?" she asked.

"I'm waiting for Evan to pick me up so we can go to his doctor's. He has an appointment today. He's a sick little nerd."

She nodded. "That doesn't sound fun. Doctors suck."

"Yeah, but they do good work." I walked past her and over to the front door to see if Evan was here yet.

I walked back up to my room and grabbed my sweater and keys. I walked back downstairs and put the sweater on. I was really just trying to stay doing something, *anything*, while I waited for Evan. He's not usually this late on picking me up for stuff.

"What are you doing waiting at the door?" my mom's voice asked from behind me.

I turned around and gave her a puzzled expression. "What do

you mean? I'm waiting for Evan. He was supposed to be here 45 minutes ago."

"Oh?"

"Yeah."

"Are you sure?" my mom asked.

Was I sure? Of course I was sure. I turned back and looked out the door. "I'm pretty sure he was supposed to be here already."

"Did you eat ravioli for breakfast?"

I turned again. "How did you know?"

"Got a little on your shirt."

I looked down and then groaned as I saw the reddish stain on my shirt. "Goddammit." I walked upstairs and quickly changed my shirt. At least I had the time to do it since Evan was clearly in no rush to pick me up. I walked back downstairs and sat back at the door.

"Spencer, you look like a lost puppy. Go sit and watch TV or something," my mom said from the kitchen.

"No. I'm okay. He should be here soon," I replied. I probably did look like a lost little puppy right now. What if something bad happened to Evan? Oh, my God, no, I don't even want to think about that.

I sat on the stairs and waited for a few more minutes until one minute left on the hour and then there was a knock at the door. Figures, he's *exactly* one hour late. I walked over and opened the door. "You're late. You're one hour late. You suck. I was waiting for an hour. Where the hell were you?"

"I said I'd be here at 9:30," he said, pulling out his phone. "And it is 9:30 on the dot."

"What?" I grabbed his phone from him. "What the hell?"

"Did you forget to set your clocks last night?"

I handed his phone back. "Set my clocks for what?"

"Daylight saving time? It was last night," Evan told me.

"What the hell?!" I shouted. "Why do people not tell me things? I am a soft and sleepy elf princess. Why do you people expect me to keep track of something as mundane as time?"

"Because you just wasted the last hour of your life waiting for me and getting mad about me being late even though, as always, I was one minute early," Evan stated. "Anyway, let's go. I got you a coffee."

"Oh, yay," I said, practically squeaking. I love coffee almost as much as I love Evan, to be honest. I followed him out onto the driveway. The drive wasn't a long one. No drive was ever that long. It never felt very long either. We were at his doctor's in the blink of an eye, but maybe that's because the coffee didn't kick in, so I probably dozed off for most of the drive. Evan needs to stop supporting my erratic sleeping patterns.

"We're here," he said as the car shuddered off.

I let out a barely audible mumbling noise.

"Um, yes?"

"Sorry," I said, yawning. "I'm just... out of it."

"Okay, well, let's get to it, then." He unbuckled his seat belt and opened his door. "Come on."

I groaned and opened my door as I unbuckled myself. I grabbed my half-finished coffee and closed the door. I followed Evan into the looming hospital. This appointment better bring us good news and not bad news, not even okay news will do. Good news or nothing.

"Whatever happens today, I just want you to know that I love you and that I'm not gonna die," Evan said as we stepped into an elevator.

"I love you too," I said. "But there's still a very real chance that you might die, Evan."

"Shut up, Spencer." His voice was firm but shaky.

"Sorry." I stayed quiet for the rest of the elevator ride. I didn't want to stress him out or anything. I'm his gingersnap, I have to make him feel at ease and calm and happy, not stressed out and cranky.

I followed him into the waiting room. He checked himself in at the desk and then we sat down next to each other and then sat in silence for a while. It was really awkward, but I think that's because both of us sort of knew what today had in store for us. It's either that Evan's cancer is in regression or that he'll likely get a terminal diagnosis at some point in the near future. I don't think I could stomach the latter.

"Do you want me to come in?" I asked.

He shrugged. "I guess."

"Okay." I looked over at him and he looked pretty nervous. I guess I would be too if I could potentially have a death sentence placed on me within the hour. This really sucks. Why can't cancer have a cure? Why can't you just take a pill and then two days later the cancer is all gone? Why? Why couldn't Evan have some other illness? Why wouldn't he just have crappy lungs and need an inhaler his whole life or something? Why does it have to be cancer? Why does cancer have to be a thing in the first place?

"Evan Fuller," a nurse said from down the hall a little.

"That's me," Evan said as he stood up.

I stood up and followed Evan down the hallway to a small room. I guess this was his family doctor or something. Last time we were here, we went to a room with a desk. But this was a room for those yearly health checks and for booster shots and stuff.

The nurse walked out as we sat down and then the second round of waiting began. I think this was one of the suckiest things about doctor visits. You have to wait for a while and then you get taken into the room to wait for a little longer and that's just not a fun time. It's even less fun when you're with someone and they're giving the world the cold shoulder.

I nudged his arm. "Evan."

No reply. He just stared blankly at the floor in front of him. I would have tried again, but I already knew he was too far gone. The doctor would come in and then they'd talk and then maybe Evan would talk to me after that.

We waited for a few more minutes until an elderly man walked into the door. He had dark skin and wiry white hair that was balding at the back. "Evan, it's been a while," he said. He had a pretty noticeable Indian accent. "Not sure why I'm the one to give you these test results. I haven't given any to you before, nor am I the one who treats you."

"So you have the results?" Evan asked, looking up.

The doctor nodded. "I do. Yes. We can discuss them in private if you'd like." His doctor eyed me a little bit as he set down a clipboard on the counter on the other side of the room.

"Why? Just like I've told any other doctor or person who tries to tell me things, she's gonna know anyway, so why not just let her know now?" Evan said.

"Evan, I am not your other doctor. And if you want these results, she's going to have to leave the room. This is an important matter for us to talk over."

"It's fine, Evan. I'll be just out in the waiting room for you," I said, resting a hand on his shoulder as I stood up. I leaned over and kissed his cheek. "I love you."

He inhaled sharply and shut his eyes. I took that as my sign to go. I made an awkward waving motion with my hand to the doctor as I walked out and shut the door closed behind me. I walked out to the waiting room and over to the little water dispenser they had. I grabbed one of the little paper cups and filled it with water. I drank a few cups of water before taking my seat where I had earlier, but this time there was no Evan next to me.

I watched the clock on the wall as it ticked. Tick. Tock. Tick. Tock. Tick. Tock. Over and over again, it repeated the same stupid clock sound. I scanned the room over to try and pass the time. There wasn't a lot of stuff here. It was a really bland office. The carpeting was a nasty grey and the walls were a weird white colour that was also somehow blue. After a while, Evan emerged down the hallway and he walked towards me with a little folder in his hands. I stood up to hear some good news, but he walked right past me. He walked by me like I didn't even exist.

I ran up to him and pulled him around to face me as he opened the door to exit the office. "What the fuck? Did you just decide I'm not worth your time or something?"

He tensed his jaw as he turned to face me. He glared down at me with a look that I never wanted to be on the receiving end of. "Spencer, what I need from you right now is some fucking space. Leave me the fuck alone." He turned and walked out of the office and left me there with my mouth agape.

"Evan!" I shouted as I walked into the hall. I looked around, but he was long gone. He walks fast. I noticed a couple spilled pages on the hallway floor and the folder that Evan was carrying. I walked over and picked them all up and put them back in the folder. It didn't feel right to read them over because I clearly wasn't supposed to know. But judging by his reaction, it wasn't good news.

I walked over to the elevators with his folder in my hands. I waited for the elevator to show up and then I went back down to the first floor. I walked out to the parking lot, but Evan was nowhere to be seen. I looked around for his SUV, but no luck on that either. He just left me here.

I pulled my phone out to call someone to get me, but then I remember that nobody else knew that Evan had cancer. I groaned and put my phone back into my pocket. Cool. I was stuck here unless I can come up with a convincing story about how Evan left me stranded here at eleven in the morning at the hospital with his cancer history in my hands.

I sighed and pulled my earphones out of my pocket. Always gotta keep a backup plan ready. I popped them into my ear and walked to the nearest coffee shop. I figured that if Evan was gonna come back to pick me up, he'd look there. It's not a very far walk, maybe ten or fifteen minutes away.

I walked there and went inside and got a coffee. I sat down at the table by the window and looked out at the traffic on the street. I set the folder down on the table and looked at it. I was really tempted to open it to find out what was so bad about that doctor's visit that made Evan storm out like that.

After a couple hours and another two coffees, the temptation got the best of me and I opened the folder. I pulled out the papers one by one reading them over. It turns out that Evan's cancer wasn't getting better. There's more cancer than there was before and it looks likely that it'll go beyond a point of no return.

Basically, it meant that Evan was on the brink of a terminal diagnosis. It really did mean that he could die if the treatments don't start to somehow magically work. I also noticed that there was a recommendation for him to change his drugs to something more powerful than the ones he had now.

I closed the folder over and sat there with a vacant expression. I couldn't think straight right now. Evan was, for all intents and purposes in this current moment, dying. I just didn't want to believe that. As much as we tell each other that it was always a possibility, I thought it was a rhetorical possibility. Like how you imagine what you'd do if a crazed gunman burst into your classroom. You talk or think about it, but that doesn't mean it's supposed to happen.

I pulled my phone out after a few minutes to try and call him, but he didn't pick up. Actually, it went straight to his voicemail, so that told me that he had turned his phone off. I guess that makes sense. He probably knew I would end up calling him at some point. I guess he wants to be alone right now. He'll call me when he wants to. No sense in trying to force him to talk to me.

I finished my coffee and walked to the nearest bus stop so I could wait for the bus. I guess it pays to have a student ID from my college. We get U-passes, so we can ride the city buses whenever. You know, for situations where your boyfriend ditches you across town.

Two buses later, I was on my street. I walked to my house and then up the driveway and noticed a lack of cars. I guess everyone went out. Good. I didn't want to get questioned about the folder. I stepped inside and hurried myself up the stairs to my room. I buried the folder at the bottom of my underwear drawer.

I showered and watched some TV until it was time for me to go to bed. I guess I'll be taking the bus to school tomorrow, unless Evan calls me in the morning, but I have a feeling he's not about to do that.

I stared up at the blackness of my ceiling and sighed.

Oh, what I wouldn't give to be back at the cottage with Evan right now, without a care in the world, just staring up at the empty night sky.

{Chapter: **Twenty-Two**}

It's been a few days and Evan hasn't called me or texted me or even shown any sign of still being alive. That appointment must have really thrown him off course in the worst of ways. I guess I get it, but he could still at least shoot me a goodnight text or something. A girl has feelings, and this girl in particular is feeling a little hurt.

I decided that today after class, I would go over to Charlotte's. And now that it is after class, that's what I was gonna go do. Of course, I had to go home first to drop off my backpack and change out of my school clothes. I wanted to wear something more comfortable. I traded my shirt for a baggier one and put on that Creeper sweater from the mall.

I walked downstairs and headed off to Charlotte's place. I first went to get a coffee though. Not for her, just for me. I walked from the coffee shop to Charlotte's for two reasons. First, I needed to walk more. I could feel myself packing away a few extra pounds that I did not want. And second, it wasn't very far away from the coffee shop I went to. See, I can be a little bit strategic sometimes.

I walked down Charlotte's street and as I neared her house, I noticed a familiar SUV parked outside her house. Evan. That rat bastard. He better not be hooking up with Charlotte or something. I picked up my pace and went across her lawn and noticed them standing in her living room. I guess her large front window was helpful today. I slinked out of view and walked over to the side window. It's usually open, and unluckily for me, it was open today. I guess it's time to eavesdrop on these little bitches.

"Evan," Charlotte's voice said sternly.

"Well, do you see any good reason as to why it makes sense to let her strap herself to a time bomb?" Evan's voice asked her. I missed his voice so much. But not now, I'm angry Spencer. Angry. Grr. There we go.

"I don't think running away is the best way to solve this issue," Charlotte stated. "You're a grown man. You can deal with this."

"Yeah, and leaving is how I'm choosing to deal with it. I just told you that."

"I can't let you do that, Evan," Charlotte pleaded. "She went through hell with the last guy and now you're gonna put her through that again?"

"It's better that it be now than later," Evan barked. His voiced cracked a little. He definitely was about to start crying. I'd go help him, but it's clear he means that he wants to leave me, so fuck him.

"Do me a favour here and don't break up with her."

Evan sighed. "It's not that I *want* to break up with her. It's just… breaking up with her is the easier thing."

"Wow, that's a coward's way of thinking right there, bud. You clearly love her, so it's not that you don't love her. I could understand it if you didn't love her and wanted to break up with her," Charlotte said. "But you do love her."

"I do. That's why I wanna do it sooner rather than later," Evan told her. "I want it to be before we fall any harder for each other."

"Asshole," I muttered. I don't even care if they heard me. Well, maybe I did care, so I muttered it instead of just saying it normally. But how dare he want to leave me over this bullshit.

"Evan, please, think it through a little longer. Think about all the little ginger babies the two of you are gonna have one day," Charlotte stated. Okay, she doesn't know about the cancer thing. There's no way she'd say that if he told her that he was dying.

"We all die at different speeds, some of us just die a little faster,"

Evan stated. "The same thing applies to relationships, the rotting of bananas, and the sunlight in the day. I didn't ask to be like this and I don't expect her to understand it. She'll be pissed and hurt and she'll hate my guts, but she'll get over it and she'll move on. She's strong and smart and beautiful and she's got a whole life ahead of her. I'm gonna be such an insignificant part of her grand story."

"If that's how you feel," Charlotte said, pausing a moment, "then I guess do it. Just… be gentle with it. Make sure you talk to her about it. She needs the closure at least. Open ends and Spencer don't make good friends."

"You're right," Evan stated. "I guess I'll figure something out. I'm gonna get going. You said that she was supposed to be heading over here soon anyway, right?"

Charlotte assumingly nodded. "Yep. So get the hell out of here."

"Right," he said. "Thanks for listening and talking to me and all that lame shit. You're a good friend."

"Yeah, sucks that we can't be friends after this."

"Why's that?"

"I'm on Spencer's side. You hurt her. I hate you. It's that simple," Charlotte told him. "Now get gone."

"Bye, Charlotte."

I heard them walk over to the door and then he came outside. I hide behind the wall as he got in his car and drove off. I waited a few more seconds and then walked over to her front door and knocked loudly a couple of times, but I ended up just walking in her house because I was too pissed off to think rationally.

"I was just about to call you," Charlotte said, looking up at me as I walked into the living room.

"What the fuck did he tell you?" I shouted.

"Whoa, calm down. I guess you saw him leaving, huh?"

I clenched my fists in anger. I could feel my blood pressure rising. "What did he tell you?"

"Nothing. We just talked about school."

"You pathetic liar. Don't cover up for him," I barked.

"What the hell are you talking about?" she asked. "I'm not covering up anything for him."

"If you don't tell me, I'm gonna kick your ass."

She cracked up a little at that. "Okay."

I glared at her for a split second and than whipped my hand across her face. "Bitch, tell me what he told you!"

Charlotte stepped back and held a hand to her face. "What's gotten into you today?"

"Tell me what he told you!"

"Stop yelling at me." She rubbed her cheek a little. "Fuck. For a little girl, you have a hard punch."

"Spirit of the fighting Irish," I told her. "Now tell me what the hell you two little shitheads were talking about."

"He wants to leave you," Charlotte said softly, still rubbing her jaw. It was red and looked like it hurt. Good.

"Why?" I asked. "What reason did he give you for that?"

"He said he's too scared to fall in love or some trash like that. I don't agree with it, but it's not my choice. I tried to tell him that he should be with you, but he was persistent."

"You still sided with him. You said you guessed he could do it. Why?"

"How do you know what I said?" she asked.

"Not important," I replied. "What's important here is that you lied to me when I asked you and that you basically did tell him to do leave me, oh, and the fact that he's actually going to do it."

"He's not gonna do it."

"He will. Why the fuck else would he have gone to my best friend and told her? He wants you to get ready to deal with the fallout."

She shook her head. "Nope. He loves you. He just needs his time to come to his sense is all."

"Oh, shut the hell up." I walked past her and sat down on her couch. "By this time next week, I'm gonna be a single ginger."

"Well, maybe you can channel that into becoming an MMA fighter because I'm pretty sure you just broke my fucking jaw," she said, sitting down next to me.

"Sorry," I said, looking up to her. "I didn't mean to hit you *that* hard. I didn't even think I was going to hit you at all. I certainly didn't come in with that idea in my head."

"Whatever. I'll forgive you because I love you and you're my friend and you're going through a rough patch right now." She rubbed her jaw a little more and sighed. "I'm gonna go get an ice pack."

I watched as she stood up and walked off to her kitchen. I can't say I regret hitting her, but at the same time, I regret hitting her. It felt kind of good to let it out, but I didn't mean to hurt her that bad. It's her fault. She provoked me by laughing at the notion that I could kick her ass. I guess I proved her wrong.

She walked back in with a bag of frozen peas on her face. "So, how's school?" She sat back down where she was sitting before she went to get the "ice" pack.

"It was fine," I replied. "Do you wanna go and get some pizza or something?"

"Are you gonna hit me again if I say no?"

I scoffed. "Nope."

"Good. I don't think I can eat anything unless it's mush now."

"I didn't *break* your jaw," I muttered. "I just hit it pretty hard. That's all."

"How do you think you break someone's jaw, then?" she asked. "By flicking it lightly?"

"If you flicked it enough times, maybe."

"Let me ice my jaw for a bit and then we can go get a pizza."

I smiled a little. "Okay, thanks. And thanks for not hitting me back."

"Why would I hit you back?"

I shrugged. "Because I deserve it."

"Yeah, well, Mindy's the only one that can hit you back," Charlotte said. "Or she'll just make you ride a dirt bike again."

"You shut your mouth," I barked. "That was the first and last time I'm ever getting on one of those goddamn things."

"Well, that's the only way I see us getting even."

"Please just punch me in the face," I said. I pushed my cheek out toward her. "Go on. Just lay one on me. Do it. Just… do it! Don't let your dreams be dreams. Do it! Yes, you can!"

"Don't quote Shia LaBeouf at me."

"I'll do what I want."

Charlotte sighed. "Okay. So this pizza. Do you want a meat lovers' or something else?"

"The more unhealthy it is, the better. I don't have anyone to look good for, so who cares if I eat a large pizza and cover myself with sweat, grease, and shame?"

"He hasn't even dumped you yet," she stated.

"But he will. So let's get a jump on the binging phase so I can get out of it early on and everyone will think I'm this tough girl that doesn't let any guys get her down."

"Should we order it, then?" Charlotte asked. "Because I don't really think I wanna be in public with you if you're planning on eating a large pizza in one sitting."

"Do I embarrass you?"

"No," she replied, "and I'd like to keep it that way. We'll *order* the pizza in a bit."

"Can I sleep over?"

She nodded. "Of course. I have some alcohol stored away for just such an occasion, so tonight we will eat pizza and drink whisky."

"Just such an occasion?"

"Yeah, if you or Mindy or I ever got dumped."

I nodded. "Right. Well, I can't go banging random dudes just yet." I joke about it, but I feel like shit. I loved Evan. I really did. I loved him so much that it's just shy of enough to run away with him and elope in Niagara Falls and then start a new life somewhere else.

"I'm gonna go get us something to drink." Charlotte stood up. "You want orange juice or milk?"

"Um, orange juice, I guess."

"Oh, you don't sound too sure. Uh-oh."

"I want the damn orange juice," I told her, kicking at her leg to make her go and get the juice faster.

She went off to the kitchen and got us our juice. She also put the bag of peas back in the freezer. We sat and talked for a little while. She helped me avoid talking about that dickhead Evan. But eventually, we got too hungry to go on living, so we ordered two pizzas. We ate those and drank a bottle of whisky between the two of us and then passed out on her bedroom floor in some kind of whisky-induced pizza coma.

Charlotte's mom unfortunately made us go to class the next morning. So I had to sit through my class with a splitting headache because my dumb ass decided to get wasted in the middle of the week.

I guess things weren't totally bad though. I had a fun night even though I learned that Evan was planning to break up with me. Maybe I could surprise him and do it myself. I'll tell him I met someone. I'll tell him that me and Collin hooked up. I don't think that would ever actually work unless I did hook up with Collin, but I could never do that because I *love* Evan. Y'know?

Eventually, the hangover faded and I went home after class and I turned my phone off and I napped all day and then slept all night. Well, I laid in bed the whole time. I don't think crying and sobbing into a pillow really counts as sleeping, but hey, it's the thought that counts.

I just knew that with every passing day, I was one more day closer to losing Evan. I'd rather him not talk to me than him not be *mine*. As selfish as it might sound, I wanted him to be all mine. Forever. It's why I turned my phone off. I didn't want him to be able to call me and make me come meet him and then him dump me. I didn't want that. Not yet. I wanted to enjoy the last few days of still technically being his girlfriend.

Oh, Spencer, what have we gotten ourselves into this time?

{Chapter: **Twenty-Three**}

I walked down the stairs and opened the door and saw Charlotte standing there. That's weird. She wasn't supposed to come over today. I mean, it is Saturday, but she still usually calls before coming over to my place like this.

"Hello?" I said as she stepped inside.

"Hey," she said, hugging me. "How's my little gingerbread girl?"

"Um, she's fine," I said as she let go of me. "She's also wondering what you're doing at her house this early on a Saturday."

"I thought I'd come by and, uh, y'know, just hang out with you," she said, stepping in and looking around as if to check if we were alone.

"Okay, you're acting weird. What's going on?"

"Nothing, homie," she said, punching my arm lightly. "So what's going on? What's new in the do?"

I cocked an eyebrow at her. "Seriously, what the hell is wrong with you? Are you high?"

"No. Why? Do you wanna get high?"

"No."

"Then why you asking?"

"Because you're acting a little bit weird right now," I said, following her into the kitchen. "So what's going on?"

"Nothing, Spencer."

"Do I have to punch you again?" I asked.

She swivelled to me and scowled at me. "Please don't."

"Then tell me why you're being so weird."

"I'm not being weird," she said. "Oh, but have you heard from Evan lately or at all?"

"No. Haven't. Why?" I asked.

"No reason."

"That's why you're here. He doesn't want to come over here and talk to me himself, so he hired you to pick me up and take me somewhere. Didn't he?"

Charlotte sighed. "Yeah. He did. Okay? He wants me to take you to some stupid bowling alley and he said he doesn't know what he's gonna do, but he just wants to talk to you."

"If he dumps me, I'm gonna break shit."

"I don't think he wants to dump you," Charlotte stated. "You know that."

"People do things they don't wanna do all the time. You get your vagina hair waxed and you don't wanna do that."

"I do though. I like how it feels all smooth and shit afterwards."

I glared at her. "Whatever. You know what I meant."

"If you're comparing him leaving you to a waxing, you're right on the money. It hurts for a little while, but you're left with something that feels fresh and new," she said. "Use it to your advantage."

"I like my landing strip, uh, Evan," I blurted out. "Okay, I need sleep and you need to change the topic. We are getting into some topics I don't feel comfortable talking about in my kitchen."

"Aww, Spencer has a little landing strip, aww, how cute," she said in a baby voice. "But let's get going."

"Whoa, he wants to talk now?" I asked. "What the hell is it with all you people wanting me to do things early in the day? How many times do I have to tell you guys that I'm a soft and sleepy creature? I need my sleep and I need to ease into my day. It's too early."

"Too bad," Charlotte said, grabbing my wrist and bringing me over to the door. "Let's go."

"I'm actually really nervous right now."

"Put your shoes on," Charlotte said, bending down and lifting my foot into my shoe.

I kicked her hand off my ankle and scowled at her. "I can put shoes on, Charlotte. I'm not a baby."

"No, no, you're an elf princess, you're the guardian of the swamps and valleys, and you're a soft and sleepy creature," Charlotte said. "I get it. I read your tweets."

"I know, but the point is that I'm not a baby."

"Put your shoes on!"

I slipped my feet into my shoes and sighed. "Okay. Let's go get me broken up with, then."

"Shut up, Spencer."

***

I looked out at the bowling alley in front of us. I didn't want to get out of Charlotte's car and go inside. I saw Evan's car parked a few spots over from us. So he was here, that much was a given though.

"So this is it," Charlotte said as she turned her car off.

"Yep." I opened the door and then froze. I didn't want to actually go through with going in there. I didn't wanna get dumped. Well, who the hell would want to?

"You okay?"

I shook my head as I shut the door. "I don't want to go in there."

"You gotta. Maybe he just wants to love you down."

"Well, yeah, I'm an elf princess. Who wouldn't wanna love me down?" I joked. "I'm still nervous."

"Don't be."

"I am."

"Don't be," she repeated. "I think things are gonna work out for you in the end. Maybe not today. Maybe he will dump you, but if he does, you gotta be strong and let him come to his senses and he'll come back to you."

"I get what you're trying to do, but I'm still not okay with what's about to happen," I stated. "I can't control my temper sometimes, and I already know that this will be one of those times that I'm gonna lose it. He hasn't talked to me in a week and I've got a lot to get mad about."

"Yeah. I can see your hair getting redder with anger," Charlotte said as she reached over and pushed my door open. "Go get him, tiger."

"I don't really want to," I muttered as I got out of the car. I shut the door and looked at Charlotte pleadingly. Maybe she would take pity on my poor soul and help me to run away on my own terms and not have to deal with Evan. Not like that would work unless I gave up on my schooling and family and friends, but maybe I could just move to Toronto and bunk with Mindy until I got a job there and met a new guy and got an apartment with him.

I shook my head a little after realizing that I had been standing, looking in through the window at Charlotte for a few seconds. I turned around and started off towards the door that Evan and I had gone into last time. I walked slower as I reached the door, almost as if the weight of the world behind me was grabbing at my ankles and begging me to stay put, to stay frozen in a moment that wouldn't be any of the ones that followed.

I took the last steps toward the door and pulled it open. I walked inside and looked around. It looked the same as it always had, I guess. It was still pretty rundown, well, except for the part that Evan's renovated. I walked in more and looked down and saw the bowling lanes lit up. I started walking towards them, trying to control my breathing as I took small steps over there. I couldn't see Evan yet, but he might be sitting down or something.

"Hello?" I called out into the empty bowling alley. I walked over to the lane that was in use and took a seat. Did Evan seriously stand me up? He's supposed to break up with me. Who the hell bails on the person they're dumping?

I debated on starting a new game to pass some time, but I opted to not do that. I'll just sit and wait for Evan to come by or for Charlotte to come in and get me, even though she hates old buildings like this.

"Hey, you," Evan's voice said from somewhere behind me.

I looked up and over to him. He was wearing a suit and had his hair slicked back a little. It's weird not seeing him in a beanie, but this suit look is a good one on him. Why's he gotta go look so hot if he's about to dump me?

"Hello?" he asked, walking over more.

"What's with the suit?" I asked.

"I have a thing later," he said, stopping in front of me and turning around to model it. "Looks good, right?"

"That's not why I'm here," I said, looking down to the floor. I sighed. "Alright, let's get it over with."

"I'm guessing Charlotte told you?"

"She didn't have to," I replied. "Between you storming out, not talking to me for a week, and me overhearing the end of your conversation with her, I sorta figured it all out."

"She told me you punched her," he said as he sat down next to me. "Did you?"

I nodded. "Yeah. She lied to me."

"Wow, I didn't know you would hit your own best friend. Badass."

"Stop," I said. "Just say what you're gonna say."

"I wanna break up," he said softly.

I nodded. "That's it. The past few months gone, just like that?"

"It's not that I *want* to break up with you, Spencer."

"No?" I asked. "Then what is it?"

"Well, you know I'm dying. I'd assume you read through the folder of papers I left in the hallway," he said. "Right?"

"Yes. I read them. I had to know why you stormed out. I mean, like, it was pretty obvious, but I wanted to be sure."

"So I'm saving you the pain of losing me for good by giving you this closure instead."

I shook my head. "This isn't closure."

"It's better this than losing me by death. I don't want you to be any more attached to me than you already are."

"What the hell would you know about what's better for me? I don't think losing you at all would be a good thing, but certainly not like this."

Evan sighed and rubbed his temple a little. "Listen, this isn't just about you, it's about me. I need time for me to cope with this."

"So I can give you space. You don't need to break up with me to get space, Evan. I'm not stupid. I care about you and I want you to be happy and I get it, I understand it if you need space and time to cope with it," I told him. "But... please... don't leave me, not like this."

"I have to," Evan said, resting a hand on my shoulder.

I swatted his hand away and glared at him. "Don't touch me. You lost those rights when you just dumped me."

"Sorry," he said, pulling away from me.

"I just don't see how this needs to even happen."

"It just does. There's no other girl or anything like that. If I was going to be with anyone, I'd be with you. I'd pick you over a trillion other girls."

I scoffed. "But apparently you can't pick me."

"Spencer, it's not like that. Just give me some time to be with myself."

"I just said you could have your time and space without breaking up with me," I barked. "Are you sure this is what you want? Because I'm not going to guarantee that I'm gonna wait around for you to come back to me."

"I don't expect you to," he stated.

"What's this really about, Evan?" I turned to face him. "Was it that I haven't fucked you yet or something? Am I not pretty enough anymore? Do you regret getting close to me?"

"This doesn't sound like the Spencer I know and love," Evan said, frowning a little. "It's none of those things. I would wait a hundred years for you to fuck me. You've always been pretty enough for me. Actually, you're too pretty for me, and you get prettier by the day. And I certainly do not regret getting close to you. You're the best person in my life, and I think that's why I need to push you away right now."

"Fine."

"Fine?" he questioned. "That's all you're gonna say?"

"What else am I supposed to say, Evan? Am I supposed to get on my knees and beg you to stay? D-do I bribe you with sex? I don't know what I'm supposed to say or do."

"I love you, y'know. I do," he said.

"No, you don't," I said, standing up. "If you loved me like you say you do, you'd hold on for me."

"I'll call you if the treatments start working or something," Evan said as he stood up.

"Don't," I said, wiping away a couple tears. "I don't want you to call me, Evan. If you let me walk away right now as a single woman, then that's it."

He nodded. "Okay. I understand."

"You're a little too cavalier about this."

"It's hard to care about too much when I could be dead in less than a year, so I'm sorry."

"Goodbye, Evan. Have a good rest of your life," I said, walking past him.

"Goodbye, gingersnaps," he muttered.

I frowned a little as I walked back towards the exit. I guess this really was it. A part of me could hope that he would run up to me and kiss me and tell me that he made a mistake and that he loves me and wants me for the rest of his life, be it for a hundred more days or a hundred more years, but all the same weight that had pulled on me and begged me not to come inside was the same weight pushing the two of us apart right now.

I reached the exit and turned to look down at where Evan was standing one last time. I could have sworn he smiled at me a little, but I guess it could have been a trick of the light. I turned and headed back outside. I walked out and the wind hit my face. It was refreshing for a change.

I think I kept myself together in there. I didn't really cry anything more than those few tears, and you'd think that I would have if I was getting broken up with, but I didn't. I guess my anger helped to keep things held down. I was more pissed off at everything than I was sad about it. I wanted to punch things and burn shit, but I figured the best way to get over Evan would be to just live life like I had been living it before Evan had come into it. I walked up to Charlotte's car and opened the door and got back into my seat. I buckled myself in and exhaled sharply. "It's over."

"It is?"

I nodded. "Yeah. It is."

{Chapter: **Twenty-Four**}

I've been single for only sixteen hours or so. I guess that's why I can't get to sleep right away. I just couldn't get my mind around the fact that the best guy in the entire world actually broke up with me today. Maybe some things really are just too good to be true. And maybe he was one of those things that falls into that category.

I rolled over a few times, trying to get myself comfortable in bed. I pretty much gave up hope that I was going to get any sleep. My mind was racing and it had no plans on slowing down. I sat up and ran my fingers through my hair. At least my hair was puffed out right now and I probably resembled a lion or something, so at least I got that going for me. I then heard some clicks on my window and turned to look at it. Not like I was going to know who or what it was by looking at a window. I got up and walked over to the window and pulled the window open.

"Oh, hey, you're up," Charlotte said.

I looked down and saw her standing in my backyard. "Dude."

"Hi," she said, smiling up at me.

"Can't a girl get some sleep around here?" I whined.

She turned her head a little in confusion. "What?"

"Evan used to do this on occasion," I told her. "What do you want?"

"I want nuggets. Come on. Sneak out for me."

I groaned. "I don't wanna wake anybody up."

"Oh, come on. You and Mindy always snuck out before. Now it's my turn to sneak you out. Let's go," Charlotte whined.

I sighed. "Fine. Okay. There's a ladder behind the shed, go get it and push it up to my window. You'll have to hold it and make sure it doesn't fall over. I don't really wanna die right just yet."

Charlotte walked over to the shed and dragged the ladder out from behind it. She lifted it up and I helped her lean it against the house without making too much noise. I went back in and put on the shoes I keep in my room for just such an occasion. I grabbed a sweater and put that on too. It was a little bit cold tonight.

I climbed out and sat on the edge of the window. "Okay, you better hold this thing sturdy. I don't wanna fall."

"I got you," Charlotte said, sounding a little annoyed that I would have assumed otherwise. "Just get down here already."

I sighed and climbed my way down. She didn't hold the ladder as sturdily as Evan does, but it didn't fall over either, so I guess I shouldn't really complain. I helped her lower the ladder back to the ground and then I followed her around my house to the street and to where her car was parked.

"So how you feeling?" she asked, pulling her keys out of her pocket.

"Besides numb and heartbroken?" I asked. "I guess I feel okay."

Charlotte smiled. "Okay. As long as you feel okay."

"Stop. Just get in the car." I opened the door and got in as she walked around to the driver side.

"Do you want to make any stops first?"

I shrugged. "I kinda think I want nuggets."

"How many nuggets do you want?"

¯_(ツ)_/¯ "Just fuck me up."

"Let's go get a whole bunch of nuggets," Charlotte suggested. "We can get every sauce and see which ones are actually any good or not."

"Spicy barbeque and sweet 'n' sour are the only good sauces, everybody knows this."

She gasped as if I had just offended her entire family. "Spicy barbeque? How dare you even suggest that that *sauce* even be put into my body!"

"Well, it's better than honey garlic or whatever the hell you were going to suggest we get the most of," I retorted.

She exhaled deeply. "This is unforgiveable. We're taking you to rehab. You need to get your taste buds checked."

"Eh, my taste buds are just fine, bud," I barked. "Yours are the ones that are messed up, okay? You don't like spicy barbeque. Who the hell doesn't like spicy barbeque?"

"Collin."

"Then Collin's as weird as you are!"

She started driving and sighed. "Okay. I'm gonna let this slide because you did just get dumped today, but if you think our friendship is gonna survive with you liking *spicy barbeque* sauce with your nuggets, then I don't know what to tell you, man."

"No. You're not leaving me over a difference in nugget sauces, you little shit. We can make this work."

"I'm from a long line of honey garlic lovers," she said. "I don't think they'd approve of us."

"But that makes it all the more fun," I said. "Come on, nerd, come to the spicier side of life."

"Not gonna happen, dude," she said. "But I can tell you what is gonna happen."

"If it's anything to do with Evan, I will not hesitate to punch you in the jaw again."

"No, it's nothing about Evan," she said. "And don't hit me again. You have a strong punch. It's still kinda sore, man. But I was gonna tell you that we're gonna go *in* on those nuggets. I'm talking a hundred and fifty each and our hands and face dripping with sauce."

"When was the last time you ate?" I asked.

She shrugged. "Yesterday. And not as in like, 'Oh, the date changed so now it's tomorrow.' It's been over 24 hours at least."

"Why?"

"I was nervous about you and, uh, a certain dickhead."

"Well, that was dumb. Eating is important, Charlotte."

She scoffed. "Don't scold me. I know eating is important. I just actually forgot to do it, okay? I was waiting by the phone in case you needed me for anything. You just went through a breakup, so as your best friend, I have to be available to you for the next week at minimum."

"No, you don't," I told her. "Who said that?"

"I did," she said. "I want to be there for you. It was just a day. We're going to eat right now. Relax."

"Okay. In case you forgot, I'm your friend too. I gots to look out for my bitch," I said.

She smirked a little. "Bitches don't likes to be called bitches."

"*Bitch.*"

She sighed and smiled a little. "I miss the old days, Spencer."

"You weren't even here for my old days."

"No, but I mean the ones with you and me and Mindy and the old barn and the staying up all night and the careless life. Everything gets so complicated the more you grow up," she explained. "I just want things to be a little less, I don't know, convoluted."

"Life just happens like that though. There's not too much we can do but adapt to the things that change around us," I said. "And as much as I would love to go back and relive those things we used to do, I still don't think I'd ever give up the person I am now for a little taste of the past. I like me. I'm smart, beautiful, and I've got the best two friends a girl could ask for."

"Right, but isn't there some part of you that yearns for it?"

I nodded. "I'm sure there is, but that part of me is suffocating under the badass woman I'm becoming."

Charlotte sighed. "Yeah, well, I guess I'm not quite on your level yet."

"You sure are," I told her. "There's nothing that would make you be any lower of a level than anyone else. Life isn't a competition. Well, it shouldn't be anyway. And you moved thousands of miles away from your home just to follow your dream and explore the world and go to college in Canada. That's pretty badass if you ask me. Now keep your eyes on the road, you're starting to drift into oncoming."

"Sorry," she said, turning the car back into our lane as she wiped some tears from her face. "I guess you're right though."

"When am I not?"

"Let me finish," she barked.

"Sorry. Go on."

"You make a good point about how I uprooted my life from California and moved here. That's a pretty hard thing for someone to do."

"Do you miss it?"

"I do," she replied, wiping a few more tears from her eyes. "I miss all my old friends. They don't even message me anymore. It's like… I left and now I just vanished from existence altogether for them. A few of them kept contact for a couple weeks and a couple of them for a few months, but after a while, everybody from back home stopped talking to me."

"Wow, they kinda suck."

"Yeah, no shit," she said. "I tried to keep contact with them. It was easy because even when I had met you and Mindy, I *only* had you and Mindy. I had two options of people to hang out with and usually it was both of you or neither of you because you guys spent a lot of time together except for when Emily was here."

"I got a little jealous," I admitted. "Mindy's my best friend. She's not allowed to have other friends."

"Yeah, but the three of us were friends and that gave me lots of time to realize how little my old friends cared about me," Charlotte said, sighing a little. "I don't think I ever really wanna go back there now."

"So don't," I told her. "Why would you go back to people who don't really care about you? You know who cares about you? Me. I care about you. One quarter is better than 25 pennies."

"You're worth a lot more than a quarter, Spencer."

"Crap, I should have said I was a dime, because let's be honest." I brushed my hair over my shoulder and looked at her with a pouty "model smile."

"Yeah, you're pretty hot, but you're still worth more than all the money in the world. You're my best friend, y'know?"

I smiled. "You're my best friend too."

"Even better than Mindy?"

"Well, Mindy and I have history, but it is hard to stay in touch with her right now because she's in Toronto and she's been keeping busy with working and banging her girlfriend," I said. "But I'm happy for her. I'm so, so, so happy for her. She followed her heart and she's living a good life right now."

"Yeah, but she cares about you. She's not like all of my old friends. Mindy's a different kind of person," Charlotte stated. "She's a good person."

"I'm sure some of your friends are. I don't know. Maybe they just got busy and then they felt like they couldn't talk to you because you had moved on and met new people or something. Who knows."

"Yeah. Whatever. Things fall apart sometimes."

I nodded. "Sometimes they do. Sometimes things fall apart to make room for better things on the way. Like the smoking hot dude in my figurative drawing class."

"Oh, shut up. You're not gonna just move on from Evan in the course of a week."

"Why not? Who says I can't?"

"I say you can't."

I sighed. "Why?"

"Because you loved the guy and he was the first one since the last one. I don't think you can just move on from that in the blink of an eye. It takes time."

"Well, *I* have lots of time," I stated. A good 60 or so more years of it.

Charlotte smiled. "You do. You're young and you have the whole world ahead of you, so slow down and enjoy things while you can. There's no sense in rushing into relationships to get back at your exes and there's no sense in wasting life on petty things. Okay?"

"Okay," I grumbled.

"But you can waste life on pretty things," she said. "Like nuggets."

I smiled widely and pointed to myself dramatically. "And like me."

"You're the prettiest of things."

"Whoa, you're not hitting on me, are you?"

She winked and clicked her tongue at me. I smacked her arm playfully and we laughed a little. And then things went quiet. I had forgotten for a minute that it was the middle of the night, to be honest. The world around us was totally silent. The only thing making noise was the few other cars and the grasshoppers in the grass hopping, well, I would assume. Why else would they be called grasshoppers? They live in the grass and they hop. Huh... I wonder if they hip.

"Do you wanna go in and eat, or should we just sit in the car and listen to the radio?" Charlotte asked as we pulled into the parking lot.

I shrugged. "We haven't dined inside at night in a while."

"Then it's settled. We're going in." She shut the car off and opened the door.

I opened the door and followed her into the place. She walked up and ordered a fairly large order of nuggets and I went off to sit down. There was nobody else in here because of how late it was, so I had the pick of the seats. I chose a table in the middle. Booths are overrated. I waited a couple minutes for Charlotte to come bouncing on over with a big smile on her face and a hundred nuggets on a tray in her hands.

We probably ate twenty each before we couldn't eat any more nuggets. We split the rest up and put our shares of leftovers into separate bags for later. I'd probably give mine to Jordan though. I don't really like cold nuggets, and microwaved nuggets are just a no.

I didn't end up getting home till almost five in the morning. Charlotte really wanted to help keep my mind off of Evan, but it's not like it was going to help, because I still had to lie in bed and try to sleep, but I'll admit that staying out that late did help me fall asleep because I did get pretty tired.

The next day, Charlotte came over. I don't know how she managed to get up early enough to come over and wake me up before noon, but kudos to her. I was pretty much tired all day, which again must be her way of helping me not think of Evan. By the time the night rolled around, I was again beyond the appropriate level of tiredness. Charlotte's a good friend, but not thinking about Evan wouldn't help me get over it. I just needed to have me a good cry about him and then move on.

He doesn't wanna be with me because he doesn't want me to feel worse if he were to die, so I guess he has a point. Crying over a breakup is a little bit easier than crying over a death. But I can't be mad at a death. I can be mad at a breakup. And right now, I was mad about it. Not sad or upset, mad and pissed off. My red hair was going to start turning white because I was actually really salty about all of this.

I guess I'll move on eventually though.

{Chapter: **Twenty-Five**}

A few days removed of Evan and I was feeling fine. I still hadn't had a grandiose cry like I should have, but I think that was because I didn't want to let myself believe that it was truly over. I didn't want to think that Evan and I weren't together. We were just on a break.

I shook myself out of my thoughts and stepped forward in line to the register to order myself a coffee. I gotta stop zoning out like that. It's a bad habit and it makes me look a little weird. People probably think I'm lost all the time the way I look around. I ordered my coffee and sat down at one of the tables with two seats so I could call Charlotte and see if she wanted to come join me. I know her class ends at the same time as mine does. I pulled my phone out and called her up.

"Hello, loser," she answered.

"Charlotte," I whined. "What are you up to right now?"

"Well, I was thinking about doing some homework. Why?"

"Well, I'm all alone and bored, so I was wondering if you wanted to come think about doing some homework with me or something."

She breathed in loudly. "I don't know, man. Thinking about homework is a solitary activity."

"Collin's over, isn't he?"

She sighed. "Yeah, he's on his way."

I groaned. "Fine. Whatever. Try not to moan out the title of your essay while he's boning you."

"Aye, aye, cap'n," she replied. "Sorry I can't do stuff tonight. Tomorrow for sure though. Okay?"

"Yeah, I guess." I started playing with the lid of my coffee cup. "I could always go make new friends that don't have boyfriends."

"No, what, no, don't do that. I love you, but a girl has needs," Charlotte stated. "And this girl has needs that other girls just can't satisfy."

I looked up as somebody sat across from me at the table. "Charlotte, I'm gonna have to let you go." I hung up the phone and set it on the table.

"Did I interrupt something important?" Evan asked.

I shook my head. "Nope."

"How are you?" he asked. The nerve of this guy. Break up with me and then ask how I am?

"I'm good," I lied.

He pouted a little. "You're not a good liar."

"Fuck off," I muttered.

"Is that a 'you need to leave' or a 'shut up'?"

"I don't know."

He sighed a little. "I just saw you over here and overheard your part of that talk and thought you might wanna hang out for a bit."

"Why would I want to hang out with you?" I asked. "It's been, like, four days since you dumped me. What makes you think I'd want to hang out with you?"

He shrugged. "No clue. Just thought I'd offer. I had to go out and do some errands and grocery shopping and I wanted a coffee and I saw you. I was going to just offer you a ride home was all."

I groaned. "Well, if you're offering a free ride home, I'll take you up on that offer. But that's all I want. I don't even know if I want to talk to you."

"You're talking to me now," he quipped.

"Because I'm telling you I don't want to talk to you when we get into your car," I retorted.

He smirked. "Maybe I wanna sit here and enjoy my coffee a little longer." He peeled the tab back on his lid and took a sip.

"I don't wanna be on a coffee date with my *ex*. Just saying."

He sighed. "Okay, let's go, then. I have to drop my stuff off at home first."

"I'm cool with that."

***

Evan pulled into his driveway and shut the car off. "I don't know if you wanna sit here or come in or whatever. Nobody else is here, so it doesn't really matter."

"I'll sit on the porch," I said, looking up at his house. It was old and beaten up. I guess it was just worn in very well. The siding was old as shit though. And at the end of the driveway was an even older garage. It was basically falling apart. The door was open a little and I could see a car that was covered with a tarp inside.

Evan opened his door and turned to me. "Well, come on. Get out."

"I'm getting, I'm getting," I whined, opening the door and hopping out of his car. I walked up the driveway a little as he went into the trunk to grab his groceries. I looked over at the car in the garage. "So, what kind of car do you got locked up back there?"

Evan walked back over to me with a stern look on his face. "Don't ask. Don't touch. Don't even look. Got it?"

"Got it," I muttered as he turned and started for his front door. "Hardass."

"I heard that."

"You were supposed to."

Evan sighed. "Whatever. Just sit on the porch. I'll just be a minute. Do you want anything to drink?"

I shook my head. "I'm okay."

He smirked at me and disappeared into his house. The door closed behind him and shut with a loud thud. I looked over at the porch. The chairs looked brand new, which was a refreshing change of scenery with everything else about Evan's house. I walked over and sat down on the swing at the end of his porch. I liked these swings. They weren't aggressive swings, just nice comfortable ones

193

that swayed gently. After a few minutes of swaying on the swing, Evan walked outside with a thermos in his hands. He walked over and handed it to me.

"I said I didn't want anything," I said as I took it from him.

He shrugged. "You like hot chocolate though."

I sighed. "Yeah. Yeah, I do."

"Seriously though, how are you?"

I shrugged. "I'm doing okay. I mean, I'm not *okay*, but I'm okay."

"That, um, doesn't really make any sense," he said, sitting down next to me.

"Does it have to?"

"Well, I think it'd make it easier to understand."

I shrugged. "Whatever. If you can't understand me, that's your issue. I understand me just great."

"Why are you so hostile?"

"It might have something to do with the fact that you dumped me but are acting as if nothing is wrong."

"Oh," he said. "I meant to talk to you about that."

"About dumping me? Again?"

He shook his head. "No. I can't dump you again. You made that perfectly clear, remember? It's just that I want to be with you—"

"So be with me," I said.

"Let me finish," he said, rolling his eyes a little. "I want to be with you, but I just don't want you to fall in love with me and then have to watch me get lowered into a dirt hole. Do you understand that?"

"Yes. I understand that. So what is it you wanted to ask?"

"Well, there's still obviously the slim chance that my treatment will start working, right? So I was going to suggest we stay in relationship limbo."

"What the fuck is that?"

"It's basically like dating, but we're not exclusive and we don't see each other all the time."

I stared at him with a perplexed looks on my face. "What?"

"Friends that go out to dinner, basically," he stated. "I want you to be my friend at least."

"I can't be friends with someone I love. It's weird," I said with a small sigh. "I mean… like, you've came in my hand. I can't go back to friends."

He let out a loud groan. "Don't make it weird, dude."

"Sorry," I said. "But it's the truth."

"Look, can we just try to make this work? Think of it like being stuck on the second date."

"We'll be going on second dates until you either get a terminal diagnosis or until the treatment starts working?" I asked. "That's kinda fucked."

"I know it is, but I've already done damage to us and this is the best way to ease back into it. It's all up to you. I totally understand if you never wanna see me again after today. I was an ass to you and this is a not very fair thing for me to do to you either."

"Yeah," I said, "it's not. But I fucking love you, Evan. You could put me through hell and back and I would still love you. You could sell me off to a pimp and I'd probably still love you."

"Friends definitely isn't going to work," he said, looking down and sighed a little. "Well, let's just start over." He held his hand out. "I'm Evan."

"We're not doing this either. You've literally had your face in between my thighs. We're not starting over."

"Stop doing that," he barked.

"I'm brutally honest and blunt about things when I'm upset. I can't help it sometimes."

"You're upset?"

I rolled my eyes a little at him. "Of course I'm upset, asshole. I love you and you tried to kick me out of your life 'cause you thought you were dying—"

"I am dying, but go on."

I glared at him for a few seconds. "You tried to kick me out of your life 'cause you *thought* you were dying, but now you want to start over on this whole dating thing. I can't do starting over, Evan. I just can't."

"Why can't we be just friends?"

"We tried that once, remember?"

"That's why I'm asking," he said.

I sighed. "I'll think about it. Until then, we're just something. Okay?"

He nodded. "Okay."

"Okay."

"I love you, Hazel Grace."

"I told you that you're not Augustus and I'm not Hazel," I stated. "I don't get why you think there is any reason for their to be any faults in our stars. Our stars are fine. There's nothing wrong with *our* stars, Evan. Our galaxies are perfectly fine."

He smiled softly. "We look up at the stars and see such different things."

"Are you quoting the book? I never actually read all of it."

"No," he said, shaking his head, "George R. R. Martin."

"He's the, uh, *Game of Thrones* writer, right?"

Evan nodded. "Well, kind of. He wrote the books that it's based on."

"Well, whatever. If you see faults in the stars, then you're looking for them. You're looking for things to fret about. You're not enjoying the glow and the twinkling lights. You want there to be faults because that somehow would make it easier for you to cope with everything," I told him. "Maybe one day you can see the stars in the same ways I do, but until then, you're always gonna want to run away from the problem at hand."

"And that is?"

"Life."

"What do you mean?"

"Well, whether or not you die in a month or in a decade or in a century, you're going to die, that is going to happen. And when you die, I'm sure I'm gonna be the one by your side," I said. "Well, I at least hope I'd be the one by your side."

"I just don't want you to become the girl with a dead boyfriend." He let out a sigh. "I don't know. I just need more time for me."

"The girl with a dead boyfriend would be happier having made her boyfriend happy until his last breath than not being able to because her boyfriend fucking broke up with her because he was dying."

"Then we're just on a break. Just friends. We're something in between that," he said. "Just let me be me and you do you and we'll figure this out."

"I think I've figured it out now." I stood up and opened the thermos. I took a sip and let out a sigh. "I think I'd like to go home now, nerd."

"Nerd?" he asked, standing up.

"I meant to say asshole." I turned to him.

He smirked at me and nodded a little as he walked by. "Sure ya did."

"I did," I said as I followed him off the porch. "You're an asshole and that's what you are to me right now. You're an asshole. Asshole."

"Okay," he said as we got to his car. "Get in."

***

"You can keep the thermos for now," Evan said as we pulled up in front of my house. He looked past me and then to me with a sort of disapproving glare. "You didn't ditch on Charlotte, did you?"

"What?" I asked, turning to see Charlotte sitting on my front steps. "She wasn't supposed to come over."

"Well, I'll see you later," Evan said.

"I wouldn't hold your breath on it," I said as I got out of the car. I shut the door and walked up to Charlotte. "What's going on? I thought you were at home waiting for Collin."

She shrugged. "He had to stay home and help his mom. He called and we arranged that he would just come stay the night, so I figured I could hang with you for a bit, but you weren't home, and that's because you were with Evan. Are you two back together or something?"

"No, I don't know. He's more confusing than anyone I've ever met."

Charlotte cocked an eyebrow. "So?"

"So I don't know," I stated. "He just said he doesn't want me to end up as the girl with the dead boyfriend. So sweet of him to think about my feelings like that, hmm?"

"No, it's confusing. Collin told me that Evan wanted to get back together with you. After that night he dumped you, he apparently told Collin that he already really missed you and regretted doing what he did."

197

"Well, he didn't tell me that," I said, sitting on the step next to Charlotte.

"Please, you wouldn't have answered his call anyway."

I nodded a little. "You're probably right about that."

"I don't know. He'll make up his mind eventually. Until then, you need to just focus on you."

"Yes, mother. I know. Thank you, mother."

"I never wanna be a mom. Kids are hard work."

I chuckled a little. "Boys are hard work. School is hard work. Life is hard work."

"Amen." She looked down at the thermos in my hands. "I don't remember you ever owning a thermos."

"Oh, it's Evan's," I told her, handing it to her. "You can drink it. I don't really feel like hot chocolate right now."

She took it and smiled. "I'd be dumb to turn down a free thermos of hot chocolate. Thanks."

"No problem. But you can't keep it. I have to give it back to him," I stated. "I'll just mail it to him. I don't really think I wanna see his face ever again."

Charlotte laughed a little and smiled as she took a sip from the thermos.

"Is something funny to you?" I asked.

"Yeah." She nodded, screwing the lid back onto the thermos. "You."

"Why?"

"Because you say you never wanna see him again, but you still let him drive you home. That's all."

{Chapter: **Twenty-Six**}

Ahh, yes, Friday night and the elf princess is all alone in her bed-room with a bowl of popcorn and a twelve-pack of root beer. Some-times I wonder why I bothered with boys anyway. This lifestyle is much more suited to me. I'd just have to go to the gym so I don't balloon out and need to buy new clothes and stuff. That's honestly the only reason. I don't care if I get chubby. Chubby girls are cute. I just don't have the funds to buy new clothes.

I tossed a finished and completely empty box of chewy cookies in the general direction of my garbage bin. I looked over to see how close I had gotten, and it wasn't very close at all. "Kobe," I muttered to myself. I sat upright and picked some popcorn out of my bra and let out a loud yawn. It's only 6:30. Why the hell am I yawning?

I reached for my phone and checked if I had gotten any mes-sages. No dice. I wasn't expecting to get any messages or calls. Mindy had a date tonight and so did Charlotte. I had a date too… if you count a hand as a date. You feel me?

I set my phone down on my bed and almost immediately after it hit my bed, it started ringing. I groaned a little as I pulled it up to my ear and answered it. "Hello?"

"Hi. Get dressed up nicely and meet me outside in five minutes,"

Evan's voice said.

"Why?" I asked before hearing the beeping dial tone. "Or just hang up on me right away, you giant assface." I climbed out of bed and put my hair up into a messy but stylish bun. I swapped my shirt and sweatpants for a sundress. It wasn't the prettiest thing I owned, but it was quick. I went to the bathroom and brushed my teeth and fixed my makeup a little bit.

I went back into my room and grabbed my phone and keys and cards and wallet and everything and stuffed it into my purse. I looked myself over and sighed. I guess this will do. The sundress I was wearing was kind of a reddish colour, or it at least looked like that because of the floral patterning. I picked up a pair of black flats and walked downstairs, putting them on as I got to the bottom. I walked over to the door and opened it and saw Evan walking up my steps.

"You're right on time," he said, smirking. He was wearing a suit again. Why?

"What's going on?" I asked.

"I'm kidnapping you."

"No, really. Why did I have to get dressed up? Where do I have to go?" I asked.

"To dinner," he said, raising my hand and kissing it. "Sorry. Clichés and whatnot. Might I add that you look very ravishing this evening."

"Um, thanks," I said, stepping outside and shutting the door behind me. "Why exactly are you taking me to dinner?"

"I thought you could use some food."

"Not to brag, but I did just go through a bag of popcorn and an entire box of chewy cookies." I nodded and raised an eyebrow at him. "Impressive, right?"

"I mean, I guess," he said, looking at me like I was the crazy one. "Let's just go get in the car, okay?"

"You haven't told me where you're taking me though."

"I told you," he said. "Dinner."

"But where are we having dinner, smartass?"

"A place," he replied.

"I swear to God. If you take me to the middle of a forest for a picnic and tell me that trees are places, I'm gonna smack you," I whined as I followed him down the driveway and to his dumb SUV. That's not fair of me. The SUV never did anything wrong to me.

Evan turned and gave me another weird look like I was still the crazy one. "That's oddly specific."

I shrugged. "I mean, I wouldn't be against it. I am an—"

"An elf princess of the forest and a guardian of the swamps and valleys. Yeah. I read your tweets."

I smiled. "Do you still?"

"Why's that any importance right now?"

I pulled my phone out and tweeted that Evan was a dork. I looked back up to him and smiled. "No reason."

He pulled his phone out for a few seconds and then looked up to me. "You're lucky you're cute. Now get in the car."

***

"Why are we at the mall?" I asked as Evan parked his car in the parking lot. I don't think I've been to the mall since we cleaned the paint up from the hardware store. I kinda liked having the mall to ourselves. Man, I miss those couple days. I'd give anything to just re-live them over and over again.

"Well, I wanted to take you to dinner, but I didn't wanna cook it this time," Evan said, opening his door. "Come on, gingersnaps."

"Don't," I whined as I got out of the car.

"What do you mean?"

"I don't want you to call me that. It's weird if we're not dating," I told him.

He stared at me with his mouth slightly agape. "We are literally on a date right now."

"Fuck." I sighed. "Still. It's too early in the night for cute nick-names and shit. Get a few glasses of wine in me first."

"Noted."

We walked into the restaurant and then we got seated and ordered our food. The restaurant looked a lot different when it was, I don't know, full of people and actually in service.

"So, I've been meaning to ask, what's with the elf princess thing?"

I shrugged. "I've always wanted to be an elf princess. I want little elf ears and I wanna talk to the woodland creatures and I wanna be one with the river and I want to rule over the land in a motherly and nurturing way."

"Ever since you were little, huh?"

I nodded. "But a princess needs a prince... or another princess. I haven't decided. Princes are buttholes."

"We're at a fine-dining establishment, you can't say anyone is a butthole," Evan muttered to me.

"Oh, right, right." I winked. "Gotcha. Princes are... something lame. They're rapscallions."

"Rapscallion?"

"It's a mischievous person. They're up to no good," I said. "Which pretty much sums up boys. Am I right?"

He shrugged. "I guess."

"I used to dream of growing up in the woods," I told him. "I used to think that if I could somehow run away to the woods, things would be okay. I wanted to be a little fairy in a cute green dress with a long flowing mane of red hair in the wind behind me. I was gonna bathe in the ponds and live in the trees. But dreams are dreams and this is my reality."

"Maybe we can get a house in the woods someday. A little getaway cabin for you to escape to," Evan suggested. "Assuming we get back together and whatnot."

"Right, assuming we do and that you live that long," I said softly.

He nodded. "Right."

"You did live long enough to talk me into getting the lasagna here, so thanks for that."

"Well, you said you wanted garlic bread and the lasagna goes well with the garlic bread. It's just common sense."

I smiled softly at him. "This is kind of really awkward, Evan."

"It's only going to get awkward if you finish that thought."

I frowned at him. "Well, I'm sure that thought was the truth at least. But maybe I was just gonna say because only one of us loves the other person."

"Right," he said, nodding. "I love you."

"Bitch," I said, looking around to make sure I wasn't getting any disapproving looks from any rich people, "you're the one who dumped me."

"You really like to remind me of that, don't you?"

"I like to remind people of their mistakes. Yeah."

He sighed. "I do love you."

"Not enough, clearly." I brushed a few strands of hair out of my face and slouched back in my seat.

"Did you really do your hair that nicely in the five minutes I gave you before getting to your house?" he asked, looking up to my stylishly unstyled messy bun.

I nodded. "I'm a pro at messy buns."

"I can tell."

"Stop it with the small talk," I said, holding a hand up. I'm sassy. "Just tell me why you randomly kidnapped me and took me on a date."

"Okay, well, I didn't kidnap you. You came willingly. You could have told me no and I would have turned and walked away and went home because I'm not a whiny bitch," he stated. "But I took you out because I wanted to."

"Did you get results back? Is the treatment working? Is it not working? Those were the two options, and I'm pretty sure our future sort of depended on which of those it was."

He shrugged. "I just missed you."

"You could have brought me a coffee and sat on my bed with me."

"Yeah, but you like going out."

"Do not," I argued.

"You do. You got all smiley when we walked in here. You dressed up within five minutes just to go out. You knew you were going out, you might not have *known*, but you did."

"Why do you know me so well?" I asked. I sighed and took a sip of my water.

He shrugged again. "I'm attentive with things that I love. Or, in this case, people that I love."

"It's annoying. I hate not being able to enjoy things in secret while openly hating them," I muttered. "I eat romantic dinners up. Both metaphorically and in twenty minutes when our food gets here."

Evan smiled. "And that right there is why I took you to dinner."

"Because I like it or because you know that I can still fit into all my clothes and that I shouldn't be able to after a breakup because I should be stuffing my face with chips and ice cream. Right?"

"You have a fast metabolism though."

"Yeah. I forgot that I had told you all that stuff about me."

He frowned slightly. "We got to know each other during the honeymoon phase of our relationship. That's why *this* first date is kind of awkward."

"This isn't a first date," I stated. "Is it?"

"It could be the first date of the rest of our lives." Evan shrugged. "I dunno. I don't really care. All I know is that I'm glad we're on this date right now."

I nodded. "Yeah. I missed being on good terms with you. We're not dating or together or exclusive, but we're on good terms. This can be a friendly date. Nothing more. Agreed?"

Evan nodded. "We can both sleep on the idea of getting back together or whatever. There's no rush. Neither of us are dying or moving away in the next month, so let's just take this time for ourselves to be with ourselves."

"You still should have just told me you needed time and space. I woulda been a lot more okay with that than with you dumping me."

"I know," he said. "It's a bit too late for that though. This is what we are now and this is what we'll stay. At least for the time being."

"You're not gonna kidnap often for dates though, right?"

He shrugged. "I haven't decided."

"I swear, you and all my friends have always done this to me. Everybody makes me go on last-minute adventures. I mean, I like it, but I'd also like being told in advance," I stated, taking a sip of water. "I'd also like it if our food got here already."

"Hungry?"

I nodded.

He reached across the table and held my hand. "Here." He reached into his suit pocket with his other hand and then handed me a chocolate bar.

I took it from him and eyed him down as he pulled his hand

back. "Why?"

He shrugged. "You like chocolate."

"I do," I said, opening the chocolate bar and stuffing a piece of it into my face. "Ugh. Why do you do this to me?"

He smiled and shook his head a little at me. I guess I looked funny with chocolate stuffed into my face. Whatever, it was good, and that's what mattered to me at this moment.

After a dozen more minutes, our food came and we ate. We talked about school and the weather and stuff. It actually did kind of feel like a first date, which was weird.

After the dinner, he drove me home and we shared a little kiss before I got out. And before I got out, I warned him to never kiss me again until I kiss him first. How was I going to be just friends with him if he's gonna keep putting the moves on me all the time? He waited until I got into my house to drive off. It's kinda cute that people wait until you get inside before they leave. It's such a small and seemingly insignificant thing, but it's really nice of them.

I turned and walked upstairs, well, I tried to go upstairs, but my mom saw me from the kitchen as I walked by it and she ordered me in.

"What's up?" I asked, sticking my head around the wall, hoping she hadn't noticed the dress I was wearing.

"Where were you?" she asked. "I specifically remember you telling me that you didn't have any plans because Charlotte was out on a date tonight. So where did you run off to?"

"I… went for coffee. Yes. Coffee. With myself."

"Why are you wearing a dress?" she asked, cocking an eyebrow at me. "You never wear dresses."

I sighed and stepped into the doorway more. "Well, I thought my pasty legs could use some air. They're pretty nice legs. I think I might wear dresses more often. I have the figure for it, right?"

"Nice cover. Who'd you have a date with?"

"Evan," I muttered.

"Evan? I thought you two were broken up?"

"We were. We are. I don't know. Boys confuse me," I whined as I walked over to sit next to her at the table.

"Well, get used to it. You're gonna have to marry one someday,"

205

she said with an empathetic look on her face.

"Maybe I like girls," I told her. "You don't know that."

"Trust me, I know you don't," she said. "If you liked girls, you and Mindy would be together right now. And you know that as well as I do."

"Yeah," I said, pouting. "She is a little ball of loveable nerd."

"Well, so is Evan."

"Not right now. He's a ball of piss-me-off and confusion."

My mom sighed and handed me a bag of gummy worms. "I picked these up for you when I was out earlier, by the way."

"Are you sure you're supposed to be giving me candy? All I've been eating for the past few days is junk food."

"I can give you carrots and broccoli if you'd prefer that?"

I frowned and took the gummy worms from her. "Thanks."

"Is there any real reason you two broke up in the first place?" my mom asked as I stood up.

"Not one that I'm allowed to talk about, no."

{Chapter: **Twenty-Seven**}

Last night was weird. Why? Because why would my ex come to my house and then take me on a date? Even if we were on the cusp of getting back together or something, it's still super weird and I don't know how to feel about it.

My phone started ringing from the kitchen, so I hightailed it downstairs. I guess my phone ringing is one way to break me out of my thoughts. I picked it up and answered the call without checking who it was. "Hello?" I hope I didn't sound completely winded from that sprint up here.

"Hey, what are you up to today and do you wanna hang out?" Charlotte asked me. Phew, it's only Charlotte.

"I'd love to. I'll go out and get myself a coffee and be right over," I told her. "I just have to find a better outfit."

"What's wrong with whatever you're wearing?"

"Well, it's a dress and I slept in it," I replied, looking down at the sundress I had worn last night on my "date" with Evan. "Eh, I'll just wear it. It looks kinda cute and I did shave my legs yesterday before getting all comfy in bed only to be interrupted."

"By?"

"Oh, I didn't tell you. Right. I'll fill you in when I get there."

"Okay, see you in a bit. You can just walk right in. We're in the living room."

"We?" I asked.

"Collin slept over."

"Wink, wink," I said teasingly. "Kudos to you for getting it in, but I'm gonna go get ready so I can get the next bus to the coffee shop, okay? Okay. See you soon, nerd." I hung up the phone and gathered my things into my purse and headed down for the door. I put on my flats again, 'cause why the hell not? I kinda liked the dress look on me. My legs did look very nice when they were shaven. They looked so soft. Elf princess legs.

I walked off to the bus stop and hopped on the bus over to the coffee shop and I got myself a coffee. Obviously, what else would I go to a coffee shop for? I then hopped on a second bus and headed over to Charlotte's house. I walked up to her door and headed right inside and to the living room where Charlotte and Collin were sitting. They were sitting next to each other on the big couch talking about stuff. I walked over to the armchair adjacent to the couch and made a coughing sound as I passed them.

"Hi, Spencer," Collin said, smiling at me.

"Hi," I said, smiling back.

"I didn't know you wore dresses in public."

I shrugged as I sat down. "I didn't either, but it looks good, right?"

"Yeah, you look great," he said.

Charlotte smacked him. "You look great, Spencer."

I smiled a little. It's cute to think that Charlotte would ever be jealous of me when she is a goddess in her own right. But guys with nose rings aren't really my type. No offence, I just find them kind of a turnoff to me. And shut up, I know I have a nose piercing too, but it's different. It's always sexy on girls. I just don't find them as attractive on guys.

"So how've you been?" Collin asked. "I heard you and Evan split."

"Well, you're his best friend, so I would have assumed you knew he was dumping me before I figured out he was dumping me," I said. "But it's a good thing you're here, because I kinda wanna talk about

Evan with you."

"He does love you, you know. He just has a shitty way of getting that across amongst other feelings he has about getting close to people and stuff," Collin said. "But any questions you have, I'll do my best to answer."

"Okay, give me your best reason as to why that little asshole would rather break up with me than confront the thing that's holding him back from wanting to be with me."

"He just wants to think about your long-term happiness. He said it'd be better to cut it off now before things got more and more serious," Collin replied. "Next."

I thought for a second. "Mm, okay. Why did he contact me the other day about wanting to be on good terms and being just friends?"

"He still loves you. He's just scared to actually give in to that feeling and he's even more scared of hurting you in the end, so that's probably why he just wants to be friends right now. He's biding time by keeping you close. He obviously doesn't want you to go on dates with other dudes and stuff, but he also doesn't want to be with you because of, well, you know. But he'll come around eventually. He doesn't shut up about you half the time."

"Okay, final question for right now," I said. "Why did he take me out on a date last night if he doesn't want us to be together again?"

Charlotte and Collin both turned to me and looked at me with a look of shock. And then they spoke in unison, "What?"

"He took me on a date last night," I stated.

"Well, that's new," Collin said. "He never mentioned anything about taking you out on a date or anything. Maybe he's already coming around."

"No. Trust me. We're not closer to being together than we were since he dumped me. I mean, we might be a little closer, but things are so goddamn confusing right now with him," I groaned. I took a sip of my coffee and ruffled my hair a little. It was in a messy bun again, but whatever. Messier bun it is.

"Evan's a goddamn mess of confusion lately," Collin said. "Like, the other night, he told me he had to go to group therapy. He didn't tell me why or what for, he just said he wanted to go for the fun of it, to see what it was like. And I asked if he wanted me to come and he laughed and then told me he had to get going. He's had weird events and stuff to go to lately and it's weirding me out."

"Yeah, I dunno what's going on with him," I lied.

"Really? He never told you about any of that?"

I shook my head. "Never even said a word of any therapy sessions or anything to me." Why was I lying for Evan right now? I hate being a good person with morals, but I find my morals conflict here. I either keep a promise to that shit stain that is Evan or I tell the truth. Well, I guess we're keeping the promise, since it was the first thing I automatically did. No matter how mad I am at Evan, I can't break a promise to him. And I promised to keep his secret safe.

"Weird." Collin shrugged. "Maybe he is going to therapy. Maybe it's for the same reason why he doesn't wanna be with you right now."

"Ha, yeah, I bet it is," I said, nearly having to bite my tongue to stop myself from saying anything more.

"I hope so." Collin reached for a cup on the table and took a drink of something, probably coffee. "You two were friggin' cute together."

"Yeah, well, that's because I'm just a goddamn ray of sunshine. You know me," I said, smiling a little. "He's the one who's losing out on me, not me on him."

"Spencer," Charlotte groaned.

"It's the truth," I grumbled. "He's a stupid, smelly guy. I'm an—"

"Elf princess," Collin said, interrupting me. "We know. We read your tweets."

"Just let me live my life, damn."

Charlotte smirked at me. "Nothing wrong with confidence, Spencer, but don't just use it as a shield to hide away your insecurities and sadness. Emotions are good."

"Okay, *mom*," I snarled. Like a dog. Picture me gritting my teeth. No don't. I forgot to brush before I left and I have coffee breath. Just picture me saying it in a surly voice.

"Stop calling me mom," she said. "It makes me sound older than I ever want to be."

"Stop trying to be all motherly with your advice and your... your face."

Charlotte raised an eyebrow at me. "Are *you* high?"

"No. I wish. That'd probably make things less confusing. Why? Could you hook me up?" I asked.

"I could hook you up easily," Collin stated. "But that doesn't mean I'm going to. Drugs are illegal and you're not the kind of girl to do drugs. Are you?"

I shrugged. "I've done 'em with Mindy before."

"Well, Mindy's Mindy," Charlotte said.

"Yeah, but I still enjoyed—" I said as I was cut off by the sound of the door being knocked upon. "Are you expecting *more* company?"

Charlotte shook her head. "I'll go see who it is." She got up and went to the door. She came back a moment later and looked at me. "It's for you, redhead with the attitude."

"It better be my boyfriend, Jerry," I said, standing up and walking towards the door. "You guys remember him. He's the guy with the thin moustache and the lazy eye." I walked out of the living room and looked at Evan standing at the door. "What the hell do you want, little dick?"

"Whoa, okay, that was uncalled for," he said, stepping outside of the house.

"You know what else is uncalled for?" I asked, following him outside and shutting the door behind us. "You taking me on that date. You coming here right now, the day after said date. And also you breaking up with me. What the hell do you want?"

"You're awfully hostile today," he noted.

I nodded. "I didn't get a lot of sleep and I haven't even finished my first coffee of the day. Of course I'm hostile." I sat down on the steps and sighed. "Sorry."

"It's okay. I kinda deserve it," he said, sitting down next to me.

"No. I'm being a bitch. What's on your mind, slugger?"

"Just life and stuff," he replied.

"We are not having a long talk about you dying. Not again. My little heart can't take that."

"No, nothing like that," he said. "It's just that last night we agreed to sleep on it and, well, we slept on it. I just wanted to know where we stood."

"Just friends, Evan. We're *just* friends."

He frowned slightly and ran a hand through his hair, taking off his beanie as he did. "I guess that's a good thing. I mean, at least you're still in my life."

"Yep. Until you go and tremendously fuck up."

"How would I do that?" he asked.

"Like, if you were to date another girl and not me, then I would want nothing to do with you. And I would tell you that. Right to your face," I told him. And I would. I'd yell at him, but I don't think I'd hit him. I couldn't hit him in his adorable little face.

"Only girl I want is you, Spencer. You know that. But I just... I don't have to even tell you. You know."

"Sadly. I do. Also," I said, looking around to make sure nobody was peeking their head out a window to eavesdrop, "why haven't you told Collin or anyone about your cancer thing?"

"Because I don't want to," he replied. "Wait. You didn't tell them or something, did you?"

"No, I didn't. I would never out you like that."

"Oh, thanks," he said, then turning his gaze to the ground at his feet. He exhaled sharply and shut his eyes.

I raised my hand to his back and started rubbing it a little. "What's on your mind, babe?"

"Dude, I'm dying."

"Yeah, I was hoping you wouldn't say that," I said, sighing a little. I pulled him over and hugged him. "I know. It's scary and I wish I could help."

"It's not scary, it's fucking horrifying. I'm not ready to die, Spencer."

"I know, Evan. I know," I said, running my fingers through his hair. This always calmed him down, to be honest. I probably should have done it more often and maybe he'd have kept his bearings a little better.

"It's not getting better," he said, crying a little bit on my shoulder. "It's just getting worse by the day."

"Hey, this is not the talk of a fighter," I said, pulling his face up so I could stare into his eyes, his stupid blue eyes.

"I'm no fighter, Spencer. I give up on everything and everyone. I don't think living is gonna be any different."

I pouted at him. "You're going to be a dad someday, Evan. You're going to have a wife and a job. You're going to own a home. You're going to get all wrinkly and your hair is gonna turn white. You're gonna live so long they'll have to revoke your licence before you die."

He smiled. "What did I ever do to deserve you?"

I smiled back at him. "You treated me like a person."

"No, there's gotta be more to it than that. I don't deserve someone as amazing as you. And you definitely deserve a lot better than me."

"I've found that you should always end up with the person that thinks they don't deserve you because that's the person that will never take you for granted," I said. "Even if they do dump you and then throw a bazillion mixed signals your way in the following days."

He looked over my face and smiled a little. "You're not wearing any makeup."

"When do I ever?"

"You do sometimes."

"Why is this the topic of conversation all of a sudden?"

"I'm trying to forget that I made the biggest mistake of my life by letting you go, that's all."

"Biggest mistake?" I asked.

He nodded. "Yep."

"Of your life?"

He nodded again. "Yep."

"Hypothetically, if we do get back together, one day you'll impregnate me, now imagine me but ten times crankier all the time. *That* would be your biggest mistake," I said, smiling softly. "Although I wouldn't mind having your baby someday. Maybe. Hypothetically."

"Well, hypothetically, let me wrap some stuff up before we talk about where the future of the two of us is heading, okay?"

I nodded. "I'm not going anywhere. I can wait a little while longer for you to figure yourself out. I love you and junk."

"Well, if you love me, please never reference my dick being little. We both know it isn't, but it still bruises my ego," Evan said as he stood up.

I stood up and shrugged. "It was supposed to bruise your ego."

"I'm gonna get going. You hang with your friends. I've got stuff to get back to," he said. He leaned over and kissed me forehead. "Goodbye for now, gingersnaps."

"Goodbye for now, nerd." I watched Evan walk across Charlotte's lawn over to his car that was parked just down the street. Collin's beautiful Charger was blocking the way for Evan to park closer. I don't know why everyone I know parks on the street instead of in the driveways, but whatever.

I walked back inside and quickly drank the coffee I had bought. It was starting to get cold and cold coffee isn't a fun time. I neglected to tell Collin and Charlotte what Evan and I talked about on the front steps. I just didn't feel like it was their business yet. Yet.

{Chapter: **Twenty-Eight**}

I tried calling again. No answer. I thought Evan wanted us to be friends. Friends are supposed to answer their phones so they can bring their other friend, me, a coffee and a bag of sour gummy worms. Stupid Evan.

I walked downstairs with my purse and sundress on. I had washed it from the other day, obviously, but I still liked wearing it. It looked really nice on me, so I was going to own it. I checked the living room and the kitchen for anybody that might be home. I groaned. I hate getting home before everyone else. Nobody's ever around to do stuff with. I sat in the kitchen and waited for the kettle to boil. I wanted to make a hot chocolate and I still had Evan's thermos from the other day. I decided that I was going to go on a walk. It was a nice day, nobody was answering their phones, and I had a nice feeling about life right now.

I filled the thermos and dumped a hot chocolate packet into it. I put the lid on and shook it up really good. I didn't feel like stirring it because all the spoons were dirty. I swear I'm the only one who ever cleans in this house. I'm gonna make such a great mom someday. I opened the drinky part and took a sip. It wasn't clumpy or anything. Good. I'm a professional hot chocolate maker. I closed the lid and picked my purse up from the table. It's weird not having all my stuff just in my pockets. Dresses are really weird, man. I'm not used to having to carry a purse around with me, but it was kind of nice. I could use it to hit Evan if I bumped into him while on my walk. I headed out and walked for twenty minutes before entering a bakery. I kinda felt like a doughnut or a brownie or something. I stepped inside and looked around.

"Hello. Can I help you find anything?" a man asked walking over. I turned and looked him over. He had light brown hair that was elegantly dishevelled. He had a plaid shirt on and jeans, duh. He also had an apron over him that had the name of the bakery on it.

"I'm just looking," I said, eyeing him a little more. "I was thinking about getting a brownie. Are they good here?"

"Of course they are. Everything's good here," he replied. "There's brownies with fudge topping. Those are my personal favourite."

"I'll take it," I said, pulling my debit card out of my purse.

He walked behind the big glass display and pulled out a box of brownies. "That'll be five dollars and 65 cents," he said as he rung up the brownies.

"I really don't think I should eat these all," I whined as I stuck my card into the little machine. I punched in my pin and sighed. "Don't judge me."

"No judgement," he replied, handing me a receipt. "See, I'm new in town and I live in the apartment upstairs, so naturally, I eat a lot of these baked goods. I've probably put on twenty pounds in the past two weeks or so."

"You're new in town?" I asked.

He nodded. "Yep. This is where I ended up after being bounced around a bunch in the last few months."

"Do you wanna get a coffee with a local girl?" I asked, attempting to bite my lip seductively. Gotta be enticing, am I right?

He nodded. "I get off in ten minutes, actually."

"You want me to wait outside?" I asked. "I'm gonna do that anyway. I don't want you to see me eat these brownies."

"Well, save a few for me," he said, smiling softly. "I'm gonna go clean up. I'll see you out front in a few."

I stepped outside and sat at one of the tables they had set up in front of the store. I ate two brownies. Just two. I had to save some for— I don't think I got the guy's name yet. Well, I still didn't want to eat the whole thing of brownies in one sitting. I've been eating so badly lately. Whatever.

After a dozen minutes, the guy came out of the store. "Hello again."

"Hi," I said, standing up from the table. "So, the coffee shop is just up the road. If you still want to go that is?"

He nodded. "I do, I do. Let's go."

"So, let's start with the basics. What's your name?"

"Carey," he said, holding his hand out. "Carey Tyler."

"Well, Carey, I'm Spencer. Spencer Everett," I said, shaking his hand. I started walking down the sidewalk and he followed. "So you're new in town, hmm? How'd you get a job at the best bakery in town?"

He shrugged. "I know some people."

"No friends here yet, huh?"

He shook his head. "I've only been here two weeks. I did want to go to college in the fall, but I'm American, so that complicates things a bit. International fees would still apply right now and I don't have that kind of money just laying around."

"Oh, yikes. Yeah. I'm wrapping up year one in June."

"Kudos to you," he said.

I pulled my phone out of my purse to check if Evan had texted me. He didn't. I let out a sigh of discontent. It was more of a groan, really.

"What is it? Friend won't text you back?" Carey asked.

"Well, I don't know what the hell we are, but whatever we are, yes, he won't text me or call me back."

"Boy troubles. Yeah, I wish I could help you with that, but I'm not exactly a guru when it comes to relationships."

"It's whatever. He just needs his time and space. We're on a break or something, but I thought we were still friends. I don't know," I said, putting my phone back. "But none of my friends seem to be around today. That's why I came out on a walk."

"To the bakery?"

I shrugged. "I guess. I didn't have a destination. I was just walking and then I wanted a brownie."

"Lucky me, then," Carey said with a little smirk. "So this coffee place, good or really good?"

I smirked. "It's really, really good."

"I look forward to it. I like coffee."

"Yeah, who doesn't?"

"I knew a guy once that didn't," he replied. "We weren't really ever friends after that. Can't have that kind of negativity in my life."

"Well, everyone I know likes coffee. I guess I can add you to the list now," I said as we sidestepped to avoid a sign on the sidewalk.

"It's nice to be going to an actual coffee shop again."

"Why? It's just up the road. I know you've only been here for two weeks, but you must have ventured out a little."

He shrugged. "I've been to the pharmacy across the street from the bakery. That's about it. I haven't really had a reason to go out beyond that. But it is gonna be great to have someone else make my coffee for a change."

"Maybe I can come over sometime and I'll make you coffee," I said. "You know, assuming this asshole doesn't wanna be with me anymore or whatever. I'd feel guilty doing it otherwise."

"I totally get it," Carey said. "We won't swap numbers or anything, but if you ever did want to talk to me again, you know where I work."

"Yeah, exactly. So I'll just shop at other bakeries if me and him get together again."

"I like being a backup option," he said, laughing a little. "Yeah, but I'm usually busy at the bakery or trying to get all my paperwork set up so I can go to school someday."

"Well, hey, at least you have a plan."

"That's the plan."

"The plan is to have a plan?" I asked.

Carey nodded. "Exactly."

"That makes a surprising amount of sense," I said, chuckling a little. "Anyway, the coffee shop is just up there." I pointed to a nice little shop that was tucked between two other stores. "See it?"

"I do," he said, looking over to where I was pointing.

I looked at my fingernails. "Blue is really my colour." I had put on a fresh layer of blue polish earlier and they looked really nice. Like little oceans on my fingers.

"Well, there's no such thing as an ugly shade of blue," Carey said, as he took the small of my back in his hand and guided me across the street. I barely noticed because I was admiring the shiny blue nails I was sporting today.

"His eyes are an ugly shade of blue," I muttered as I stepped up the curb on the other side. "Okay, that's a lie. I'm just salty."

"Should we rock-paper-scissors to see who's gonna pay?" Carey asked as we stopped up at the door to the coffee shop.

"Look at how cute my nails are," I said, raising my hand to his face.

"I'll pay," he said with a small smile as he pushed the door open.

"Oh, I want a double-double. Thanks," I said, turning and taking a seat at a little window booth. See? Pretend to be infatuated with your nails and then he'll just buy you the coffee. I set the brownies down on the table and took one to eat while I waited for Carey to get our coffees.

"Here you are," he said, walking back over and setting the coffee down in front of me as he slid into the booth on the other side. "So why are you so obsessed with you nails today? Or are you obsessed with them every day?"

I shrugged. "It's just today. I dunno. I think they look nice. My toes match, but I'm not taking off my shoes to show you. I really like this blue colour."

"It's remarkably bright and poppy," he said, grabbing my hand and looking at my nails. "I think it'd look nice with a green polish that has little gold flecks in it. It would match your eyes that way."

I pulled my hand back and thought about it a sec. "Maybe. I'll think about getting some. I know I've seen one that was pretty much exactly my eye colour before. I'll investigate."

"You should."

"I will."

"Good." He pulled the tab of the lid back and took a sip before putting the coffee right back down. "Okay, it's too hot to drink."

"No shit."

"Don't sass me," he barked.

"I sass what I want when I want to sass the things I sass."

"That's one."

"One what?" I asked.

"Right, see, I do this thing where I keep track of when people don't make sense. You're at one now."

"What? I said that I sass when I want to sass. I made perfect sense!" I protested.

"Eh, I dunno about that," he stated. "You said it in a nonsensical way."

"Shut up," I whined. "I made sense."

"You sound like this girl I used to date," he said. "Her name was Brooke. She always said the same thing to me when I added another nonsense to the nonsense counter."

"Brooke, hmm? Tell me about her," I pried. "I mean, if you want to. Don't do it if it makes you uncomfortable."

"No. We had to split under circumstances," he said. "I still love her and I'd wager that she still loves me."

"Okay, I'm intrigued. Tell me."

"She's this cute girl with nice sunshine hair and she wears a beanie. She has the prettiest eyes and the most beautiful smile," Carey told me. "She's kind of a dork though. She sometimes talks in third person. Instead of saying 'I want this,' she'll say 'Brooke wants this.' It's pretty cute though. It makes her unique."

"More, more!"

"She's also pretty smart. Smarter than me, that's for sure. She's also pretty caring. I remember this one night when I got jumped by this other guy that wanted to be with her and she got her parents to take me to the hospital. She held my hand the whole way there."

"Do you miss her?"

"Of course," he replied. "I miss her every day, but I can't talk to her. She went off the grid after I left. And I can't talk to her anyway. It'd be in breach of agreements, but let's not get into that in detail because that would also breach the agreements."

"Gotcha, I'm a pro at secrets."

"Good to hear." Carey smiled. "Anyway, there was this one night I went and visited her and there was a storm. And because there was a storm, I stayed the night. And because her parents weren't home, I woke up a man."

"Were you a girl before?"

He glared at me a little. "You know what I meant. We did the adult thing. It was the best night of my life because, well, I loved her."

"Do you think you'll see her again?"

He shrugged. "I'd like to think that if two people are meant to be, then things will somehow work out for them in the end."

"Yeah. Maybe things will."

"I hope so." He rested his head in his palms as he rested his elbows on the table. "Does doing this make my face look chubby?"

"Well, kinda. It pushes all of your cheeks upward," I said, looking at him. He looked dead tired right now. "You should get going home soon. I think you could use a nap."

"Yep," he muttered. "Wanna join me?"

"Sorry. I'm still putting my cards on the table for the asshole to love me again, you know?"

"Two. That didn't make any sense, but I still get it."

I scoffed. "Yeah, well, shut up and eat a brownie. If you have a frownie, eat a brownie."

"That's a cute slogan," he said, cracking a smile as he took a brownie from the box. Half of them were already gone because of me and my gluttonous need for more sugary goods and pastries.

"You can use it if you want."

"I might have to," he said, taking a bite out of the brownie. "Man, these things never get old to me. They're always so goddamn good."

"Well, please eat more of them so I don't end up eating them all."

He smirked. "That I can do."

{Chapter: **Twenty-Nine**}

I woke up to knocking at my bedroom door. I rolled over and rubbed my eyes as I looked at my younger sister Jordan walking over to me. "I just noticed that your eyebrows are actually just a little bit darker than your hair. It's not normal to have red eyebrows," Jordan said as she handed me our cordless house phone.

"You have red eyebrows too, dummy. We're redheads," I said to her as I took the phone from her.

"I'm gonna dye my eyebrows. Red eyebrows are just weird."

I scoffed. "They're part of our beauty, Jordan. Now get out of here so I can answer this call in peace."

"Yeah, yeah," she said, turning and walking out. "Later, dork."

"Hello," I said as I lifted the phone to my ear.

"Dude, why don't you keep your phone on?" Charlotte asked.

I groaned as I reached for my phone on the nightstand. I clicked the button and the dead battery thing popped up. "Ha, my phone's dead. Look at that. I forgot to charge it last night."

"It's two in the afternoon."

"I like sleep," I whined. "What do you want?"

"I just wanted to see if you wanted me and Collin to pay you a visit."

"I guess. Just give me a few minutes to get pants on."

"You need a few minutes to put pants on?" she asked.

I sighed. "It's hard to get out of bed when the world feels like it's trying to suffocate your happiness."

"Okay, right, well, take your time. We're gonna grab you a coffee and then we'll be right over." She hung up the phone and it made the dial tone start beeping in my ear. Lame.

"Rude," I muttered as I put the phone on the nightstand. I spent the next three minutes trying to will myself to get out of my bed. It was so warm and cozy in these blankets.

I rolled over and plopped down to the ground and then pushed myself up before plopping down again. I really need to go to the gym. All this junk food has made me weak. I tucked my arms in and rolled over to my closet and pulled out a pair of jeans. I slipped into them and groaned as I got them to my waist. I collapsed out on the floor and left the button undone because I was lazy. I reached up and pulled a red plaid shirt off a hanger from the closet. I pushed myself to a sitting position and put the shirt on. I buttoned it up and fixed the pocket on my chest. It was inside out and now it's outside in. Wait. That doesn't make any sense. It's inside in and outside out now that I fixed it.

I pulled myself using my dresser as a balance so I could stand. I stood up and stretched out and yawned. I buttoned my jeans and grabbed a belt. "Nothing like waking up at two to start your day." I pushed the belt through all the little loops of my jeans. I went downstairs and got my sister to put my hair into a single long braid. My hair wasn't that long. It was only down to the middle of my back. So now I had one long and thick braid of luscious orange hair down to the middle of my back. I probably looked a little country with the braid and the plaid and the jeans. At least I don't own a single pair of tan-coloured boots.

"You better not just take the braid out and put your hair in a bun like you do every other time I braid it for you," Jordan said when she finished braiding my hair.

"I won't," I whined at her. "I like it. It can stay for at least the rest of the day."

"Good. I hate braiding your hair and having you take it out an hour later."

"I know, I know," I said, standing up. "I'm a jerk. I get it." I walked over to the door and looked out the glass. I opened the door and smiled at Charlotte. "Hola, friend."

"Good timing," she said as her and Collin walked past me and into the house.

"Evan call you yet?" Collin asked.

I shook my head. "We're on week three of no contact. I'm getting used to him not being around though. I guess we're just *over*. Y'know?"

Collin shrugged. "I guess."

"Do you know something that I don't? Tell me. Are you allowed to tell me? Is it about Evan? What happened to him? Is he okay? Tell me!"

"If you'd slow down a minute so I could actually talk, then I might tell you," Collin stated. "But I don't think you want to hear it."

"Tell me what's going on," I whined as I followed the two of them into the living room.

"I think I'm gonna wait a little bit," he said. "There's not sense in getting into the serious stuff. We just got here. Let's hang out for a few minutes first."

"Right. Makes sense." I sat down on the couch and Charlotte took a seat next to me. Collin took a seat on the recliner chair that was off to the side. He dragged it a little closer to he could actually face us properly to converse with us.

"You really just got up when I called, didn't you?" Charlotte asked.

I nodded. "Affirmative."

"Did you put your phone on the charger?"

I shook my head. "Negative."

"You probably should have."

"Why?" I asked. "In case Evan comes and takes me on another random and completely unasked for date? I'll tell him to take a hike."

"I doubt you would tell him that. I was just saying you should charge it so it'll be charged for when you wanna use it."

I scoffed at her idea. "My charger reaches my bed, dude."

"You're officially the laziest person I know," Charlotte said with a smug frown on her face.

"I'm just doing what Evan's doing. I'm taking some time for me."

She sighed. "I don't think putting on five pounds in brownie weight is how you're supposed to do you."

"I actually haven't gained any weight. Thank you very much," I said, furrowing my eyebrows at her a little.

"Seriously?"

"Not even a pound," I told her.

"Dude, you eat junk food all the time and stay in your bed most of the day. How are you not putting on any weight?"

I shrugged. "I have been blessed, not only with good looks and smarts, but with a beautiful body that refuses to be tainted."

"Maybe it's because you're an elf princess. I hear elf princesses have bodies that are very good at burning unneeded calories to prevent the body from putting on too much empty weight," Collin said.

I smiled at him. "He gets it."

"I do. You're an elf princess. The magic in you keeps you nice and healthy no matter what."

"Don't encourage her," Charlotte barked. "Spencer, I get that you're bummed out about Evan, but eating your weight in gummy worms is never gonna help you get over him."

"I don't need to get over him. I need to eat good food because it makes me feel good," I told her.

"You can't just eat away your feelings. That's definitely not a healthy habit, Spencer. Stop being a knob about this."

"I'll beat you up," I said, pouting at her. "I like brownies and gummy worms. Let me enjoy my shit."

"Enjoy it in moderation," Charlotte said. "Your body needs to be taken care of just as much as your mind does."

"I hate that you're always looking out for me," I muttered. "Why can't you just aid and abet my bad habits?"

"Because I care too much about you," she stated. "And I hate seeing you eating all day and hiding away in your room like that. It sucks that Evan's a little shithead, but you gotta get out and live life."

"I took a walk the other day."

"And?"

I shrugged. "And that's it. I met a guy who worked at a bakery and we had a coffee and we ate some brownies. The point is, I went out and did something."

"You should go have another coffee with him sometime," Charlotte said.

I raised an eyebrow. "Why? Did Evan tell you that he's not ever gonna get back with me or something? I would have thought you'd tell me that Evan's gonna come back or something."

"It's been two weeks since he talked to you and, well, other stuff."

"Other stuff?" I questioned. I looked over to Collin. "What other stuff?"

"Um, I guess I should just tell you, then," he said. He coughed a little to clear his throat. "Right, so, our dear friend Evan has decided to start romancing another young lady."

"He's dating?!" I shouted. "What?"

"That's just what he told me," Collin said. "Don't take my word on it. You'd have to go and talk to him about it if you want answers. He doesn't like to let me in on too much of his personal life all at once."

"He's fucking dating?" I asked, starting to tear up again as I look to Charlotte. "Why would he lie to me? He told me he loved me. You don't tell someone you love them and then start dating someone else two weeks later. What the fuck is wrong with him?"

Charlotte moved over and let me sob onto her shoulder. "I don't know, Spencer. Boys are stupid."

"Hey," Collin protested. "Evan's stupid. Not me."

"Boys are stupid, Collin. You're just one of the few that seems to not be stupid," I said, looking over to him. "At least for now."

Charlotte used her shirt to wipe away tears from my face. "Cry. Let it out."

"I don't wanna cry!" I shouted into her embrace. "I want it to stop. Make it stop, Charlotte. I fucking hate crying." I pulled away and sniffled loudly. "Look at this. I'm a mess. I'm all covered in tears and my nose is all snotty and I hate Evan. I'm so mad at him right now. Why would he go date some other girl?"

"I don't know," Charlotte said, wiping more tears from my face. "I guess he just thought you were done with him. You did tell him you were done with him, remember? Back at the bowling alley?"

"I wasn't serious. He should have known that. He knows me. I think everybody that knew either of us knew that I was in love with that huge pile of shit. I hope he does die now that stupid asshole."

"Okay, simmer down," Charlotte said, grabbing me and pulling me into another hug. "You don't mean any of that. You're just upset. I get it. Just cry, okay? Get it all out and we'll go talk to him."

"I don't think hearing it from him is gonna be any better for me," I stated. "It's just gonna make everything so much more real and shitty."

"Trust me," Collin said, "you're gonna want to go talk to him."

"Let me compose myself first, damn. Do you not see my clammy eyes right now? I can't go anywhere right now," I said, wiping tears off of my face with my hands. Gotta admit though, it felt nice to finally let it all out and have a good cry. I hadn't cried once since the appointment where he had stormed off on me, but something about crying right now made me feel a little better, a little more human in a way.

Charlotte kissed me forehead. "I'm gonna go make you a hot chocolate, okay?"

I nodded. "Thanks, Charcoal."

"You haven't called me that in a while," she said with a small smile as she stood up.

"Evan does love you," Collin said. "He just has a shitty way of showing that he loves someone. He's scared of it or something."

"That's not it, Collin," I said, wiping tears from under my eyes with my fingers. "He's a complex mess of scared and confusing. I don't think he knows much more about what he's going to do next than we do. It comes with the territory."

"The territory?"

"Yeah. I can't tell you, but I know what's going on and I know why he's being stupid with everything," I replied. "And please don't ask him about it."

"I can do that. I mean, like, I won't ask him about this."

"Thanks. I think I should go talk to him. I just—" I took a deep breath and exhaled just as deeply. "I just need to calm myself down a little first."

"If he really does have another girlfriend or something, I'm sure she's way shittier than you are," Collin said. "I dunno if you could tell or not, but Evan's pretty lame."

"Oh, I know he is," I said, smiling a little. "That's one of the reasons I fell in love with him. He was a dork, but he was *my* dork."

"Well, when you go talk to him, I guess you'll know for sure what's going on. Personally, I think he's just trying to blow smoke up his own ass in a way. I doubt he'd get another girlfriend. I doubt he'd even find a girl just to have sex with once as a coping mechanism," Collin stated. "He's not that kind of guy, and frankly, he couldn't pull a better girl than you."

I scoffed. "Yeah, okay."

"I'm serious."

"I'm not that pretty or great or whatever."

Collin smirked. "Yes, you are. You might not feel it right now because the crying, but you know you are. You've said it yourself. Evan's said it a bazillion times. Hell, Charlotte even told me that Mindy wanted to hit it once."

"She did?"

"Did you not know that?" he asked.

I shook my head. "That's kind of flattering. My mom told me not too long ago that she could see me and Mindy having ended up together if I was on her team, so to speak."

"See, everybody thinks you're a right cute little princess," Collin said with a small smile. "Just get ready to make sure Evan knows what he's going to miss out on if he does have another girlfriend."

"Oh, I will. I'll make sure he realizes that he'll never get me back and that I'm taking you with me and he'll have nobody there to lean on," I said. I knew that wasn't fair and that I'd never have the balls to do that to him, but it felt kinda nice to say.

Collin smirked at me as Charlotte came back into the room with our hot chocolates. I think Collin's a pretty good dude. But I just couldn't help but wonder why Evan doesn't tell anybody the whole story. Collin seemed the type to pry a little bit if it came down to it. Evan would end up caving, especially if it was his best friend prying at him. Or maybe Collin did know everything. Maybe the two of them were up to something sneaky instead.

{Chapter: **Thirty**}

I sipped the last bit of hot chocolate and stood up. I let out a loud belch and smiled triumphantly about it.

"Nice one," Collin commented, standing up and letting out his own loud belch.

Charlotte shook her head at the two of us. "You two are gross, but at least you're bonding."

"Bonding? I've always liked Spencer. She's pretty awesome," Collin said. "We went bowling once."

"Oh, yeah, we did, didn't we?" I let out a sigh. "Simpler times."

He laughed a little. "Yeah. But I'm glad about some of the stuff that happened after that night. I'm glad I met Charlotte, that's for sure. This little dork is one of the best things to ever happen to me."

"That's good. You hurt her and I'll hurt you," I warned him. "I don't think I've given you this spiel about hurting her, but to keep it short, I read an article about castration once, and I will put that knowledge to use if you break this dork's heart."

"I'm not a dork," Charlotte protested.

"You kind of are."

"Am not!"

"Are too!" Collin and I shouted in unison.

"Fuck both of you," she growled as she stood up and took our empty mugs from us.

"Well, you can fuck him, but not me," I said as she walked out of the living room.

"You wanna get going over to see Evan soon?" Collin asked as he sat down.

I shrugged. "I guess I should go do it so I can be back in time to get a nap in before my midnight snack."

"You've really let yourself go, huh?"

I scowled at him. "Piss off, man."

"Do you want us to drive you over there?"

I shook my head. "I'm gonna walk. I need the exercise."

"Spencer, his house is a two-hour walk from here," Collin stated.

I shrugged. "Like I care. I've got nothing to do all night."

"Your phone isn't even charged. What if you get into trouble?"

I shrugged again. "I'm short and fast. I'll find a way to escape."

"Fine, fine. I'm not gonna waste energy trying to talk you out of it. In my experience, gingers are pretty stubborn."

"That is *our* word. How dare you use that word."

"Sorry, I meant to say redheads."

I smiled. "Better. The only people who can call me a ginger is Evan and Mindy, but only if he's referring to me as his 'gingersnaps' or something like that."

"Got it," Collin said, holding back a laugh. "You should really get going."

I nodded and walked over to the front door. I slid my shoes on and sighed. "Charlotte, I'm going for a walk. I'll be back at some point." And I walked outside before she could even answer me.

I took off running for the first few blocks. I slowed to a casual jog for the next couple blocks. And the rest of the way, I just walked at a normal pace. I wasn't in a rush, so I had no idea why I even bothered running or jogging. I guess I just wanted to see if I still could, since I did stay in bed for hours a day in the past few weeks.

I made it to Evan's in an hour and a half. I think that was pretty decent time for someone on foot. I headed up his driveway and noticed the garage door was open and the car was uncovered. I couldn't see much of it, the hood was up and Evan looked to be working on the engine or something. I walked up and made a soft little cough to get his attention.

He turned to see me and then shut the hood of the car. He came out of the garage and closed the door behind him as he walked out. "Spencer."

"You're a goddamn asshole, Evan." My jaw tensed up and my eyes started to water slightly.

"You would think that," he said, smirking at me.

"Stop smirking," I demanded. "Collin told me you had a girlfriend. I thought you said that if you got news back on your cancer that you would be with me again. You can't just let me get my hopes up like that, Evan. That's even more fucked up than you being scared of being with me because you're dying."

"He told you. Good. I told him to tell you."

"So it's true? You got another girlfriend? Why? Why the fuck do you continue to do this shit to me?" I asked, holding back tears. "God, to think I wanted to ever sleep with you."

"Spencer."

"What?"

"It was a lie," he said, walking over to me and kissing my forehead.

"Which was a lie? The girlfriend or you loving me?"

"The girlfriend," he replied.

"Oh, thank God." I hugged him and rested my head on his chest. It felt like the weight of a thousand galaxies had been removed from my chest as he collapsed his arms around me. "Why did you tell Collin to tell me that you had a girlfriend, then?"

"I needed a sure-fire way to get you over here."

I sighed. "Why not just, I dunno, call me and ask me to come over?"

"You and I both know that you wouldn't have answered my call," Evan said, picking me up and hugging me tightly. "I missed you, gingersnaps."

"I missed you too, bubbercup."

Evan put me down and looked at me with an odd expression on his face. "Bubbercup?"

I nodded. "Is there a problem with that?"

231

He smiled. "No. I think it's actually pretty cute."

"I thought so too."

"I missed you so much, Spencer. I'm sorry for being such an ass this past month, but that's all done now. I'm here for you, every day and every night," Evan said. "Well, if you still want me to be here for you, that is."

"I do," I told him. "The past little while has been the shittiest time of my life. It's been almost as bad as the thing with my old flame. The virginity story, you know, I've told you."

"Yeah, you have."

I nodded. "Anyway... where do we stand now? Are we still just friends?"

"Yes, but we're not talking about this right now. We're talking about us later on."

"Do you wanna talk about if your cancer is getting better yet?" I asked. "Do you know if it is or not?"

He shrugged. "I don't care at this point, but it's the same as before. It's stagnated. That's what my doctor said anyway."

"That means the treatments are stopping the spread, right?"

Evan shrugged. "We don't know what it means yet. When I know, you'll know. I don't wanna talk about all this serious stuff right now. We have all night for that."

"All night? I can't be out all night. I didn't tell my mom where I was and I don't have my phone with me," I said.

"Why?"

I sighed. "It died yesterday and I was too bummed out to care about recharging it."

"Wow."

"Don't judge me," I barked, looking past him to see a little brown glass bottle on the floor of the garage. "Have you been drinking?"

"Slightly," he replied. "And before you ask, no, you can't have one."

"Why?" I whined. "It's not like we're gonna try to have a baby in the next week. Let me have one."

"Well, we can make a baby next month. But I'm still not giving you a beer."

"You suck."

He shrugged. "What can ya do."

"It's funny, we started going out by being sarcastic assholes to each other." I sighed. "Good times."

"How is that good times? You used to beat me up."

I shrugged. "I'm feisty, but it's not like I ever hurt you. And you were always welcome to hit me back and start a little fight with me."

"I didn't want to beat you up," he said, shrugging.

"Bitch, please." I scoffed. "If either of us could beat up the other, it'd be me beating up you."

"It's good to see that you're still delusional," he said, smiling at me widely.

"I'ma smack the smirk right out of you."

He winked at me. "Try it."

"Okay, come here," I said.

He stepped closer to me and I pulled his head down. I pulled my hand back as if I was about to smack him and he closed his eyes. Perfect. I leaned in and kissed him on his dumb lips. I hadn't done it in ages and I missed kissing him. Kissing him made me feel sparkly inside and I needed that feeling again. He was noticeably shocked at first, but he raised a hand and cupped my cheek as he kissed me back.

I pushed him away from me and smirked. "See, now I'm the one who gets to be all smirks."

"Still me," he said softly. "Fuck, I missed that."

"So don't give me up, asshole."

"No serious talk right now. Keep it light. We have all night."

"Right," I said. "I forgot that you like to kidnap me."

"I did that once."

"You and Charlotte still need to get got for doing that," I said with a pout. "I hate you. That was seriously scary as shit."

"Well, you did punch her in the face."

"That was for lying to me, not kidnapping me," I reminded him.

He sighed. "You know what I meant."

"Yes, I did," I said. "So, why did you want me to come over here right away? Is there any real reason? Or did you just miss me? Missing me is a pretty good reason."

"I did miss you, but that's not the whole reason why I wanted you to come over," he said, nodding for me to follow him as he turned around headed to the garage. "Remember how you told me you wanted a 'Cuda?"

"I do remember this," I said, following him up to the garage.

"Well, over the past couple months, I've been putting her back together," he said as he opened the garage door. "And she's ready for you."

I look at Evan and then to the car sitting in his garage. I looked it over. It was a bright purple colour with black detailing. It was clearly a Barracuda, probably a late-sixties model. I looked over to Evan. "You can't be for real."

"You told me you wanted one. I had one," he said, smirking at me. "I guess the smirks are in my court again."

"Evan, this is not real." I ran my hand along the shiny new paint as I walked along the car looking at it. The interior was made to look all black and intimidating.

"It's real, Spencer."

"Why would you build a car for me?" I asked, looking over to him from across the hood of the car.

"Well, I love you. You're my girl. I gotta get my girl stuff she wants. That's my job," he replied as he ran a hand over the hood.

"Can we drive it?" I asked.

"You can," he said. "I've had a couple beers, remember?"

I nodded. "Right. Well, where are the keys?" I walked around the car and jumped on him a little in excitement. "Gimme, gimme. Let me drive it."

"It's stick. Can you drive stick?" he asked.

I nodded, smiling widely. "I was friends with Mindy, remember? She taught me how to do all the *boy* stuff."

"Right, Mindy was the tomboy of your group," Evan said as he dug around in his pocket. "And you were the nerdy bookworm."

"Shush."

He kissed my forehead. "Now, before I hand over the keys to this car that I've spent months repairing for you, I have to ask you something."

"Yeah. I can do that for you later, just let me drive the damn thing," I whined.

"Do what?"

"What?" I asked, raising an eyebrow.

"Nothing," he said.

I sighed. "Just ask me the question."

"Can you even legally drive?"

I opened my mouth in shock. "How dare you assume that I can't drive. Is this because of my height?"

"No, it's because I've never seen you drive."

"I can drive," I stated. "Legally."

"Let me see your licence," he said, holding his hand out.

I groaned. "You're kidding, right?"

"Nope. Let me see."

I made a whining sound as I reached my hand into my pocket to pull out my wallet. I handed it to him and he inspected my licence.

He looked it over and then back to me. "Are you sure this is you?"

"It's me, dumbass," I said as I put the licence pack into my wallet.

"You're a lot prettier in person," he said, smiling softly at me.

"Yeah. I don't feel like it today, but thank you."

"So you wanna drive it?"

I nodded. "Yes. Giveth me the keys."

"Hold your hand out and close your eyes."

I sighed. "This is so cliché and lame." I put my left hand over my eyes and stuck my right hand out with my palm facing the sky and waited. I waited a little more. I groaned and glared at Evan. "Dude."

"Okay, cover your eyes again. I'll give them to you this time."

I did as he said and covered my eyes again. I held my hand out and this time he actually did place the key to the car in my hand. I curled my fingers around it and smiled at him as I uncovered my eyes. "This is real."

"The door's unlocked. Get in," he said as he stepped out of the way.

I moved over and opened the door and got in the car. I sat down in the driver's seat and felt the steering wheel in my hands. I fit perfectly into this car. My feet reached the pedals and I could see over the dash just fine. I closed the door and gripped the steering wheel at the ten and two positions to really get a feel of it.

Evan got in on the other side and shut his door. "How's it feel?"

I turned to him and smiled. "Like home."

"That's a good thing to hear." He leaned over and took the keys from my hands and put them in the ignition. "You have to start the car to drive it, by the way."

"I know that," I said, glaring at him. "I just wanted to enjoy the moment."

"Let's go. I'll give you directions to where we're going."

I sighed. "Okay, okay. Don't get us lost."

"I won't."

"You might," I said as my hand found the keys. I took a deep breath and turned them. The engine roared to life. And I do mean roar. This fish has some serious pipes, man.

"Turn right when you get out of the driveway," Evan said, looking over at me.

I nodded. "The car sounds great, bud." I turned to him and smiled widely. "Thank you."

He smiled at me and then leaned over and kissed my forehead.

"I love you so much," I muttered under my breath. It was half to Evan and half to the car, so…

Yeah, but anyway, I then pulled out of the driveway and we were off into the evening. I guess it would be the night, since he did tell me that we had all night to talk. I really wished people would just plan things for during the day. But I guess this new car sort of makes up for the bad planning.

{Chapter: **Thirty-One**}

I followed Evan's directions until we reached a small highway on the outskirts of town. I don't know what the hell we'd be doing all the way out here, but I don't think I cared. I had an excuse to drive this car, and that's all I really cared about right now.

"So, I never asked, but what year is this?" I asked, glancing over at Evan to make sure he didn't fall asleep in the last five minutes or something.

"It's a '69 'Cuda," he replied. "Hemi."

"Beautiful. It's what I've always wanted."

"It was lucky that we kept this thing. We were gonna sell it because it's a pretty nice car. I've seen these things go for a couple hundred thousand at auctions before."

I cocked an eyebrow at him. "You mean we're sitting in a car worth as much as a house."

"Probably," he said. "But you are *not* selling this thing."

"I wouldn't dream of it."

"Good. You would not believe how annoying it was to get the parts for this thing to be in working order."

"Well, you did it. And I'm grateful."

Evan pointed to a little road up ahead. "Take that turn there."

"It says dead end on the sign," I said.

"Just go up there and go slowly when you get to the top."

"The top?" I asked.

"Yeah, the road goes up a hill. Be careful. I don't want you driving off of a cliff or anything," Evan stated. "I just don't want anything to happen to us or the car on its first night out."

"Pfft, I got this," I said, making the turn and heading up the gravel road. I drove up the road in silence with Evan. It's weird how he was being so quiet right now. He usually talks more than not at all. I sort of ignored it and enjoyed the purr of the engine as we drove up the gravel street. After a little while, the trees around us made way for an impressive view of the night sky and the area below the hill. I stopped the car and looked over to Evan.

"I know, it's cliché to bring a girl to a kissing cliff or whatever, but you drove, so you technically brought me here," he said as he unbuckled his seat belt and got out of the car.

I sighed and shut the car off. I got out and walked over to where he was standing. "Why did you bring me here?"

"I thought we could go to some place that was better than the roof of a mall for a change," he said with a small smile. "Look at the view. You can see the whole city over there and the ocean right everywhere else."

I looked around and saw the grid of city lights and the darkness of the ocean beyond the coast. "I guess this is pretty cool."

"Pretty cool?"

"I guess this is *really* cool."

He smirked. "That's the spirit." He walked back over to the car and opened his door and reached into the back and pulled out a bag. "Here." He pulled out a thermos and tossed it to me.

"I still haven't given you the other one," I whined.

He shrugged. "Keep it."

"How do you have so many of these things?" I asked as I opened it to take a sip of the hot chocolate inside.

He shrugged. "Your guess is as good as mine." He pulled a thermos out for himself as he sat down on the edge of the rocky cliff.

I sat down next to him and rested my head on his shoulder. "It's not gonna rain or anything tonight, right?"

"I would assume not, but I'm not a weatherologist."

"That's not what they're called."

He raised an eyebrow at me. "No? Then what are they called Mrs. Smartypants?"

"They're called meteorologists."

"They study weather though," he said, looking deeply concerned about this.

I rested a hand on his shoulder as I took a drink from the thermos. "It's one of life's many wonders."

"I guess. Kind of like you."

"Aww. You little cutie, you," I said, playfully punching his arm.

"Okay, so I figure now is a good time to ask."

"Oh, uh-oh, we're gonna get deep right now, aren't we?"

He nodded. "Probably."

"Good, that's the shit I came here for. Ask away," I said.

"What are we?"

I shrugged. "What do you wanna be?"

"That's what I was asking, or trying to."

"Oh," I said, nodding a little. "Right, well, me, personally, I want to be your girlfriend again. I feel like that would make my heart do the happy thing and I would smile and I would actually not spend eighteen hours in bed every day."

"Eighteen hours? Impressive." He raised his hand for a high five, so I obviously slapped him five.

"I know. Charlotte doesn't think it's impressive though."

Evan shrugged. "Eighteen hours of anything is pretty impressive."

"Okay, so what do you want to be?"

Evan sighed. "I don't know. I was kind of thinking about asking out this one girl. You don't know her, she's *way* too cool for you."

"Oh? Is that right? What's her name?" I asked him.

"Her name is Spencear... Yeah, Spencear."

"Spencear." I smiled at him. "You're such a goddamn dork."

He shrugged. "I do my best."

"So does this mean you want to ask me out? Because that's what I'm waiting on now, bud."

He nodded. "I do, but I want to really stress that there's a high chance of me being dead in the next three or so years."

"That's if treatment doesn't work, Evan," I stated. "And treatment will work. Believe me. Trust me. Trust yourself. You're gonna fight. You promised."

"I am fighting," he said, scowling at me a little. "Are you under the impression that I've packed my bags and I'm ready go over and hug the reaper and have a tea party with him? I don't *want* to die, Spencer. You've given me a reason to want to stay alive."

"Then don't leave me. Ever. Never again."

"I won't. That was a mistake the first time. I just needed my space and I did it in the wrong way and I apologize for that and I want to start over," he said. "But I don't want to start over. I want to just love you. I just want to be in love with you and that's it."

"So be my boyfriend again."

"Spencer Everett, will you take me, Evan Fuller, to be your newly reinstated boyfriend?"

"I do," I said, turning to him and smiling. I leaned over and kissed him. "Never break up with me again. I will not wait around for you next time."

"Understood," Evan said, nodded a little.

"And the dying talk needs to stop. I know it's a very real possibility, but I honestly just want to focus on how much I love you."

He nodded. "Right. But I still could die. We'll have to face that."

"We'll have to face that when it comes," I said. "I have a gut feeling that tells me that you're gonna be okay. You're gonna beat it."

"I'm just gonna have to believe you on that, because I have no goddamn idea what to think about anything anymore. I just don't know, Spencer."

"I know," I said, rubbing his back. "But the less you think about it, the more you'll know."

"That doesn't make much sense."

"Ignorance is bliss."

He nodded in understanding. "Now I get it. I don't necessarily agree with that though. Imagine how shitty things would be if you had that attitude."

"What do you mean?"

"If you thought that ignorance was bliss, you wouldn't have gotten me out of that boiler room for one."

I shrugged. "I dunno. I think I saved you because you sounded kinda cute."

"I sounded cute?"

"Yeah, you were like a hot little damsel in distress."

He pouted a little at me. "I'm not a damsel."

"You're right. I'm the damsel. Marry me already, dang."

Evan gave me a questioning look. "What does marriage have to do with being a damsel?"

"A damsel is an unmarried woman," I told him.

"Really?"

I nodded. "Really."

"Hmm, I'll make you a deal," he said.

"Oh, I hear a proposition coming up."

He nodded. "You are correct."

"Okay," I said, sipping from my thermos, "lemme hear this deal you wanna offer me."

"After we're finished college, I wanna marry you. I do. I think I can safely say that if I live that long, I will want to marry you and spend the rest of my life with you."

"Is that so?"

"Yes, that is so," he said. "And with the stars out tonight as my witness, I love you, Spencer."

"I love you too, Evan," I said, leaning over and kissing him. "So what age are we thinking here?"

"I dunno, around 21 or 22 would be ideal."

"Agreed."

He stood up and looked out over the view. "You can see your house from here."

I stood up and looked where he was looking. "No, you can't."

He pointed from just over my shoulder. "Right there."

I pushed him off me and looked where he had pointed. "I can't see shit. Are you talking about that light over there or the other fifty thousand lights?"

"The other fifty thousand," he said from further behind me than he just was.

I turned around and didn't see him immediately until I looked down and saw him on one knee. "No. Oh, my God. No. Evan." I scanned over the little box in his hand, the diamond of a ring catching the moonlight and shimmering every so slightly.

"Spencer Marie Everett," he said.

I cringed a little. "I forgot that I told you my middle name."

He glared a little at me for ruining his moment. "Spencer Marie Everett, you nerdy little ginger, over the past six months that I've grown to know you, you have proved to me that you are more than a temporary girl, and you have proven yourself to be more amazing with every passing day, and I just want to ask, will you let me make you my wedding bride?"

"Was that a *How I Met Your Mother* reference?" I asked, wiping away a couple of joyful tears from my face.

He nodded. "Yeah. I thought you'd like it."

"I did."

"Is this a yes?"

I nodded. "Of course, you dumbass."

He stood up and stuck the ring on my finger before picking me up and kissing me like he hadn't seen me in three years. I let him squeeze me as tightly as he wanted to. I couldn't care less about the air in my lungs right now. Tonight has been the best night of my life thus far.

I wiggled free and he set me down. I looked over the ring on my left hand and smiled widely. "This is not real."

"It's real," he replied.

I looked up at him and smiled. "Evan... buddy... you're my fiancé."

"I know," he said, smiling back at me. "And I've brought something to celebrate the occasion." He walked over to his bag and pulled out a bottle of champagne.

"I guess neither of us are driving home tonight."

He shook his head as he pulled out two plastic wine glasses. "Neither of us are driving home tonight." He pulled a blanket out and tossed it on a part of the ground that had grass on it.

I walked over and sat down next to him on it and smiled at him. I looked back down to the ring as Evan popped open the bottle of champagne. "Evan, how the hell did you afford this?"

"Remember how I told you that your car could be worth a few thousand at an auction?" he asked, handing me a glass of champagne.

I nodded. "I remember you saying that."

"Well," he said, sitting down properly next to me with his glass of champagne in his hand, "we did have two of them."

"You sold one to pay for the ring?"

"Yeah, and to pay for the car repairs on the other one."

"I love you. Have I told you that? Because I love you."

He smiled. "You better not love me just because I have a couple tens of thousands in my bank account."

"No, I loved you before that anyway," I told him. "I'm also gonna love you all the way until you die. And then I'm gonna love your memory beyond that."

"Whoa, hey, whoa, what makes you think I'm gonna die first?"

"Well, odds are, we're gonna have a kid someday, and that means I have to get pregnant, and if you make one fat comment, I will remember, and then I will kill you when we're in our fifties."

"Long time to hold a grudge," he said.

I shrugged. "You'd be my husband. You can't escape my wrath."

"Oh, boy, what have I gotten myself into?"

"Hell, my boy. You've gotten yourself into hell," I said with a smirk. I think I'd make a good wife. I mean, the only difference between girlfriend and wife is that you have the option to take his last name if you're his wife. I don't think I'd want to do that. Maybe I'll hyphenate the last name, not too sure yet, but we have time to figure that out.

"You know, even if I do die in a couple of months or something, I think I'll be okay so long as you love me right up until the end," Evan said, sipping some champagne.

"I promise, no, I *vow* to love until you're dead, you know, at, like, eighty or something," I stated.

Evan smiled. "I wish I could have another sixty years with you. That would be the best sixty years in the history of forever."

"Yeah, there you go. Maybe even longer."

"You know, a long time ago when I was a wee lass, I wished upon a star," Evan said. "You wanna know what that wish was?"

"Well, I'd guess that even if I don't, you're still gonna tell me. So of course I wanna know what that wish was. Lemme hear it."

"I wished to have the love of a beautiful woman someday," he said, smirking a little at my remark.

"Sorry to disappoint," I said, pouting a little bit.

He flicked my cheek. "I meant you. I just wanted to thank you for making that wish come true. I know you didn't do it on purpose because you didn't know about it, but I did, and so did the heavens, so I just wanna thank you for that."

"Well, you're welcome."

He smiled and pulled me over so I could rest my head on his shoulder. I think things were finally how they were meant to be. Evan and I sitting on the cliff, watching the stars and the city lights, talking about a future life we wanted to have one day. There was obviously mention of his death a few more times, but I shut him up pretty quickly by kissing him. That always works.

He told me some bedtime stories as we watched the skies. He pointed out constellations and I played with the ring on my finger, rotating it around and around. We ended up falling asleep on the hood of his car, curled into one another. And I'm pretty sure he fell asleep after me, but we could have fallen asleep together at the same time.

Y'know, the last month may have been really shitty, but the next lifetime is gonna be amazing. Tonight was the start of that. I had fallen asleep on the hood of my new car with my fiancé, listening to him tell me lame stories until I fell asleep.

Life is strange, but life is good.

{Chapter: **Thirty-Two**}

I woke up to the sound of a bird chirping. It sounded really close to me. I opened my eyes and felt a little bit of pressure on my chest. I opened my eyes and expected to see Evan's hand there, but instead of that, it was a little plump bird. I looked at it and it chirped at me cheerfully. It had a white belly and light brown feathers. It looked really chubby and had a thin little beak.

"Evan," I whispered. I kicked his leg and he stirred awake.

"What?" he groaned as he looked over to me. "Oh, my God, Spencer, there's a bird on you."

"I know, dude. There's a bird sitting on my right now."

"Hey, little bird, those are my boobies," Evan said to it.

I shot him a look and he dropped his smirk. "Take a picture or something. This is the cutest thing ever."

Evan pulled his phone out of his pocket and took a picture of the little bird sitting on my chest. "What are the odds of waking up to this?"

"My guess is slim to none," I said, slowly moving my finger up to the bird. It nuzzled my fingertip with its beak and I pet its little head lightly. "I told you I was the elf princess of the forest."

"I read your tweets," Evan said. "I get it."

"Shut up," I muttered to him.

The sound of a loud engine suddenly overtook the peaceful quietness of the nature around us. The bird flew off and I sat up to looked what was making the sound. I rolled over and saw Collin's car pulling up across the little clifftop clearing.

I hopped down from the hood of the car and walked over to the two of them as they walked over from their car. "What the hell, guys?" I shouted at them. "You ruined a perfect moment."

"Were you and him kissing or something?" Charlotte asked.

"Better," I barked. "I woke up and there was this little bird sitting on my chest. It was the cutest little bird and it was on my chest, staring me right in the face with its cute little eyes."

"Sorry," Collin said. "We were supposed to come meet Evan here. He texted us the details last night. I'm to the understanding that you guys are back together."

I nodded as Evan came over and rested his arm over my shoulder. I put my right arm around him and held up my left hand. "We're actually engaged, believe it or not."

Charlotte's eyes widened in shock as she caught a look at the ring on my hand. "Holy crap." She stepped over and looked at it. "You guys are seriously engaged?"

I nodded. "He proposed, I said yes, and he put the ring on me. That's usually how people end up being engaged."

"So all is right with the world," Collin said with a smile. "Congrats, bro. And congratulations to you too, Spencer. As Evan's future best man, I have to say, you're making a total mistake in wanting to marry him, but as long as he's a mistake that will do his best to make sure you wake up with a smile on your face every day, then I think it'll be a successful marriage."

"Guys, we're still young. I don't wanna get married for at least another three years or so," I told them.

"You want to be married at 22?" Charlotte asked.

I shrugged. "If it's to the right person, of course." I looked up to Evan and smiled. "And I don't think I have to worry about finding the right person 'cause he's right here by my side already."

"So my best friend just got engaged."

I nodded. "I did."

"I hate that stupid deal we made with Mindy," Charlotte whined.

"Oh, right, where I be your maid of honour, you be hers, and she's mine?"

Charlotte nodded. "I wanna be your maid of honour."

"We can arrange it so you can be mine and I'll be hers and she'll be yours. That works just as well, right?" I suggested.

"Okay, so I'm guessing neither of you brought breakfast," Evan chimed in.

Collin shrugged. "Nothing's really open. It's still pretty early." He nodded over to the rising sun as it loomed over the ocean.

"Oh, yeah," Evan said as he turned to look at it. "My bad. We can go for breakfast a little bit later on."

"Breakfast sounds nice," I said, rubbing my stomach. "I'm kind of hungry."

"I got you," Evan said. He walked over to the bag by the car and pulled out something. He walked back over and handed me a bag of sour gummy worms.

"My favourite," I said. I pulled him down and kissed him. "Thanks for supporting my snacking habits."

"You're a bad influence on her, Evan," Charlotte said as the four of us walked over to the edge of the cliff.

Evan laughed softly. "Get used to it. She wants me for *life*. And life lasts a lifetime."

"You guys are gonna have a big wedding, right? I want to wear a pretty dress and stuff my face with *hors d'oeuvres* and wine."

"You're gonna be doing a fair bit of planning," I told her. "Evan's shit at planning and I just simply don't want to. And the bride is always right. Oh, guys, I'm gonna like being engaged. Now I can pull the bride card whenever the fuck I want and there's nothing that anyone can do. And then when I'm married, I can use the wife card on Evan. Life is good, you guys."

"Hey, so I was thinking that we take your sweet new ride out for a test race," Collin said, interrupting the wedding talk. Charlotte shot him daggers. He sighed. "I'm sorry. I just hate all the wedding talk. I'm a man, okay? I like monster trucks and beating up hitchhikers."

I laughed a little. "Alright, look, I'm game for a little racing. Where can we do it without getting arrested or ticketed?"

"There's a four-lane highway nearby. It's usually empty during rush hours, so it's probably really empty now. We can use that and just gun it back and forth for a little while," Collin stated. "And then we can get some breakfast, 'cause I'm also kind feeling the urge to get my snack on."

"I hope you like chasing taillights," I teased, smirking at him.

"Oh, somebody thinks they can beat me," Collin said, looking around as if talking to a bigger crowd of people. "Had a car for one night and now you think you're a big shot, huh?"

"You're gosh darn tootin' right about that one," I said in the most shucksy-doodle accent I could.

"Never do that again, or I will revoke the engagement ring," Evan said, glaring over at me.

"You're dating a girl that fishes popcorn out of her bra for fun," I said. "You ain't getting the ring back, bud. You knew what you signed up for."

"What about when we get some nice wedding rings though?" Evan asked. "Are wedding rings a thing?"

Collin nodded. "I believe they are. Yes."

"Well, shut up. I still think Collin needs to get his butt whooped in a race by Team Princess."

Evan groaned. "Team Princess? Really?"

I turned to him and stared at him sternly. "I am a princess. We are naming the team after me."

"Fine," he groaned.

"Should I call my team something lame too?" Collin teased.

"You're just asking for a fistfight," I said, turning and walking up to him and getting in his face.

"I'm too hungry for this shit," Evan whined, grabbing me by the braid I had in my hair and pulling me back.

I smacked his hands away and put my braid over my shoulder. "Don't touch my braid. My sister did good work on this."

"I wonder what's gonna happen in our futures," Charlotte said as she sat down on the rocky ledge of the cliff.

I sat down next to her and put my arm around her. "Good things."

"You think so?" she asked.

I nodded. "I know so. Look, even if things do become shitty, we'll find a way through. As long as we have each other and Mindy, we'll always find a way through."

"Oh, you need to tell her you're engaged."

I nodded. "I know. I'm gonna go visit her and I'll tell her then."

"Good."

"But back to the future thing. The future is gonna be fine, Charlotte. Nothing's really gonna change, at least not for a couple more years," I told her. "And then if they do change, it's gonna be because we're gonna go off and do amazing things."

"Like?"

"Like write a book," I said. "I've always wanted to."

"I dunno, writing isn't my strong suit," she said.

I smiled. "It's not mine either. The point I'm trying to make is that we're gonna grow up and we're gonna get married and we're probably gonna have kids and life is just gonna pop up and we're gonna have fun with it."

"It's just that everything feels so mature now that you're engaged to Evan. I dunno. It's a dumb feeling, but it's how I feel. I've always been nervous about the future, you know that. All this makes adult life feel so imminent."

I smiled at her and rubbed her back a little. "Charlotte, my sweet little American, life is going to be a wonderful journey for you. You are beautiful and smart and talented and you shouldn't even need to worry at all about this."

She nodded. "You're right. Day by day, we're still young."

I smiled at her. "There you go. Now you're thinking." I stood up and stretched out. "Okay, well, let's go get this racing done with. I'm pretty hungry, but don't think that means I'm gonna go easy on you."

Collin smirked. "I don't want you to go easy on me. I want you to give me your very best."

"I will. Promise."

"Okay, think you can keep up with me?"

I nodded. "I'd get there before you if I knew where we were going."

Evan walked over and picked up his bag and tossed it into the car. I watched as Collin and Charlotte got into Collin's car and then I turned and got into my car. Evan was already waiting in the passenger seat for me. He smiled at me and kissed me on the cheek and told me how beautiful I looked and made a joke about how we're gonna whoop their ass in the race.

There was clearly no doubt in his eyes when we started following Collin down the gravel road and towards the four-lane highway. I pulled up next to them and we all traded glances with each other. None of spoke any words, but Evan put his arm out the window and used his fingers to count down from three. Three, two one. And then the sounds of two cars doing a burnout took over the silence of the nature around us. And soon after that, the sound of wind flushing into the car replaced the sounds of everything else. It was a numbing sound, but one that made me focus on the things around me all that much more. Evan rested his hand on top of mine and helped me switch gears as we picked up speed along the highway.

***

I know that not everything can be butterflies and rainbows all the time, but I don't really think I care about that right now. I know that the life I'm setting myself up for is gonna have a tremendous amount of good days in it. And all of those good days are going to far outnumber the bad ones.

Every day that got me to where I am now, in this car with Evan going down the highway, wind in our hair, is a day that I don't regret. I don't regret the crying or the confusion or the anger or anything. If everything led to this exact moment, I would do it over and over again. Evan is the only thing that keeps me hopeful for the future.

Not everything would be perfect in the years to follow though. Charlotte and Collin ended up heading to the west coast and leaving us all behind. It was kinda sucky, but that's whatever. Evan and I got married before they left though. We all had a pretty good time. Evan and I honeymooned in London, England. After a while, we decided to move to Toronto because we wanted a change of scenery and because Evan had gotten a job there.

It was a good move for me too. I had become a game designer

and there was more work in Toronto for me. I also started writing novels on the side, with one of my books series becoming a mild success before I turned 25. It was only a matter of time before offers for the movie rights to the series started to come in, but that could wait. At 25, my life was pretty good. I was living in Toronto at that point, living with Evan in an elegant condo in the city. We had friends and we had happiness. It was great.

But back to the car for now, the car that was driving down an empty highway. We had our two best friends in a car right next to us and they were all smiles too. This was the first day in a pretty long time that I felt truly *free*. Something about going 160 kilometres per hour makes you feel like you're on top of the world.

Evan always talked about how we all die at different speeds. I think what he made me realize is that we have a say in how fast we go. Maybe it's not that we die at different speeds, we just run out of gas at different times. Some of us like to go fast and live recklessly and risk dying early on and others like the slower routes, but the end is always the same. We all crap out on the side of the highway at some point or another, whether it's for a few minutes or forever. Evan really taught me that we do die at different speeds, but not in the way he thought he meant it. Evan thought it had to mean that his time on Earth was shorter than anybody else's, but it wasn't. He was so scared of dying that he missed the part of living that made him be alive. He said I helped with that. He told me later on that I had helped him realize that life and death don't have to coexist as much in his head as they had since he got his diagnosis. And that year was a rollercoaster for him, but we got through it.

And beyond that year, nobody ever found out that Evan *had* cancer. If you ever ask him about it, he'll deny it tooth and nail. To him, it never happened. And to me, well, I'm just glad that it's behind us now. I'm looking forward to living a long life with Evan by my side.

About the **Author**

Darren Richardson is, at the time of writing this, a student at Durham College. He enjoys writing, napping, gaming, drinking coffee, staying up late, and learning things.

When it comes to writing Darren likes to write about teen fiction, teen romance, young adult fiction, general fiction, fantasy, crime, and really anything he feels up for. He finds the most challenging part of writing to be getting the motivation to keep going when you're already halfway through a novel.

When Darren gets older, he hopes to still be writing and creating things in every facet of media and art that he can. His advice for writers, young and old, is to just keep writing. Even when it feels like you're completely tapped out of words, keep trying to get something written. Every word is one step closer to a finished product.